LITTLE,
BROWN

LB

LARGE
PRINT

DEADLY
CROSS

JAMES
PATTERSON

LITTLE, BROWN AND COMPANY

LARGE PRINT EDITION

Copyright © 2020 by James Patterson

Little, Brown and Company
Hachette Book Group
1290 Avenue of the Americas, New York, NY 10104

First edition: November 2020

Little, Brown and Company is a division of Hachette Book Group, Inc. The Little, Brown name and logo are trademarks of Hachette Book Group, Inc.

ALEX CROSS is a trademark of JBP Business, LLC.

The Hachette Speakers Bureau provides a wide range of authors for speaking events. To find out more, go to hachettespeakersbureau.com or call (866) 376-6591.

ISBN 978-0-316-42025-9 (hardcover) / 978-0-316-54176-3 (large print)
LCCN 2020932323

10 9 8 7 6 5 4 3 2 1

LSC-C

Printed in the United States of America

DEADLY CROSS

CHAPTER

1

DEVON MONROE TORE HIS EYES off the two dead bodies in the powder-blue Bentley convertible, top down, idling not twenty yards away, and glanced at his best friend.

"No movement," Devon said.

"Lights out," said Lever Ashford, nodding.

"I don't know, Lever. This is high profile. Know what I mean?"

Lever said, "C'mon, Dev. It's a once-in-a-lifetime, straight-up gift from God on top of everything else. We slip in. We slide out. See Waffles. No one knows."

"I'm telling you, damn white folks get hung for less. Now let's get out of here."

Lever snarled, "You owe me, brother, or have you forgotten?"

The young men were both sixteen, African-American, and had their dark hoodies up. It was four fifteen in the morning, and they were standing in the shadows cast by the Harrison Charter High School in Garfield Heights in Southeast Washington, DC. The parking lot behind the school was dead silent except for their whispers.

Devon grimaced, struggled, but finally said, "Just don't get prints on nothing."

"Why we got them," Lever said, smiling as he groped in his back pocket for two pairs of thin surgical gloves.

They put them on, scanned the area, and saw no movement anywhere around the school, not in the parking lot or on the track and football field.

"Forty-five seconds and we're gone," Devon said. "I'm serious."

Lever bumped his fist. "Forty-five."

They walked right up to the Bentley, Lever at the driver's door, Devon going around to the other side. He skidded to a halt by the passenger door, feeling not fear but horror. "I don't know if I can do this, man."

"Do it! Take what's rightfully yours, brother!"

CHAPTER

2

DEVON FELT LIKE HE MIGHT puke but took one step, leaned over, and reached into the back seat, not letting his shirt or pants touch the Bentley in any way.

He tried to keep his eyes off the woman sprawled there, half naked and dead. Lever, however, stared right into the eyes of the dead man lying next to her as he slipped his surgical-gloved hand into his tuxedo jacket. He looked at the man's pants around his ankles, sniffed disdainfully.

"Freak bastard," Lever said. "Serves you right, getting shot like this."

On the other side of the Bentley, Devon smelled a coppery odor and it sickened him. *Blood*, he thought, trying not to breathe through his nose as he felt for the woman's hands, found a big-rock ring, and worked it off her finger.

The bracelets, two on the left, one behind the watch on the right, came off quicker than he'd expected.

Devon was about to call it good when he saw the pale glow of the pearl necklace around her neck. He tilted her head forward, found the clasp, slipped it off, and slid it into his pocket.

"Thirty-eight seconds," Lever whispered from the other side of the car. "I'm done. Watch and wallet."

"Right behind you," Devon said. He tugged the pearls from the dead woman's ears and laid her head back on the seat.

"Alley now," Lever said, pivoting.

They heard scuffling in the gravel behind them. They took off at a sprint and dodged through a hole in the fence into a dark alley, where they stopped to look back. Someone was heading toward the car.

They ran the length of the alley, slowed to a walk across Alabama Avenue, then kept on at a faster pace toward Fort Circle Park. Forty minutes later, as the boys were reaching home, they heard sirens begin to wail back at the school.

CHAPTER

3

IT WAS SEVEN THIRTY IN the morning, and I was standing at the bottom of a granite cliff on Old Rag Mountain in Shenandoah National Park, looking dubiously up at the cracks in the wall and the ropes dangling beside them.

"Biggest one yet, Dad!" said my ten-year-old son, Ali, who stood to my right wearing a white rock helmet and a climbing harness over his T-shirt and shorts.

"You think?" his sister said. Jannie, my seventeen-year-old, was kneeling to my left, retying her climbing shoe.

The man beside her, who was going through a knapsack, said, "Definitely. It's six stories and technically more challenging. And the rappel down's a screamer."

"It's a screamer, Dad!" Ali said.

"No screamers," I said. "As far as I'm

concerned, if you're screaming, you're falling, so no screamers."

"Sorry, Dr. Cross," the man said, setting the bag down. "It just means you can take bigger leaps before you tighten up on the rack coming down."

"I'll be good, Tom, and locked into my rack, thank you," I said.

Tom Mury grinned and clapped me on the back. "It's just cool to see someone like you willing to go on rope."

"Someone like me?" I said.

"Six two? Two twenty-five? Forties?"

"With all the hiking we've been doing, I'm two twenty."

"It's still impressive to see a guy your size going up."

"He is at a disadvantage," Ali said. "So is Jannie."

"Nope," my daughter said, standing. "I'm stronger and got longer arms and legs than you do."

"Helps to be small and crafty if you want to be a human fly," Ali said.

"Sometimes," Mury said. "Who's up first?"

For the past four days, we'd been taking a course with Mury, who was a certified rock-climbing instructor. It was Ali's idea, of course, the newest of his obsessions, and Jannie had expressed interest in it right away.

To be honest, I had been less enthusiastic,

but with Jannie entering her senior year of high school in two months and her college years looming, I was trying to lead a more balanced life, focusing more on my family and less on murder and mayhem. So I agreed to join them.

We'd been bouldering and climbing less sheer rock for the past two days. Though we'd all spent time prior to the course learning the basics in a climbing gym in Northern Virginia, this would be the first time we had climbed an actual cliff.

"I'll go!" Ali said, stepping forward.

"Sisters first," Jannie said.

"Dad?"

"She's up."

While my son pouted, Jannie went to the rope and watched Mury intently as he linked her to the line with a small mechanical device called a jumar that was already tied to her harness. The jumar would allow the rope to slip through only when Jannie ascended. If she fell off the rock, the device would lock her in place on the rope.

"Just like we talked about yesterday," Mury said. "We're not trusting the jumar, are we?"

"I'll work the Prusik knot, too, and the cow's-tail all the way up."

He picked up the other rope and called, "On belay."

Jannie turned all business, said, "On rope. Climbing."

CHAPTER

4

WATCHING YOUR CHILD CLIMB A sheer face, even roped in, is an experience somewhere between breathtaking and panic-inducing. At least that's how I felt seeing Jannie boldly ascend the cliff, sure with her hands and feet, using her safety gear exactly the way Mury had taught us.

"Great job!" Mury called when she disappeared over the top.

Ali and I clapped and whistled, and unseen high above us, Jannie let loose a scream of triumph.

"I'm on now!" Ali said.

My son was less sure as he climbed, but every time he stalled and tried to figure out his next move, Mury would shout up some encouragement or instruction. Twenty minutes after he began, Ali disappeared over the top.

"I am the human fly!" I heard him shout.

Mury laughed. "Your kid's a piece of work, Dr. Cross."

"Call me Alex, and he is that." I chuckled. "He never ceases to amaze me."

"Ready, Alex?"

My stomach did a little flip-flop, I'll admit it. Heights aren't my thing, but once I commit to something, I commit.

"As I'll ever be," I said, going to the rope.

Mury helped rig me. As I climbed, I'd work the jumar on the main line and the Prusik knot on the rope beside it. Like the mechanical device, the knot allowed a rope to pass through only in one direction. Any weight on the safety rope attached to my harness, and the knot would cause it to cinch tight. In the unlikely failure of the jumar, the Prusik would save me a long and potentially fatal fall.

"Enjoy yourself, Doc," Mury said. "On belay!"

"On rope!" I called back. "Climbing."

I made it to the top, and I wish I could say it was through a series of well-calculated and smoothly executed moves, but it wasn't. My climb was tentative and clunky, and I was immediately aware that my hip and shoulder joints weren't as loose as they needed to be.

"You're killing it," Mury called to me when I'd gotten up twenty feet.

"Doesn't feel like it."

"What do you need?"

"How about a crash course in yoga?" I said, sweat pouring off me.

"Look for hand- and footholds in your range of motion," he said. "Remember, not everyone climbs the exact same route. This is about you adapting to the wall."

"C'mon, Dad!" Ali called.

"You got this!" Jannie cried.

I looked up to see them still some three stories above me, peering over the edge of the cliff. They had such joyous grins on their faces that I was inspired to keep climbing, slow and steady, trying to do everything by the book.

At forty feet, I said, "My hands are cramping. Gimme a second to rest."

"Use your cow's-tail," Mury said. "Tie into that wall nut on your right."

I reached around, grabbed the short rope with a carabiner dangling off my right hip, and clipped it to the loop of steel linked to a block of steel jammed into a crack in the cliff. Now supported by three lines, I could relax a minute and stretch my fingers and knead my palms.

"How's the view?" Mury said.

I looked over my shoulder at the lower flanks of the Blue Ridge Mountains, a perfect sea of midsummer green shimmering in the morning light behind and below me. It was kind of thrilling, I decided, to be dangling off the side of a cliff for no reason, enjoying the beauty of nature. I smiled, looked down, and said, "Okay, I'm starting to get the attraction of this."

Our instructor threw me a thumbs-up, said, "I told you—it's an acquired taste and then an addiction."

I doubted the latter would be the case, but I enjoyed the rest of the climb, finding myself thinking more about the mechanics of it than the dangers. A half an hour after I left the ground, Mury's assistant, Carley Jo Warner, helped me up over the edge.

"Well done," she said.

"I almost dislocated my hip a few times, but thanks," I said, gasping. I sat still as she disconnected me from the ropes. When she was done, I lay down on my back with a silly grin on my face.

"Wasn't that great?" Ali said, giving me a high five.

"Not at first," I said. "But yes, eventually it was fun."

"I can take you to a yoga class, Dad," Jannie said.

"I'm not exactly built to be a human pretzel, but I'll think about it."

Before either of them could reply, my cell phone rang, which surprised me, as we'd had no service at the bottom of the cliff.

I got it out of my shirt pocket and saw my wife, Bree Stone, was calling from her DC Metro

Police phone. Bree was chief of detectives and had been under a lot of stress lately.

There'd been a string of unsolved rapes and murders in the DC area, and in just the past week, in two separate incidents, two vocal and well-connected lobbyists had been shot at in Georgetown. To make it worse, there was a new commissioner of police, and everyone's job, including Bree's, was on the line.

I got to my feet and answered on the third ring. "Human fly here."

Bree said, "We've got a double homicide, and I want you involved."

"Why?"

"You know both victims," she said, and she gave me their names and location.

I felt my stomach lurch and my knees wobble in disbelief and grief. In my mind, I saw them both as I'd last seen them, felt their loss like a blow to the head.

"I'm sorry, Alex."

"Thanks. I'll use the bubble and be there in two hours, tops."

"I won't be there. Another meeting with the commissioner."

"Hang tough. You're still the woman for the job."

"We'll see," she said, and she hung up.

I looked at my kids. "Sorry, guys."

"It's okay," Jannie said. "We've had three and a

half days and lots of fun." Ali nodded, and somehow their understanding made me feel even
worse about cutting our time short.

"We will be back," I promised, then I looked
at Mury, who'd just reached the top. "Can you
teach us how to do screaming rappels? We have
to go."

"Screamers." Mury smiled. "I can do that."

CHAPTER

5

THE FEELING OF LEANING AWAY from the cliff, pushing off the rock face, releasing my grip on the rappelling rack, falling a good fifteen feet before my boots hit the wall, then starting the whole process over again was still with me when I got out of my car and headed up the block toward the police lines.

It was July in DC, but it was strangely cool, low seventies, low humidity, with a brisk breeze. The school came into view, shut and empty for the summer. Jannie went to Harrison, and when I saw the circus of media satellite trucks around the school grounds, it made the scene that much more upsetting.

I skirted the trucks and pushed my way through the onlookers, hearing but trying to ignore the vicious gossip and speculation already spreading about the victims and the heinous crime.

In the past I had been both an FBI agent and a DC Metro Homicide detective, and now I was a consultant for both agencies. I showed my identification to the uniformed officer restricting entry to the crime scene, and he let me duck under the tape.

I made it fifteen yards before an FBI agent asked me for my ID. I gave him my FBI contractor's badge, and he waved me through. John Sampson, my best friend and former partner at DC Homicide, came around the corner.

"FBI?" I said.

"Given the victims, not surprising."

"Right, but who's in charge?"

"Mahoney. He wants you to look at the bodies before they're moved."

"How bad?"

"They weren't shot in the face. You'll recognize both."

We walked around to the lot in the rear of the school, and I saw an FBI forensics van and a DC medical examiner's vehicle parked by the football field and track where my daughter had run some of her finest races. There were at least twenty agents prowling the lot, looking for any and all evidence. I could see a team of them on the field.

"Who found them?" I asked.

"School security guard," he said, gesturing toward dumpsters with yellow police tape around them. "They're out back."

I said, "Time of death?"

"ME says four a.m."

We went over to the dumpsters to find the familiar powder-blue Bentley convertible cordoned off by more police tape, and agents, criminologists, and police detectives milling around the area.

FBI Special Agent in Charge Ned Mahoney, my old partner at the Bureau, separated himself from the pack, came over, and shook my hand. "We've been waiting on you, Alex. It's been photographed but not scoured by forensics yet."

"Okay," I said. "Can I get some breathing room?"

Mahoney clapped and yelled, "All right, now, everyone back off, we need the scene to ourselves for a moment."

We got odd glances, but they walked off.

I took in the Bentley convertible and the victims in the back seat, and part of me wanted to sit down and cry. But I'd spent the majority of my adult life confronting murder, and there was only one way to do it well: divorce yourself emotionally from the victims. In this case, that was going to be difficult.

Mahoney, seeming to read my thoughts, said, "You sure you're up to this?"

"I'll deal with it," I said as I walked around the car toward the female victim.

I wanted to treat her as an object to be studied

and evaluated, but I was having a hard time taking my eyes off Kay Willingham's face. She was one of the most striking, most interesting women I'd ever known, and here she was dead, sprawled next to a man who had apparently been her lover, unlikely as that seemed.

I had to force myself not to look at her blank expression and instead focus on the two bullet wounds about four inches apart and two inches above her bare left breast. Her rose-lace bra was on her lap; her black dinner dress was tugged down around her waist.

"No sign she had her hands up in a defensive posture," I said. "I'm thinking she never saw her killer."

"Neither did he," Sampson said from the other side of the car. "I think they had other things on their minds."

Only then did I look at the male victim. He was turned slightly toward Kay, his head slumped on his right arm, which was extended over the compartment that held the convertible's retracted roof. His pants and boxers were around his ankles. Blood from two chest wounds had drained across his left thigh and pooled between his legs.

"The press is going to have a field day with this," Sampson said.

"For way too many reasons," Mahoney said.

I didn't reply, but Ned and John were right;

there were so many reasons for this to blow up, and in ways we couldn't predict.

Kay Willingham was a vivacious Georgetown socialite, a Southern heiress and power broker who had, until two years ago, been married to J. Walter Willingham, the current vice president of the United States.

The man with her, Randall Christopher, was the founder and principal of Harrison Charter High, a charismatic man rumored to have his eye on the mayor's office and, if that went well, higher political aspirations. Christopher was African-American and married with twin girls who were sophomores at his school and friends of my daughter.

"Look at that," I said, shaking my head.

"What?" Sampson and Mahoney said.

"We might be witnessing the birth of a perfect shitstorm."

CHAPTER

6

BEFORE EITHER OF THEM COULD respond, two men in dark suits and shades ducked under the tape.

"Spin around, whoever you are," Mahoney barked. "And get off my crime scene."

They both held up badges. The taller of them, the one with the buzz cut, said, "Donald Breit, U.S. Secret Service."

"Lloyd Price, U.S. Secret Service," said the other, who was built like a brick with powerful legs and arms. "You are?"

"FBI Special Agent in Charge Mahoney," Ned snapped. "Now get off my crime scene."

Agent Price took off his shades, his face softening. In a quieter voice, he said, "Please, sir, and no disrespect, but Kay Willingham is—was— our boss's ex-wife."

Agent Breit removed his sunglasses as well,

revealing bloodshot eyes. "He's crushed, the VP. I've never seen him like this. As soon as he heard, he asked us to come down. To find out what we could, Special Agent Mahoney. I know it's crazy…but he still loves her."

Mahoney hesitated for a moment, and then in a reasonable tone he said, "I'll share what I can once I know where the vice president was last night, the entire night."

"So, what, you think J. Walter killed them?" Agent Breit said. "Are you insane?"

"Answer the question," Mahoney said.

Agent Price said, "The VP was seen last night by five hundred people at a ten-grand-a-plate fundraiser at the Hilton. He left at ten thirty-seven on the dot, and I personally drove him home to One Observatory Circle, where he went to bed and remained *all night.*"

"You have documentation?"

Breit nodded. "Every minute of that man's day is accounted for."

"Glove up," Mahoney said. "You can take a look. Dr. Cross will brief you."

"Alex Cross?" Agent Price said.

"That's right," I said, shaking his hand.

Agent Breit said, "The boss will be happy you're on the case. He's heard of you."

"I'm flattered," I said and shook his hand as well. "Do you want to take a look? Maybe you'll see something we've missed."

The Secret Service agents nodded and followed me to the blue Bentley. They both stopped and lost color when they saw Kay.

"Jesus," Breit said.

Price said, "I don't want to be the one to tell him."

"Too much?" I said.

"No," Breit said. He walked closer, saw Christopher's pants down. "What? Jesus."

"She's not wearing jewelry," Price said. "That's wrong."

Breit nodded. "Kay was a jewelry nut, and she's got no jewelry on. Look at the dress. She should be decked out in diamonds and pearls. And his watch is gone. Check his breast pocket."

Mahoney did, then shook his head.

Sampson said, "No phones. Either of them."

"Well," I said. "That complicates things, doesn't it?"

CHAPTER

7

WE SEARCHED THE CAR AND the bodies but found no cell phones anywhere. After the medical examiner removed the corpses from the scene, Special Agents Breit and Price left to brief the vice president, and forensic techs went to work on Kay Willingham's Bentley.

An FBI blood-spatter expert soon determined they were shot from less than twenty feet. A tech who specialized in bullet trajectory said the killer probably stood ten or fifteen feet away from the front bumper and was tall enough to shoot over the intact windshield.

"Brass?" I asked.

The tech shook his head. "Smart shooter. Picked up after himself."

"Does that say *I'm a hophead*? Killing two people to grab diamonds and pearls, money, and phones?" Sampson said.

"A hophead wouldn't care about brass," I said. "So scratch that killer profile. And even if Kay was wearing one of her really big necklaces, I'm having trouble seeing a pro killing her to get it."

Mahoney nodded. "Why not just a holdup? Her boobs are out; his pants are down. They'd be compliant."

"Right," Sampson said. "So this is made to look like a robbery gone bad."

"Maybe," I said. "Or maybe a scavenger passed by after the killer left."

"And maybe the scavenger saw the shooter," Mahoney said.

"I like that maybe," Sampson said, pointing at Ned. "I'm gonna work my sources on the street, find out where a scavenger would go to fence jewels in this hood."

"Good," Mahoney said, then he looked at me. "After Christopher's office, I'll need you at Kay Willingham's place."

I said, "Let's not forget there's another possible classic-killer profile here."

"Which one?" Mahoney asked.

"The vengeful wife," I said. "Where's Mrs. Christopher in all this?"

Sampson left. Mahoney and I entered the high school and got the janitor to open the principal's suite of offices, which were dark. We passed the secretary's desk and went through a door into a nice large office with Christopher's framed diplomas, citations, and family photographs on the walls between the bookcases. The desk was remarkably tidy.

A door stood ajar on one side. I found a switch, turned it on, and saw a much smaller second office that looked more used. There was a printer but no computer, although there was space for a laptop on the desk crowded with books and correspondence. This was where he'd really worked. "We'll need agents to go through the mounds of stuff and find his computer."

"Probably at his house—" Mahoney started. His phone buzzed before he could finish. "Great. I have to brief the media."

"How fun," I said. "I'm going to go to Christopher's home and talk to the wife, then I'll go to Kay's house in Georgetown."

When I left, I noticed a gap in the school perimeter fence, and I went through it so I could skirt the media circus.

When I was almost to my car, a man called out, "Dr. Cross? I thought I'd find you somewhere about."

I knew that whiny, nasal voice and waved my hand without slowing. "No comment, Sparkman."

"No comment? I haven't even asked a question."

"See there?" I said, reaching my car. "I'm saving you the time and effort."

"Oh, I think you'll want to comment," he said, and I finally looked at him.

Clive Sparkman was in his early forties, disheveled, and generally a rude pain in the ass who made a very comfortable living running a highly clicked-on website that spread news, gossip, rumors, and outright lies about power brokers of all persuasions in the nation's capital. He also published lurid stories about murder cases, which was how we'd become acquainted.

"I know this case is a twofer for you, Sparkman, politics and homicide," I said. "But I'm not answering any questions about an ongoing investigation. You want to know something new? Go listen to the FBI briefing in ten minutes."

Sparkman cocked his head knowingly. "I'll be there listening to every word, but I'll know something no one else does, something I'm considering publishing on my site tomorrow morning—a little nasty sidebar about this case for the rabidly interested."

I opened the car door, started to get in, said, "I've got places to be."

Sparkman said, "Actually, it's about you, Cross, and...Kay Willingham?"

I froze but looked at him dispassionately.

He took off his sunglasses and smiled. "Did you have an affair with the vice president's wife, Alex? Were you the cause of the divorce? I've seen a photograph of you two together, and I must say, you're awfully chummy. Care to comment now?"

"Go to hell, Sparkman, and write anything you want," I said. "But make sure you're accurate in that rumor or you will hear from my lawyer. His name is Craig Halligan. You remember him, don't you? The guy who sued you for libel, took you for four million?"

Sparkman looked like he'd swallowed a parasite.

"Thought so," I said. I shut the door and sped off.

CHAPTER

8

IT ACTUALLY TOOK A BIT of digging to figure out where Randall Christopher lived. The name on the lease of his rented home, it turned out, was Elaine Paulson, Christopher's wife. I rang the front-porch bell on the left side of a duplex on Tenth Street between F and G Streets, but no one answered.

I rang the neighbor's bell next, and a big woman, mid-forties, wearing hospital scrubs and looking weary, opened the door a few inches but left the chain on.

"Yes?" she said.

"I was looking for Elaine Paulson?"

She grimaced. "She's gone."

"Do you know when she'll be back?"

"No idea."

"Who are you?" I asked.

"Who I am is none of your business," she said, and she started to close the door.

I put my fingers on it, said, "I work for the FBI and Metro Homicide, ma'am. This is a murder investigation."

That stopped her. "Murder? Who was murdered?"

"Ms. Paulson's husband," I said. "Randall Christopher."

Her left hand lifted slowly to her mouth. "Oh God," she moaned. "Oh God, don't tell me that."

"It's all over the news. Or will be, and I need to talk to his wife sooner rather than later."

"I think I'm gonna be sick. Can you come back?"

"Uh, no, this is a murder investigation, and we need your help."

She didn't appear pleased about it, but she slid back the chain and opened the door.

I held out my hand. "Alex Cross."

Her eyebrows raised in interest, and she shook my hand. "I recognize you now. From the news. I'm sorry. I'm Barbara Taylor."

"Nice to meet you, Barbara," I said. "May I come in?"

Taylor closed her eyes for a moment. "I'm going to get sucked into this, aren't I?"

"I just need to ask you a few questions."

"My ex got me sucked into things I didn't want any part of."

"Mr. Christopher is dead. You can help."

She hesitated, then stood aside. "Can I get you a cup of coffee? Some iced tea?"

"The iced tea sounds great, thanks," I said, and I followed her through a tidy living area into a tidier kitchen.

We spoke for a good forty minutes. A surgical nurse at Georgetown Medical Center, divorced, and the mother of two college students, Taylor had befriended Randall Christopher and his wife the day they'd moved in. The twin girls were nine or ten then, and Elaine Paulson had her hands full while her husband founded and built the charter school from scratch. Taylor described Christopher as "single-minded and evangelically passionate" about his work, starting the school in a small building and then, as enrollment increased, taking over and refurbishing an existing school structure.

"What about the marriage?"

The nurse chewed her lip. "My judgment might be clouded here, given that my husband left me for a twenty-six-year-old, okay?"

"Okay."

Taylor said the marriage seemed loving and supportive in the first couple of years. But as Christopher got involved in various civil crusades, his star began to shine and people in the community began to look to him for leadership on everything from education to addressing the series of rapes and murders that had taken place in Southeast DC over the past fifteen years.

"As a result, Randall was away often," Taylor said. "And there were fights when he was home. Nothing physical, not that I ever saw. But there was a lot of shouting, and I heard her crying more than once."

"Police ever have to get involved?"

"Not to my knowledge. I never called them, anyway."

"Did she confide in you?"

The nurse gave me a strange look. "If I tell you, I'm not keeping her confidence."

"I gather that's a yes."

Taylor did not respond.

I said, "I'm going to ask her these same questions when I find her."

Still no response.

"Have you considered the possibility that Elaine Paulson and her daughters might be in danger? And that they might need the FBI's protection?"

The nurse thought about that, then swallowed hard. "Please, I adore Elaine as a person, and I would not want to jeopardize our friendship."

"I just want to understand the situation, ma'am."

"All right," she said, relenting. "They hadn't made love in months. She suspected an affair. She considered hiring a detective to follow Randall."

"Did she hire one?"

"I don't know."

"When was the last time you saw her and the girls?"

"Tina and Rachel? Fourth of July, before they went off to camp. They're counselors."

"Is that where they are now?"

"Until mid-August."

"When was the last time you saw their mother?"

Taylor licked her lips and looked ready to cry. "This morning," she said in a soft voice. "Early. Twenty to five? I thought I heard her moving around next door even earlier, when I was eating breakfast. But as I was going out the door for my shift, I saw her coming in from a run, climbing the porch steps drenched in sweat. She looked like she'd been crying."

"Early run and crying," I said, estimating the distance to the school at roughly two miles. "Describe what she was wearing, please."

Taylor said Christopher's wife had on blue running shorts, a long-sleeved white T-shirt, a reflector vest, and a pack with a hydration pouch.

"Did you talk to her?"

"Just to say hello and ask if she was okay. She said she'd been having trouble sleeping, that she was emotional with the girls away, so she'd gone for a run."

"What else?"

"She said she'd decided to go somewhere for a few days and think things through."

"She say where?"

"No."

"Do you have her cell phone number?"

She nodded and went to her phone. She choked as she read the number to me, then she threw her hand up to her mouth and said, sobbing, "You don't think she killed him, do you, Dr. Cross? The Elaine Paulson I know is such a sweet, sweet soul."

CHAPTER

9

AFTER TRYING ELAINE PAULSON'S PHONE unsuccessfully several times, I drove to Kay Willingham's brick home in Georgetown. She'd bought two old townhomes decades before and merged them into a small mansion. As I parked, I noted that the front door was still deep green and the brass knocker was still polished to a high shine. A riot of flowers spilled from window boxes to the left and right.

It was so familiar.

I remembered a night, years before, when Kay had had too much to drink at a fundraiser and I'd given her a ride home. I was working a brief stint as a private investigator at the time, and I was single then, a widower. The socialite had gotten her high heel stuck in a crack in the brick sidewalk; the heel broke, the shoe slipped off and landed in a puddle, and she tripped. I'd caught her before she hit the ground. She'd been gasping and afraid and suddenly there'd been this intense moment of attraction between us that I'll never forget.

Shaking the memory off, I got out of my car and walked to the broad-shouldered young man in a dark suit and glasses standing at the low iron gate across the short path to the front door. "FBI?" I said.

"Special Agent Aaron Tilden," he said, nodding. "I recognize you, Dr. Cross. I heard you lecture several times at the academy."

"I hope I was coherent."

"Very, sir," he said, holding out his hand. "It's an honor to meet you."

I shook his hand, saying, "The honor's all mine, Agent Tilden. Has anyone been inside?"

"Not since my partner and I arrived a half an hour ago. Bill's in the alley. Doors are locked. No one is answering when we knock. Do you have a key?"

"No, uh…we know the location of the spare," I said, feeling a little flustered. I motioned him aside. "Any media been by?"

"Cameraman from CNN," Tilden said. "He shot the front of the house and stayed about two minutes."

"She lived alone," I said, putting on latex gloves. I reached over the iron railing left of the door to the brick face of the house, counted two bricks in and two down, then pressed on that brick. A small door levered open, revealing a shallow slot and the key.

"That's neat."

"Her idea, evidently," I said and unlocked the door.

"Do you need help, sir?"

"I'm sure I will, Special Agent Tilden," I said as a hollowness formed in my stomach. "But I'd like to take the first look around alone."

"Of course," Tilden said.

The door opened on oiled hinges and shut behind me just as quietly. I had not been in Kay's two-hundred-year-old Georgian town-home since that night long ago when she'd tripped and I'd caught her and she'd invited me in for a nightcap.

But standing there in the foyer that met the long center hallway of her home, I felt like it could have been yesterday. I could smell her scent. I could hear the echoes of her laughter in the air.

I walked down the hall, passing the various paintings on the walls, and stopped at the entrance to what had been Kay's grand salon. Then I stepped inside the long rectangular room and took it all in with a sweeping glance.

The floors were two-hundred-year-old plank-board interrupted by tasteful squares of cream-colored carpet. The furniture was early sixties

glamour, from the Kennedy era; "pieces of restored Camelot," Kay had called them. The
couches were upholstered in wide stripes of
indigo blue and mouse gray. Some of the overstuffed wingback chairs were blue, and others
were gray. All so familiar I could not help
replaying that night in my mind.

We had met at a fundraiser for victims'
rights. This was years ago, when her husband
was the governor of Alabama and they were
separated and contemplating divorce. The car
service that normally picked Kay up was late;
she'd had a few drinks, and I'd offered her a ride
home in my car.

I'd be lying if I said there was not a genuine
spark between us after I'd caught her when
she fell. That sense had continued inside the
house.

I accepted a brandy. I couldn't remember
what music she'd put on, but it was perfect.
She'd danced away from me, twirling across the
floor and the carpet, barefoot, totally free, and
laughing.

"God, she was something," I said to myself and
walked over to a built-in shelf in the corner that
was crammed with pictures of moments in Kay's
remarkable life.

I found one that she'd shown me that night,
a framed snapshot of an eleven-year-old Kay
cheek to cheek with an African-American girl,

both of them wet from swimming, both of them grinning with love.

"That's Althea," Kay had said softly. "Best friend I've ever had. Only person I've trusted completely in my entire life."

"Where does she live?"

"Here and there," she'd said. Her phone rang. She picked it up, listened, and said, "Walter, I'm home before curfew, and yes, I've had a few drinks, but I'm going to bed now. Does that work for you?"

She listened again, her brows tightening. "Good night."

Kay hung up the phone and stood there a long moment as if in a trance. When it broke, she looked at me sadly. "It's time for me to say good night, Alex."

Whatever spark there was between us out on the sidewalk had died. I set my untouched brandy on the coffee table, said her house was beautiful, and got ready to leave.

"Could you check around the house? That's what my driver usually does before I set the alarm and go to bed. Thank you for not letting me fall out there," she said. "I'd have probably broken something irreparably."

CHAPTER

10

THE BIG APARTMENT BUILDING ACROSS the street from Harrison Charter High School was being totally renovated, so no one lived there at the moment. It was surrounded by a high chain-link fence to keep people out of the construction site. John Sampson noticed two security cameras mounted on the fence posts and aimed at the street.

He went to the supervisor at the site and asked for copies of the feeds from midnight on the evening before but was told the cameras had been down since the big lightning storm a few days earlier. Frustrated, he walked up the street, looking for more security cameras. His cell phone rang. His wife, Billie.

"Hey, baby," he said. "How you feeling?"

"Better every day," she said.

"What we love to hear. What's up?"

"I didn't get a chance to see you this morning and I wanted to tell you I love you before I go get Willow from camp."

Sampson softened and slowed down. "That's the best news I've heard all day. I love you too, baby."

"Big case?"

"Big as they come," Sampson said, quickening his pace. "I'll tell you what I can when I get home. Make sure you get your rest, hear?"

"I hear you," she said and clicked off.

Beyond a vacant lot to the north of the apartment building, on the northeast corner of the block, there was a two-story white structure that housed a small bodega and a laundromat at street level. Two cameras were mounted below the second floor and aimed out at the street and school grounds, but because they were painted the same color as the building, Sampson almost didn't see them.

He went inside the bodega and regretted it the moment he did, finding it packed with scruffy types buying provisions for the media people camped out around the crime scene. Thankfully, none of them seemed to recognize him as they chatted and traded unsubstantiated rumors about the case.

"Kay knew too much," he heard one kid say. "Mark my words, she knew too much."

"I dunno," said another. "Randall rubbed a lot

of folks hard. Especially in this neighborhood. Drug dealers and such."

Sampson listened without judgment. He pressed his hand against his jacket to cover the badge on his hip, picked up a Diet Coke and a bag of kettle potato chips—his secret vices— and got in line to pay for them. Two people were working the registers: a grinning, homely, redheaded guy in his late forties and a girl in her late teens with green hair, tats, and piercings, all of which went well with her miserable mood.

When Sampson reached the front of the line, he got the Goth; her name tag read LUCY. He set the chips and the soda down.

"That makes no sense unless your goal is blimpdom," she said, managing to sound bored, mildly disgusted, and sarcastic at the same time. She gestured at the chips and soda.

"Excuse me?" Sampson said.

"The combo. The diet soda's supposed to make you lean, but it actually makes you fat. The chips are supposed to make you fat, and they do it double time."

Irritated, Sampson opened his jacket to show her his badge and gun. "Do I look fat?" he asked quietly as he leaned forward.

"No," Lucy said, drawing back. "This about—"

"It is," Sampson said, still talking low. "Who's the owner?"

Lucy pointed her thumb at the other cashier,

who was engaged in pleasant chitchat with a woman from the neighborhood. "Mr. Peters."

Sampson paid for the chips and soda. "Lucy, after I leave, tell Mr. Peters quietly that I am a detective and I would like to speak to him outside."

Lucy looked indignant. "I'll be swamped."

"Better than having me lock the doors and Mr. Peters and you making no money," Sampson said. "I'll be outside."

A few minutes later, Peters came out, looked around, saw Sampson, and beamed. He rushed over, extending his hand. "Ronald Peters, Detective…"

"Sampson," he said, showing him his credentials. "Metro Homicide."

Peters's smile faded, but his gaze stayed steady on Sampson. "I heard. Mostly from the reporters. Is it true? Randall Christopher? And the vice president's ex-wife?"

Sampson nodded.

"Jesus," Peters said, shaking his head. "You never know, do you?"

"You knew Christopher?"

"Yup," he said. "Came in every so often to pick up a few things, make sure I wasn't having any problems with his students."

"Did you have problems with his students?"

"Not one," Peters said, nodding. "That guy ran a tight ship. His kids were always polite. Not even a shoplifting attempt, which is a miracle."

"That's saying something."

"It is, which is a shame," Peters said, looking toward the high school. "Randall Christopher had it, you know? It? I mean, the way he helped organize the searches for those missing girls, it made you want to be part of it."

"You helped search?"

"As much as I could," he said. "Mostly I worked the phones. I'm a busy guy. I own four other small businesses besides the store and the laundromat. What's going to become of them, the students? The school?"

"Questions I can't answer, sir," Sampson said, then gestured up at the security cameras mounted high above the bodega. "We're going to need the feeds from those."

"Last night's?"

"Midnight on, for now," Sampson said.

Peters nodded. "Megan, my store manager, is out sick, but I think I can get it for you. Can I copy it to a thumb drive? Will that work?"

"If it's time-stamped."

"By the second," Peters said, then he looked over as two more customers entered his store. "Need it now?"

"I'm standing here," Sampson said.

Five minutes later, the bodega owner came out and handed him a thumb drive. "From midnight up to when you entered the store," he said.

"When will I see you arrive?" Sampson said.

"Five forty-five," Peters said. "On the dot. I usually get here before Megan to help out before we open at six fifteen."

"Appreciate it, sir."

"Anytime, Detective. Believe it or not, with all the bad press lately, we're a neighborhood of good people here. Or trying to be."

CHAPTER

11

THAT EVENING, IN OUR KITCHEN at home on Fifth Street, Bree peered at my phone and a picture of Elaine Paulson that Barbara Taylor had sent me. She'd taken it right before the twins boarded the bus to camp.

In the picture, Randall Christopher's wife had her arms around her daughters. The three of them were smiling, but their grins looked forced, as if they all had other things on their minds.

Bree said, "Where's Dad in the pic?"

"Well, exactly," I said.

"You've called her number?"

"Ten times," I said. "It goes straight to voice mail. I've got Rawlins at Quantico watching for any calls from her number or charges on her credit card. We'll find her. Given what we found in the house? We have to."

After looking through Kay Willingham's home,

I'd returned with a search warrant for Randall Christopher and Elaine Paulson's duplex. The place was spotless, with vacuum tracks on the rug and all the trash cans empty; it looked like Christopher's widow had gone to a great deal of trouble cleaning the place. Upstairs in their bedroom, however, in a nightstand, I'd found something that she'd neglected to clean. I'd taken a picture of the small, open, empty gun vault, and now I showed it to Bree. "Pistol is missing. Recent gun residue inside."

Bree shook her head. "Mom kills Dad because he's having an affair."

"Looks like it."

After a long silence, she said, "Too bad. I liked Randall Christopher. He was never afraid to dive in and help a good cause."

"Wasn't for him, you wouldn't have had so many people looking for Maya Parker."

"Or Elizabeth Hernandez."

Maya Parker and Elizabeth Hernandez were the most recent victims in a series of rapes and murders in Southeast DC that went back fifteen years. The early crimes had gone largely unnoticed by the media because of the long gaps between the attacks and because the victims were all either Hispanic or African-American.

Then, last year, seventeen-year-old Elizabeth Hernandez disappeared. Less than three days later, her body was found dumped in the

Potomac. Eight months passed before sixteen-year-old Maya Parker vanished; soon after, her body was discovered floating in the Potomac. The autopsy determined that she had been beaten and savagely raped. That was a little less than four months ago.

It was obvious to law enforcement that the killer was losing control because the gaps between his attacks were growing shorter. As a result, Bree, who was chief of detectives for Metro PD, was under tremendous pressure to catch the fiend. Most of that pressure came from the new commissioner.

"How's that going?" I asked.

"We could use you and Sampson."

"I can't speak for John, and I'm a little over-extended at the moment, but I'll get there."

Bree smiled. "Thank you. Want to see something interesting?"

"Always," I said.

She led me out of the kitchen, past Nana Mama, my ninety-something grandmother, who was peering into the oven at a meat thermometer buried in the thigh of a roast chicken.

"Dinner in twenty minutes," Nana said as we left.

In the front room, Bree opened her briefcase and retrieved a small box marked BOND ARMS. She lifted the lid.

"That is interesting," I said.

"Isn't it?" she said, pulling a small, modern, nickel-plated derringer from the box. She handed it to me. "They call it 'the backup.'"

"Appropriate," I said, bouncing the stout little gun in my palm. "Nice weight. Easy to conceal. Double barrel over and under."

"And a forty-five-caliber," she said. "It packs a wallop. And look."

She showed me a small holster attached to an elastic sleeve through which she slid her left arm. She took the derringer from me, slipped it into the holster, and rotated it so the little gun rode snugly beneath her forearm. "Put a jacket with loose sleeves on and no one would know," she said. "Or I can put it around my ankle with an accessory, but I kind of like this idea. I don't have to bend down for it."

I nodded. "Just reach up your sleeve. Where did you find it?"

"A rep from the company gave us a demonstration today. He asked me to try it for a while. If I like it, I'll buy it."

"Sounds like you're already sold."

When we returned to the kitchen, Nana Mama tapped a wooden spoon on the side of a saucepan, covered it, and clicked on CNN.

"It smells amazing, Nana," I said.

"I should hope so," she said, then she moaned sadly and gestured at the screen, shaking her head.

CHAPTER

12

BREE AND I LOOKED AT the TV to see Anderson Cooper doing a standup in front of the yellow tape blocking access to Kay Willingham's Georgetown mansion. On the screen, over Cooper's left shoulder, there was a picture of Kay from several years before, beaming and waving.

"Kay Willingham died today at fifty-two, shot to death in her powder-blue Bentley convertible in the middle of a tryst with her latest political protégé and apparent lover, Randall Christopher," Cooper said.

A montage of video clips and images of Kay with many of the most powerful people in the country began to play. Cooper went on in voice-over. "She inherited her family's millions and moved from Alabama to the nation's capital, where for years Kay was Washington's socialite queen. She was more than just beautiful and rich. She spoke five languages and had several degrees from schools all over the world, but she also possessed that rare ability to relate to almost everyone she met with warmth and genuine interest. She was known as a political mentor and an advocate for social justice—until she became better known as the angry ex-wife of the sitting vice president of the United States."

The screen cut to Kay in a video clip from when she was in her late thirties. "I genuinely like people," she said in her soft, familiar drawl. "Every soul who appears in front of me deserves my love and attention. But I know that to have real impact while I'm alive and kicking, I have to curate the souls I spend time with. Hence the parties. They're good for me."

The screen cut to a female columnist from the *Washington Post.* "Kay Willingham honestly never met a stranger," she said. "She was giving and glamorous and passionate, and she was not afraid to show it—especially, unfortunately, when she had a few drinks in her."

The footage cut again to Kay, older now, dressed for a ball and not quite three sheets to the wind as she smirked into the cameras, winked, and said, "This is what three political fundraisers a night will do to a 'Bama gal, boys. Please be gentle with me. The headache I'm facing in the morning will be punishment enough."

The screen cut back to Cooper in standup in front of the Georgetown mansion. "Long before she married J. Walter Willingham, a rising political star in her home state, Kay lived here in the nation's capital and entertained her way to power. Her Georgetown parties were private, the conversations completely off the record. The gatherings were legendary, partly because they were safe places where people from all walks of life with radically opposing views could come together and talk frankly about the pressing issues of the day—if they could get an invitation."

The screen jumped back to the *Washington Post* columnist, who was smiling. "Kay understood exclusivity and kept those parties small, forty guests tops. So people who wanted power as well as people who didn't want to lose their power asked to come, but she'd turn them down if the space was full or if it wasn't the right mix."

With more video and commentary, the piece then dug into Kay's marriage to Willingham. They were married a few months before he ran for the governorship of Alabama. Unconventional as always, Kay had refused to leave DC and move back home, and she split her time between Alabama and Washington while her husband led the state and then ran successfully for U.S. Senate.

The feed cut to Willingham with Kay six or seven years ago, sitting for a formal interview.

He was smiling as he said, "Our marriage is a little unconventional, at times rocky. But it's always worked for us."

Kay, I noticed with twenty-twenty hindsight, seemed cool as she agreed with her husband. Not surprisingly, the story then veered ahead a few years to the ugly end of her marriage, when her drinking surged and she made wild, unsubstantiated accusations about her husband, now a vice-presidential candidate, publicly filing for divorce four and a half days before the general election.

"Willingham survived, and he and the president won the election," Cooper said, returning to the screen. "Voters seemed to feel sympathy for him. In exit polls many of them said that they'd personally seen what drugs and alcohol had done to their own families and dismissed the things Kay had said to reporters in a drunken state."

Cooper went on to note that shortly after the election, Kay's mother had become terminally ill. Kay went back to Alabama and disappeared from the Washington, DC, scene. When she returned, stone-cold sober, she quietly began trying to pick up her life as a single woman.

But within a year, she was testing the social waters, appearing at a few events and parties, though still solo and sober. At one gala, she met Randall Christopher, a telegenic married

African-American educator who ran an innovative school in DC and was interested in a political career.

"They evidently became lovers at some point," Cooper said, again in standup. "They died together earlier today, shot at close range.

"So far Vice President Willingham has not spoken publicly about his ex-wife's murder. His office did release a statement to us saying he was, quote, 'shocked and beyond saddened by Kay's death. My ex-wife had fought long and hard to conquer her demons and we'd made our peace with each other. She deserved a much longer life. The world would have been better for it.'"

CHAPTER
13

THE SEGMENT ENDED. NANA MAMA shut the TV off, but I kept staring at the screen, seeing images of Kay Willingham barefoot, laughing, and twirling away from me.

In addition to being a shrewd and skilled detective in her own right, Bree has always had an uncanny ability to read me, to sense things I might not even be consciously thinking about.

My wife tugged on my arm. "What's going on? You couldn't take your eyes off that story about Kay Willingham."

"Well, I am working the case and there were things I'd never heard before."

Bree wasn't having it. "There's more to it, Alex."

I sighed, glanced at my grandmother. "There is. Clive Sparkman."

Bree rolled her eyes. "What crackpot conspiracy theory is he pushing now?"

"He's threatening to publish a story saying that Kay Willingham and I had an affair a long time ago."

Bree stared at me, then burst out in nervous laughter. "You're kidding."

"Wish I was."

"There's nothing to it," she said.

"I know."

Nana Mama put her hands on her hips and sputtered, "This is what's wrong these days. No one knows what's true or not. Anything that gets thrown up there on the internet, people take as fact and gospel truth. No wonder the country's in the state it's in. Everyone's hating on everyone, and nothing gets done because no one can agree on basic reality, even if you put the evidence right in front of their noses."

Bree got angry then. "What can we do about it?"

"Until Sparkman publishes, nothing," I said. "But I told him I had Craig Halligan on retainer if he chooses to post a libelous story."

"Do you?"

"I met him last year and gave him a dollar in case I ever needed his services."

"Really?"

"Uh-huh."

She gave me a hug. "You never cease to amaze me, Alex Cross."

"Get a room, you two," Nana Mama said. "But before you do, I need someone to set the table."

As we did, I told Bree what Barbara Taylor had said about Randall Christopher's wife suspecting he was having an affair.

"She mention evidence?"

"Just that they hadn't made love in months."

My grandmother had the oven open and was peering inside at the roast chicken. "That's the first real sign of relationship disintegration," she said. "If a man isn't looking to his wife in the bedroom, he's looking in some other bedroom."

Both Bree and I stopped setting the table to gape at Nana Mama. We were still staring when she set the chicken on the stove and turned to us.

"What are you two looking at?" she asked.

I smiled. "Nothing, Nana. It's just not often I hear someone in her nineties talking about that kind of thing."

She shot me a withering look. "Shows how much you know. It's all most eighty- and ninety-year-olds talk about because they spend so much time watching daytime television and that's all that's talked about on daytime TV."

"C'mon," Bree said.

"It's true," she said. "Don't believe it? Look up the rise in the rate of sexually transmitted diseases among octogenarians."

"I'd rather not," I said.

"Sky-high," Nana Mama said. "Especially in those assisted-living facilities."

My son Ali came into the room. "What's sky-high?"

My grandmother frowned. "A subject not for young men."

"I'm ten," he said indignantly.

"Nana Mama was talking about the number of people who make it to ninety these days," Bree said.

"Oh," he said, then looked at me. "Were the murders of Mr. Christopher and the vice president's ex-wife professional hits, Dad?"

Ali, in addition to rock climbing, had long been interested in detection. At times, in our opinion, that interest had been borderline unhealthy. I said, "You know we can't talk about active cases."

That irked Ali, but he said, "There are all sorts of theories already on the web."

"You want to try to ignore the internet," Nana Mama said. "It's for idiots."

"Well, the idiots all think that Mrs. Willingham is to blame because Mr. Christopher was such a good guy."

My daughter, Jannie, came into the kitchen, upset. "He was a great guy. I can't believe it. Everyone's talking about it. Tina and Rachel are destroyed."

My stomach sank. "They heard up at camp? Did their mother break the news to them?"

She shook her head, on the verge of tears.

"They found out on Facebook hours ago, Dad, and they can't find their mom. They said she's not answering her cell."

"She'll call in soon, I'm sure," Bree said.

The doorbell rang and Sampson called out, "Hello?"

I called back, "We're in the kitchen, John."

Sampson, his wife, Billie, and their seven-year-old daughter, Willow, appeared in the doorway. "Smells good in here," John said.

Billie, ordinarily one of the most vivacious women on the face of the earth, nodded and smiled weakly. "It always smells good in here."

"Just like I like it," Nana Mama said, turning from her stove. "How are you, Willow?"

"Good," Willow said, looking at my grandmother's cookie jar.

Nana Mama winked at her, then turned to Sampson's wife. "And you, Billie?"

"Getting better every day, Nana," Sampson said, wrapping an arm around her shoulder. "She walked two miles this morning."

"Two miles," Bree said. "That's huge!"

Billie smiled broadly. "I just wish I could do it without feeling so tired afterward."

Sampson said, "The cardiologist said that will pass. He said in two weeks he'll be taking the gizmo out of her chest."

Billie had been stricken with Lyme disease that went undiagnosed long enough to precipitate a crisis in the emergency room when her heart rate dropped to twenty beats per minute. Luckily, a sharp ER doc had questioned Sampson about her exposure in the woods. It turned out that Billie had gone hiking in Pennsylvania a month earlier. Even before the blood test came back positive for Lyme, the doctor was pumping her full of the antibiotics that saved her life.

"Have you all eaten?" Nana Mama asked.

"We don't want to impose," Billie said. "Just stopped in to say hi, though I think John wants to talk with Alex."

Sampson nodded.

"Nonsense, you're family," Nana Mama said. "Ali, can you set three more places? We need to fatten Billie up a little."

"Can you make mine and Alex's to go?" Sampson asked, and he looked at Bree. "I want to tell Alex what's going on with my end of the Willingham case, and I might have something on the Maya Parker case that should be checked out sooner rather than later."

I smiled at Bree and said, "See? We're already on it."

CHAPTER

14

AS SOON AS SAMPSON AND I walked out the front door, he told me he'd spent much of the day canvassing the neighborhood around Harrison Charter High and looking for security-camera footage.

"Any luck?"

"A little," Sampson said, getting into his car. "And that's the problem."

I got in on the other side. As he pulled away, he explained, "Due to lightning, we have no operating cameras on the apartment building opposite the front of the school. I got solid footage from the security cameras on the bodega on the northeast corner across from the school, but—"

"Did you get it from Ronald Peters?"

"Yes, you know him?"

"Enough to say hello," I said. "I used to use his laundromat. Have you looked at it?"

"Yes, and I found nothing, but that's not the point," Sampson said impatiently, waving his hand at me. "The point is there were nine other cameras around the perimeter of the school, including our two CTs on the west side of the campus."

"The school faces east. So our traffic cams are behind the football field?"

"Correct. At the cross streets north and south."

"Okay."

"Both our cameras were shot out an hour before the crime," Sampson said. "The other cameras facing the campus were all small, personal-surveillance types with strong lenses, and those lenses were smeared with Vaseline before our cameras were shot out."

"This is not some junkie, then."

"And this was not a rip-and-run deal gone bad, Alex. This was cold-blooded murder."

I thought of my son Ali and wondered at his instincts. "By one or more professionals," I said. "How did they miss the bodega cameras?"

"I almost missed them," he said, smiling. "They're painted white, like the building, every-thing but the lenses." He slowed, pulled over, and parked on a street of row houses in DC a mile from my home.

"What are we doing?" I asked.

"Maya Parker went to Bragg High, but she had friends all over Southeast through her community-service work. One of them lives here. Her name is Dee Nathaniel. She evidently told someone that there was a creep after Maya in the weeks before she disappeared."

He took us to a brick building badly in need of repointing and knocked on the door. A tall, strikingly attractive African-American woman in her early forties answered the door on a chain. She was wearing a navy business suit and no shoes.

We identified ourselves and said we were hoping to talk to Dee Nathaniel.

"I'm her mother, Gina," the woman said, concerned. "What's this about? She hasn't done a thing wrong, not that girl. She's a straight arrow."

"Yes, ma'am," I said. "But we heard she was a friend of Maya Parker."

Gina Nathaniel's face fell. "She was. That hit my baby and me very hard. We helped search for her for days."

"Would you mind if we spoke to her?" Sampson said. "It might help us."

Mrs. Nathaniel hesitated, then said, "We don't need an attorney, right?"

"We just want to talk," Sampson said, holding up his hands. "If Dee's a straight arrow, I can't imagine she has anything to say that requires a lawyer."

After a beat, she nodded. "But I'm listening in.

Come in. You'll have to excuse the minor mess, but I only just got home from work."

After shutting the front door behind us, she called for Dee up a flight of stairs and got no answer. She asked us to wait in the kitchen and went up the stairs to get her.

We walked down the hall and into the kitchen, where the morning's breakfast bowls were still in the sink. Two of them. Mother and daughter.

Dee came in a few moments later, a younger version of her mother, wearing shorts and a T-shirt. She walked with an awkward gait, her arms loose and swingy; her mother followed behind her. Dee looked at us uncertainly. "Mama said you want to talk about Maya?"

"That's right," I said and introduced myself and Sampson. "How did you two know each other? Through school? Bragg High?"

Dee shook her head. "I go to Stone Ridge."

Her mother said, "It's a Catholic school in Potomac."

"We know it," Sampson said. "So where's the connection?"

"I knew Maya before, in middle school," Dee said. "We stayed friends even though she went to Bragg and Mom made me go to Stone Ridge."

"C'mon, Dee, do we have to go there?" her mother said.

Her daughter sighed. "No." She looked at us.

"It's not that bad except for the zero social life. You know, the things normal kids do?"

Gina Nathaniel rolled her eyes. "It's not like I keep her in a cage, Detectives. I let you go to the Bragg spring formal with Maya and her friends, didn't I?"

Dee shrugged and nodded glumly. "That was the last time I saw Maya alive."

"When was that?"

"March twenty-seventh? It was a Friday."

"They had a limo that I helped pay for," Mrs. Nathaniel said.

Dee described the evening as fun except for the limo driver, who she said was creepy. There was a roll-up window between him and the kids. They asked him to keep it up, but he kept cracking it to look at the girls and make comments.

"Especially to Maya," Dee said.

Sampson did not react, but he wagged his pinkie finger, a signal we used during interviews when someone tells us something we did not know before.

"Do you know the name of that limo service?" I asked.

"No," Dee said. "But the driver's name was Charley. We joked about him, called him Creepy Chuck."

"You didn't tell me that," her mother said. "But I think I have a card from the limo service somewhere."

She went to a drawer and began rummaging around. She returned with a card for Capital City Limo, which I took a photograph of. Sampson took the business card and left the room.

I asked Dee, "And that was the last time you saw Maya? In the limo?"

"When they dropped her off here," her mother said. "Right?"

Dee nodded, tears welling in her eyes. "Maya didn't deserve it. She was one of the good ones, you know?"

"Your mother said you were part of the search for her," Sampson said.

"Everyone was part of it after Randall Christopher got involved."

Her mother shook her head. "It's a damn shame a fine man gets shot to death like that. We knew him. I mean, he was the one who assigned us our search areas and we reported back to him."

"We didn't find a thing," Dee said, growing angry. "That's why I wished me and Maya had done that TFT course. If she had been trained, that guy would be dead, and she'd be alive." Dee explained that Maya had told her she wanted to take a self-defense course called Target-Focused Training taught by a former hand-to-hand combat instructor for the Navy SEALs.

"They teach you targets on the body that can incapacitate someone," Dee said. "Like their eyes or kneecaps or groin or the side of the neck, and you learn to see them and to hit them. Lots of girls and women have used it successfully."

Mrs. Nathaniel said, "It also cost more than two thousand dollars."

Dee gritted her teeth. "That's exactly what Maya's mother said, Mom."

CHAPTER
15

OUTSIDE THE NATHANIELS' HOUSE, AS Sampson and I were walking to the car, I said, "Home?"

Sampson shook his head. "Good as that sounds, I called Capital City when I left the room. Turns out Creepy Chuck's name is Charles Kendrick, and Mr. Kendrick has a sheet. Ex-con. And he's done with his shift in twenty minutes."

We sped back through the city and were at Capital City's location off New York Avenue in Northeast DC with five minutes to spare. The night manager said, "What's Charley done? We took a chance on him and I need to know."

"Nothing that we know of," I said. "We just want to have a chat with him about one of his rides."

A limo came into the garage and parked. "That's Charley," the manager said. "Have at him."

We walked toward the limo as Charley

Kendrick, a long, lanky white guy with a hawkish nose, flecks of gray at his temples, and an ill-fitting dark suit, got out. He saw us immediately, studied us, and his expression toughened.

"Whoever you are, I know for a fact you have no reason to be here," he said.

We held up our identifications. I said, "We want to talk about Maya Parker."

Kendrick looked puzzled. "Who?"

"The girl murdered and dumped in the Potomac about four months ago," Sampson said. "She was one of your rides the week before."

"Hey, hey," he said, holding up both palms. "I have no idea who you are talking about. I don't read newspapers. I don't listen to the news. My counselor told me to lose all media and social media contact for a year, said it would be better for my head. It's the truth. Call her."

I held out my phone and showed him a photograph Dee Nathaniel had given us from the night of the formal with all the girls dressed up in the limo. I blew up Maya's face. "Recognize her now? Her friend said you took the picture."

Kendrick got out reading glasses, studied it, and smiled. "I remember her now. The whole bunch of them. Little hellions!" Then he sobered. "You said she's dead?"

"She is," Sampson said. "And her friend said you were being creepy the night you drove them all to the dance. Lowering the window to spy on them, especially Maya."

"More likely I was making sure they weren't blowing dope or anything harder back there," Kendrick said. "Company policy."

"What did you do time for, Charley?"

He took a deep breath, closed his eyes, and said, "Embezzlement from a nursing home. I have no history whatsoever of violent crime and I'm hardly the sort to obsess over a teenage girl."

"So what sort are you?" I said.

"The gay and cross-dressing sort," Kendrick said, raising his eyebrows and pursing his lips. "Honestly, I was simply admiring Maya's dress and hairdo that night. Nothing more. When did she disappear?"

"April fourth," Sampson said. "Eight days after you drove her."

He got out a phone, said, "When? Night? Day?"

"She was last seen around six thirty in the evening," I said.

Kendrick thumbed the phone, looked up, and smiled. "What I thought. I was gone that entire day and the two days after, a three-day gig in New York City driving for the Landreys, a nice, rich old couple from Georgetown who wanted to see if a limo was more fun than the train. Go ask Marty, my boss. He can confirm it."

CHAPTER

16

I DIDN'T SLEEP WELL; I had terrible dreams about Maya Parker and then Kay Willingham. In one, Kay was walking away from me, in and out of fog and mist. Occasionally she'd look over her shoulder or make a half turn and beckon me closer.

But every time I took a step her way, even when I ran toward her, I could not close the distance between us. She'd fade away, wrapped in the fog, and I'd start calling her name, waking myself up.

At ten minutes to five, I was groggy but awake for good. Bree appeared deep in the land of Nod. I eased out of bed, got on my running gear, then slipped from the room, went down the stairs, and walked out onto the front porch.

The air was thick; it was in the seventies, even at that early hour. I did some ballistic stretches

Jannie had taught me, then set out at a slow jog that soon quickened into a nice steady pace. Ordinarily, running is a time for me to work my body and empty my mind. But I couldn't empty my mind that morning. Kay Willingham kept barging in. So did Randall Christopher.

When had they met? And how? And where was Christopher's wife? Did she kill her husband and his lover in a jealous rage?

Though I'd spoken to the principal five or six times over the years, I'd mostly seen him from a distance, heard him speak at parent-teacher events and whatnot.

Christopher was strikingly handsome, and at six foot two and weighing about one ninety, he was still built like the basketball guard he'd been at the University of Maryland. And yet the physique and good looks weren't what I remembered about him. It was his palpable charisma, the sense you got the moment he opened his mouth that you were about to hear something both challenging and profound. He was smart without being a show-off, compassionate with the students, and naturally funny.

And he wasn't afraid to be of service to the community, just as he had been during the early days of both the Parker and Hernandez disappearances, volunteering to help us organize the big civilian searches. I considered the possibility that he was involved in the rapes and killings because serial killers have been known to try to insert themselves into investigations.

Could Christopher have been involved? Were he and Kay killed for it?

I could not see it, at least not based on the evidence at hand, but I decided not to close the door on the possibility, unlikely as it was, that Kay had been wrong about Christopher, that her legendary instincts about political talent were off the mark.

The fact of the matter was that the principal had made concrete improvements in his students' lives. I'd seen how much Jannie and her classmates had grown as people in his school. That had to have made Christopher attractive.

Was it what made him attractive to Kay?

Of course it was. His infidelity with her aside, on paper Christopher was just the kind of project Kay liked to take on: a political diamond in the rough that needed to be cut and polished so it would gleam brilliantly.

After all, didn't she do that for her ex-husband? I thought as I ran up the sidewalk toward St. Anthony's. I meant to head home. But when I came abreast of the church, I felt compelled to stop and go inside.

With a good forty minutes until morning Mass, the church was empty. I crossed to the rack of devotional candles and fished around in my back pocket for the five-dollar bill I always stuck in there in case I wanted to stop for water during my run. I slid it into the box, took a long stick match, and lit two candles, one for Christopher and the other for Kay. As the flame on her candle began to dance, I remembered watching the news after coming home from the Capital City Limo garage the evening before and feeling horrible at the way some in the media were treating her.

Alive, Kay had had most journalists in Washington eating out of her hand, but now they were tearing her to shreds. The rumor mills had been grinding out nonsense, filling the airwaves with snark and innuendo that smeared both victims' reputations, but especially Kay's. The socialite, it was suggested, had had a wild side before and after her marriage to the vice president. Kay allegedly had a series of torrid affairs over the years and at one time or another she'd been linked romantically to a wealthy Wall Street investor, an actor young enough to be her son, and an editor at the *Post*.

But thank God, not to me.

How long will that last? How long before Clive Sparkman gets into this mix and decides to sling some mud my way?

CHAPTER

17

I STOOD THERE LOOKING AT the candles, then I closed my eyes and tried to tune it all out for a moment, tried to see the Kay Willingham I'd known.

Her husband at the time, J. Walter Willingham, had been the governor of Alabama when I first met her at a charity function for victims' rights nearly a decade ago, well before Bree came into my life. That was the same night I'd driven her home and she'd broken her heel and tripped.

After that there'd been no contact for almost two months. Then she called me and asked me to meet her for lunch at a restaurant in DC; she said she had a personal request. She wasn't the kind of woman you turned down, so I agreed.

At that lunch, Kay asked me to look into the conviction of a killer on death row in Alabama who had written her asking for help.

"Most people like you would push a request like that to the corner of the desk or drop it in the trash," I said after she set a bulging legal-size envelope in front of me.

"I'm not most people, Alex. I actually care about wrongfully convicted prisoners. And it's not because of the privileged life I've led. If I see an injustice, I try to right it."

I studied her. She was so much more than beauty, poise, and wealth. "Okay, I'll take a look at this, see if there's anything I can do."

"Thank you, Alex," she said. "I can't tell you what this means to me."

Her smile was dazzling and pure. Her eyes sparkled with empathy.

I swallowed hard, looked away, and gestured at the envelope. "What makes you so interested in this case? These usually go to the governor."

Her smile faded. "Before we married, Walter was the prosecutor on this case. It was the one that helped launch his political career."

"And you're questioning the conviction?"

"No, I just want there to be zero doubt going forward. Between you and me, Walter is thinking of running for national office, and despite our current difficulties, I want no skeletons in his closet, no stone unturned before he launches his next campaign."

Standing there in the church, I opened my eyes, remembering how I'd looked at the case only briefly because, with Nana Mama's help, I was caring for three young children. I couldn't run off to Alabama to learn more, so three days after she offered me the job, I turned it down. She'd accepted my decision gracefully when I explained about the kids.

My attention drifted from Kay's candle burning in the church to Christopher's.

Maybe he was the one, I mused. *Maybe he was the love she'd been looking for.*

I'd no sooner had that thought than a ball of emotion swelled in my throat. I tried to stay in control, tried to swallow it back down deep in my gut.

But the enormous, irrational grief I felt for Kay and the weird jealousy I felt about Randall Christopher was too much. I felt a tear roll down my cheek for everything that had been lost when someone put multiple bullets through both of their hearts.

CHAPTER
18

I RAN UP OUR PORCH steps ten minutes later, drenched in sweat but feeling lighter for having visited the church and expressed those conflicting emotions. Inside the house, the air-conditioning made me shiver. I went into the kitchen to find Bree and Jannie cooking breakfast, Ali sitting at the counter typing on his laptop.

"Where's Nana?" I said.

"Feeling under the weather," Bree said, scooping scrambled eggs into a dish. "She wanted to sleep in."

"Fever?"

"Just tired and listening to her body," Jannie said. "Isn't that what you told me to do when I had mono?"

"I did."

Bree scooted past me, bringing the eggs to the table.

"What, no kiss?" I said.

"The way you smell?"

"I'm not that bad."

"Yes, you are," Ali said, waving his hand in front of his nose.

I threw my arms up in defeat. "Save me some."

Upstairs, as I showered and shaved, I felt slightly rudderless, not quite knowing what move to make next. While I dressed, I decided to call Mahoney, and I was about to do that when Bree walked into the room.

I went to hug her, and she pulled back slightly to study my face. "Why were you out running so early?"

"Couldn't sleep and I figured a run would help me understand why. Turns out I needed to purge something."

She smiled quizzically. "You want to explain—" Her work cell rang. "Duty calls," she said; she turned away from me and snatched her phone off the bed. She looked at caller ID and groaned. "It's Commissioner Dennison." She pecked me on the cheek as I left the bedroom, then answered the phone while shutting the door. "Yes, Commissioner. How can I help?"

In the hall, I almost knocked on Nana Mama's door, but if she needed rest, she needed rest. Downstairs, Jannie was on her way out of the house with her workout bag over her shoulder.

"Training?" I asked.

"Core and agility."

"Have fun."

"Always."

I gave her a hug and watched her go. My daughter was tall, strong but not bulky, and very, very fast. According to the many NCAA track coaches who had tried to recruit her, Jannie possessed athletic skills that had made her a top prospect as a four-hundred-meter runner and a potential heptathlete.

I went into the kitchen and found the plate Bree had set aside for me wrapped in foil. My phone rang before I could take a bite. Mahoney. I snatched a piece of bacon to munch on before I answered. "Ned?"

"You still have your security clearance?"

"Yes."

"We've been granted an audience with Vice President Willingham on Thursday."

"*We?* As in me too?"

"He specifically asked that you be there."

"The vice president did?"

"As I understand it. He wants Sampson too, since he was first on the scene."

"What time?"

"Eight a.m. sharp. His residence. One Observatory Circle. Bring two forms of ID to show the Marines."

Bree walked into the kitchen, still on the

phone. "Dr. Cross is on the Maya Parker case as well as the Willingham case, sir. I don't think I can…yes, Commissioner Dennison. I hear you loud and clear."

"I'll call you back, Ned," I said and hung up.

Bree hung up as well, then looked at me, perplexed. "He drives me nuts with this micromanaging stuff. You have to help me out here one more time, Alex."

"I just agreed to work the Parker and Hernandez case for you," I said.

"I know," she said, holding up one hand. "Just go talk to this guy at some point today. He's a big-time tobacco and food-additive lobbyist. He was shot in the ass with a twenty-two last night outside a restaurant in Georgetown."

"Shot in the ass?"

"You heard me," she said. "And someone spray-painted *Shoot the Rich* on the wall of the alley that the shooter likely fired from."

"Okay?"

She sighed. "Two other wealthy people have been shot at in DC in the last month. The shooter missed both times, breaking things right next to them, but the same *Shoot the Rich* graffiti tag was present."

"I didn't hear about the graffiti tag."

"We've been trying to keep it quiet," she said. "But he hit this lobbyist guy. And the lobbyist guy is a friend of Commissioner Dennison somehow. It could get some of his heat off my back if you go."

"I promise I'll try to get to him at some point today," I said. "I have a noon client here. And Ned wants me on Kay's case, and Sampson and I wanted—"

"Kay's case?"

"You know what I mean."

"You don't see it, do you? This lobbyist wounded? Two others shot at? *Shoot the Rich*? What if it's the same shooter who killed Kay and Christopher?"

"No graffiti tag that I know of."

"Just the same."

I blinked, said, "I think I'll go visit that lobbyist before my noon appointment."

CHAPTER
19

AN HOUR LATER, JOHN SAMPSON and I were riding an elevator in the Watergate complex. He yawned.

"Didn't sleep well?" I asked.

"I stayed up looking at the video from the bodega's security cameras again," he said and shook his head. "Nothing that I can see that's relevant, and I scrolled through it for hours."

"Because the killer or killers came from the west," I said as the elevator doors opened with a ding. We stepped out into a small round foyer as a door on the opposite side was opened by a maid.

She led us into a stunning penthouse condo with a huge living area and floor-to-ceiling windows that offered sweeping views of the Potomac River and Northern Virginia.

We found the owner in front of the windows, but he wasn't enjoying the scenery. Phil Peggliazo was facedown on a massage table, covered by sheets and moaning as a concierge doctor and a nurse tended to a series of monitors and IVs hooked up to him.

"Can you boot up the drugs, Doc?" Peggliazo said.

The doctor stopped scribbling on an e-tablet. "Can't do that for another hour."

"My ass is on fire here," the lobbyist complained.

A polished blonde in her forties came into the room, filing her nails with an emery board.

"Phil, you're being a child," she said in a soft Texas drawl. "The ER doctors told you it's a miracle that the bullet missed all major organs. Be thankful."

"My ass is a major organ, Priscilla Mae," he grumbled.

"No, it's not," she said. She looked at the nurse and the doctor. "Right?"

"Right," the nurse said.

The doctor nodded. "A set of gluteal muscles does not constitute an organ."

"I may never take a dump sitting down again," Peggliazo whined.

Priscilla Mae rolled her eyes. "My daddy says you should be grateful that bullet didn't go right through your ass and into your gut."

She seemed to notice us just as Peggliazo said, "Your daddy can kiss my—"

"That's enough, Phil," she said sharply. "We've got visitors with badges. I told you Vanessa Dennison would come through."

A bear of a man with a blocky head, a full mane of silver hair, and two days' growth of beard, Peggliazo propped himself up on his elbows on the massage table and twisted around to peer at us.

"About time someone showed up. You catch him yet?"

"No, sir," Sampson said. "We just wanted to ask you some questions."

"I'm gonna spend my life facedown with a blowtorch coring out both cheeks," he said. "That should answer most of your questions."

"Phil!" his wife said, then looked at us. "I'm so sorry. He's not himself. They've got him on drugs."

"Not enough drugs!" he shouted before settling back onto the massage table, face in the ring. "You want to ask me questions, you come around here and lie on the floor so I can see you."

"They're detectives, for Christ's sake. They're not lying on the floor. All last night you kept saying, 'How come no one's come to get my statement? Call Vanessa.' I did. So here they are."

"And here I am, Priscilla!" he roared. "Unable to sit up for their questions!"

I said, "It's okay, Mrs. Peggliazo, we can lie on our backs to talk to him."

"See there?" Peggliazo said as we walked to the head of the massage table and started to get down on the floor. "These people are willing to cooperate."

"Who's not cooperating?" his wife asked.

"Mirror, mirror on the wall," he said.

"I'm glad you got shot," she said. "But I can't believe the bullet missed your head. I mean, it had to have been up your ass like it always is." She stormed out.

Peggliazo was chuckling when Sampson and I rolled over on our backs and looked up at the wounded lobbyist's face.

"That was a good one," he said. "Can't believe he missed my head, she says! She's good. Tough but good. Like Kate, you know, in *Taming of the Shrew*."

"I'm not touching that one," I said. "Tell us what happened."

"I'm seeing you upside down."

"It's either that or the side," Sampson said.

He grimaced, then said, "I'm telling you, neither of you has ever had a pain in the ass like this pain in the ass. Unless you've been shot there?"

"No, sir," I said. "I haven't had that pleasure. Tell us what happened."

The lobbyist said he'd been saying goodbye

to his guests outside Argento, an upscale Italian restaurant off Prospect Street, when he was hit.

"Never heard the shot, but I went down like *boom*," he said. "Felt like fire and then both of my legs were funny-boned, you know?"

"Any idea who'd want to shoot you?"

"Other than cigarette- and Dorito-haters, I can't think of anyone offhand."

Sampson said, "So you've gotten threats before?"

He chuckled again. "With predictable regularity. They've threatened to put enough nicotine in me to stop my heart while stuffing me with enough preservatives and food additives to damage my brain."

"But no specific threats about shooting you?"

"Creative haters. What can I say?"

Before we could answer, he winced again, said, "Doc? How much more time?"

"Fifty minutes."

"Aw, c'mon. I'm having a lava eruption back there."

I started getting up and motioned for Sampson to do the same.

"Hey," Peggliazo said. "Where you going?"

"To try to find whoever shot you in the ass," Sampson said.

CHAPTER

20

TRAFFIC WAS SNARLED DOWNTOWN AND I made it back with just ten minutes to spare before my noon appointment. In addition to my law enforcement consulting, I tried to maintain a small client base in my private psychotherapy practice because the work gave me much fulfillment.

That day, however, I felt harried and on the verge of being overwhelmed by the three hot cases on my plate. But I was, if anything, a professional, and even though the client I was about to see was connected to one of the cases, I needed to shift into a completely different way of thinking. I pulled out Analisa Hernandez's file and almost immediately felt my mindset change from detective to healer.

A knock came at the basement door about five minutes later. I left my office, opened the door, and found a Hispanic woman in her forties who had been seeing me on and off for a while now smiling at me.

"Dr. Cross!" she cried as she hurried in. "I miss you!"

I grinned. I never knew what I was going to get when Analisa showed up for counseling. One day she could be bubbly like this and the next distraught, so I was happy when she walked into my office with a big smile on her face after she'd spent six months working in Guatemala.

When I shut the door to my office, she sat down on the edge of her chair, smiling eagerly, and said, "So how are you?"

"In demand," I said.

"I hear this, yes," she said. "Tell me about Maya Parker."

"You heard?"

"Even in Guatemala there is internet," she said, her smile fading. "It's him, yes, the same one who killed my Elizabeth?"

I nodded. "We think so."

"Where did she go to school, Maya?"

"Bragg," I said.

"And Elizabeth was at Anacostia. But all of them from Southeast."

"All eight."

She looked away from me, her hand going to her lips, and her right knee began to jiggle nervously, signs I'd seen before when her mood was becoming darker. "Did he make a mistake this time?"

"If he has, we haven't found it yet."

She shook her head, then pounded her fist gently on her thigh. "How can this be? I ask myself. How can he be so much like the ghost?"

"We believe he prepares extensively," I said.

"Prepares," she said and tears began to dribble down her cheeks. "What makes this kind of monster, Dr. Cross?"

We'd had this discussion several times, but I indulged her. "Probably a lot of things," I said. "One damaging incident after another, probably as a young child and in puberty, possibly involving abuse by a female about Elizabeth's age. That abuse festered in his brain until the brain was literally changed. The chemicals, the wiring, it's different for these kinds of men."

"Not human. A predator," she said, staring off into space.

I handed her a box of tissues. She took one, smiled weakly, and said, "Elizabeth would have been twenty soon. Maybe she would have given me grandchildren. And maybe I'd be happy at least some of the time." She wiped her eyes and then blew her nose.

"You've told me you are happy in the work you do in Guatemala," I said.

"This is true," she said grudgingly. "I like working with girls that age, Elizabeth's age. They never listen to their mother, but I am like their aunt."

"They listen to *you*."

"They do," she said, smiling outwardly again.

"Then the meaning you're giving Elizabeth's death is different than before. She's the reason you can talk to those girls. You know that, don't you?"

Analisa nodded and then burst into tears again. "Every day, I feel Elizabeth with me when I am teaching those girls. Every day, she works through my heart to reach them."

I said nothing for a moment, then smiled and said, "I can't imagine a more wonderful legacy and meaning for Elizabeth's life."

She sighed and looked at the ceiling before taking another tissue. "I know you are right, Dr. Cross. But I still have anger in my heart. And I still want you to catch him before he can do this to any more girls."

"Maybe you can help with that," I said. "Randall Christopher?"

Analisa's face fell and she made the sign of the cross. "That poor man. I know he cheated on his wife, but I believe he was a good man."

"He organized the searches for Elizabeth and Maya Parker."

"Yes. I did not know about Maya. Her parents?"

"Her parents are devastated. They moved to Florida to get away from here."

"I don't blame them."

"But refresh my memory," I said. "How did it work? The search for Elizabeth?"

Analisa thought about that. "Well, the police, Metro, they searched first. But Randall thought it was not enough and he knew how to get everyone involved."

"He was a great organizer," I said. "But why Christopher's interest?"

"Well, I suppose because he'd known Elizabeth since she was a girl."

"Really? How's that?"

"When he started the charter school, it was in a building I used to clean at night. After my husband left, I used to bring Elizabeth there to study while I got my work done. Like I said, a good man."

Analisa left soon after and I was back in my office writing up my notes on our session when my cell phone rang, a call from a number I recognized. "Rawlins?"

"She made a mistake," said Keith Karl Rawlins, who employed his formidable skills as a computer scientist consultant to the cybercrimes division of the FBI. He had the odd habit of assuming you'd already heard the story he'd been telling himself in his head.

"Who made a mistake?" I said.

"Elaine Paulson," he said. "Randall Christopher's missing wife."

CHAPTER
21

THREE HOURS LATER, AS DARK clouds were rolling in and the breeze was stiffening, Sampson, Mahoney, and I stood at the front door of a little bungalow on Chincoteague Island in eastern Maryland. Mahoney rapped hard.

Keith Rawlins had tracked Elaine Paulson, Christopher's wife, to this bungalow through the IP address assigned to the router here. She'd signed on for barely ten minutes, but Rawlins had picked her up and traced her in less than seven.

No one answered the door. Mahoney had a search warrant with him and he was starting to pick the lock when a locomotive of a woman in pink Bermuda shorts and a sleeveless white blouse shouted at us from across the street that she was calling the police.

When we told her we were the police, she

relaxed and became cooperative. Her name was Adele Penny, and it turned out she was the bungalow's owner.

"What's she done?" she asked when we told her who we were looking for.

"We just want to talk to her," Mahoney said.

"What about? Her marriage?"

"What about her marriage?" I said.

"She said it was over. Ended badly. That's why she's out here, taking time to figure things out."

"You don't know anything about her?"

"No. And I didn't ask."

"Why is that?"

"She said her husband beat her, and she paid cash."

Showing her the search warrant, Mahoney said, "We need you to open the door. When did you last see her?"

"An hour ago. What is this about?" Mrs. Penny said, rattled. She unlocked the door and pushed it open.

"A murder investigation," Sampson said, stepping past her.

"No," she gasped. "My God. She's so…murder?"

"Any idea where she might have gone?" I asked her as Mahoney went inside.

"I don't know for sure. But she's been going to the spit off Toms Cove in the afternoon, sitting on the dunes, watching the waves. She said it's been calming."

"Alex!" Sampson called.

"Excuse me," I said and I went inside to a tiny and tidy living area with a wicker love seat and a chair. Sampson and Mahoney were putting on latex gloves at the counter that separated the living area from the little kitchen.

"There's a sealed envelope here," Sampson said. "Addressed to the daughters."

"Open it," I said, already feeling queasy at what it might contain.

Mahoney slit it open with a knife, pulled out a single piece of paper, and unfolded it. I looked over his shoulder and read *Dear Tina and Rachel, I love you more than life itself. I'm sorry that it has come to this. I'm sorry about all of it...*

I didn't need to see the rest. "She's going to kill herself."

It was all I could think of as we raced in Mahoney's car down the narrow road toward Toms Cove, ignoring the traffic trying to leave the area ahead of the coming storm.

The cove itself was west of the dunes that separated it from the National Seashore. We pulled into a parking area at the visitors' center and spotted the blue Nissan Sentra with Pennsylvania plates that Mrs. Penny said Elaine Paulson was driving.

Against a stream of people heading the other way, we walked toward the dunes and the ocean, the wind building and thunder rumbling behind us.

Big waves were crashing up and down the beach. To the north, the shore was wider, with extensive dunes behind it. To the south, the sand narrowed to a long spit with barely a necklace of dunes separating it from the cove.

While the beach was largely devoid of swimmers and vacationers now, there was still a smattering of hard-core fishermen and surfers. We split up; Sampson and Mahoney headed for the spit, which seemed the more deserted place, and I ran toward a cluster of fishermen, older men with an elaborate array of surf-casting rods and pails of bait. I showed them a picture of Elaine Paulson and asked if they'd seen her, but they shook their heads and said they'd only just arrived.

I went up the beach several hundred yards, seeing fewer and fewer people ahead of me; the dunes appeared empty. When the wind started to throw grains of sand that stung my cheeks, I turned my back to it and debated whether to leave.

That's when I realized that, looking south, I had a much different perspective on the beach. A few seconds later I spotted Elaine Paulson sitting in the seagrass about three-quarters of the way up the flank of a dune back toward the parking lot. I had walked right by her because it looked like she'd sat down and tucked herself into the dune.

Or she died in that position, I thought as I cut hard and fast due west into the dunes and then hooked south. Creeping up the north side of the dune where I'd last seen her, I kept peering ahead through the waving seagrass.

I was almost to the crest before I spotted her through the grass around the front of the dune, about thirty feet ahead. She was turned slightly away from me, directly facing the water. She had a green windbreaker on, hood up, and was sitting in a kind of depression in the dune, her spine to the wall of sand and grass behind her.

No wonder I missed her on my first pass, I thought, watching her as I crouched and moved closer. *She blends right in.*

My attention was fixed on her hood, which hadn't moved. Was she sitting there or was she slumped there?

I'd no sooner had that thought than her shoulders began to tremble. She pulled back the hood with her right hand and, with her left, pressed a nickel-plated revolver tight to her temple.

CHAPTER

22

I TOOK TWO LONG STRIDES toward her, threw myself to my knees well within her line of sight, hands up, and shouted over the wind, "Think of Tina and Rachel!"

Whether it was my sudden appearance or my bellowed reference to her daughters, the late Randall Christopher's wife startled and pulled the gun two inches away from her temple. I could see she'd been sobbing and was not seeing me well; she was still clearly in the waking trance that people intent on killing themselves get into.

"Please put the gun down, Elaine," I said. "Please. My daughter knows Tina and Rachel. They're schoolmates."

That further interrupted her suicidal spell. She squinted at me as her hand relaxed. The angle of the revolver's muzzle shifted clear of her skull, but it lingered about four inches above her left shoulder.

"Who are you?" she asked.

"Jannie Cross's father," I said. "My name is Alex."

Her jaw quivered as the handgun's muzzle angled back toward her head. "I know who you are, Dr. Cross. I know why you're here."

"Right now I'm just a father to a young lady who adores your daughters. And I don't want to see Tina and Rachel exposed to any more pain than they're already feeling at the death of their father."

"And his older whore," she said bitterly. "His older socialite whore."

Christopher's widow had the gun pressed back against her temple again. She gazed my way with watery, bloodshot, and soft-focused eyes.

"No matter what I do or say now, I've seen how this machine works," she said, a quiver in her voice. "They won't see me as a victim. They'll crucify me, sacrifice me because of who she was. They'll throw me in a hole and I'll rot, and my babies will have to suffer every day for as long as I'm alive. It's better to save them the longer-term pain."

It is remarkable what people in deep turmoil will tell you if you truly listen to what they are saying. More often than not, they will spill some of the pattern of repeated dark words, thoughts, and fantasies that have been spiraling in their heads so relentlessly, so furiously, that they have entered a trance that has eliminated all other thoughts. If the spiral continues without break, they will essentially talk themselves to the point where the pain of dying seems less than the pain of living.

That's how suicide works.

Her unfocused gaze had traveled by me and out toward the crashing waves and the sea beyond; she was back in her trance again. "They'll pin it on me. The spurned wife."

I sensed the muscles in her forearm start to tense.

"Elaine, Elaine, look at me!" I shouted, trying to break the trance. "I promise you, I am not part of any machine except justice. I promise you that I have no bias or interest in throwing you in a hole. No interest in making you rot there just to clear a case. All I'm interested in is seeing you in your daughters' loving arms again."

For a long moment, Christopher's wife stayed with the gun against her head, dwelling on the ocean. Then raindrops began to fall.

"Believe me, Elaine," I said. "If you know who I am and what I do, I am going to hear whatever you have to say without prejudice or filter. Do you understand?"

I could see the struggle in her face as the repetitive thoughts and emotions of the suicidal trance fought against this new story I was telling her. And then it came to me. Suddenly, I understood a part of the death spiral that she hadn't yet revealed. And even though the first cut would be cruel, I used it against her.

"I know Randall didn't want your love anymore and that made you feel destroyed inside, as if you'd never love or be loved like that again. But that is not true, Elaine. You are loved."

She shook her head, her lower lip trembling. "No."

"I can prove it to you," I said. "I've seen the picture of you with the twins the day they left for camp. My wife did too. She said the love you have for them and the love they have for you is so powerful, it just radiates right out of the picture. I agree, Elaine. Do you see the beauty in that? In that picture, part of your heart has been broken and yet you are blooming with love for Tina and Rachel and they're blooming with love for you. Do you really want to end something so beautiful?"

Her shoulders began to shake.

"Please, Elaine," I said. "Put the gun down for Tina and for Rachel or they'll never know that kind of unconditional love again, their mother's beautiful love again, your beautiful, limitless love again."

That broke her.

Christopher's widow burst into gulping sobs

and let go of the gun, which fell in the sand. I scrambled forward and snatched it up even as she said, weeping, "He didn't care about me or the girls or anyone anymore. All he wanted was Kay."

CHAPTER

23

THE RAIN CAME IN A patter that surged to a downpour after we'd put Elaine Paulson in the back seat of the car and Sampson started the drive back.

"Am I under arrest?" she said when Mahoney put handcuffs on her wrists.

"In federal custody," Mahoney said. "Pending interrogation."

"And psychological evaluation," I said. "And weapon testing."

"Why?" she said, looking at the rain splattering against the windshield.

I studied her, wondering about her mental state and her guilt or innocence. I said, "After your husband and Mrs. Willingham were murdered with a thirty-eight-caliber pistol, you ran, hid from law enforcement, and were at the brink of killing yourself with a thirty-eight-caliber pistol, Elaine. That's why."

"Don't you have to read me my rights?" she asked, still not meeting our eyes.

Mahoney nodded and read them to her. "Do you understand your rights?"

Elaine nodded dully. "I do. I'm going to remain silent now because that's what they always say to do." She snorted with rancor. "Even Randall always said it. You talk to a lawyer first."

As the rain drummed on the roof, she raised her head and looked at each of us in turn before shutting her ravaged eyes and sleeping the rest of the way back to DC. She woke up when we pulled into the hospital parking lot.

"What's this?" she asked.

"Elaine, we're taking you in for evaluation, remember?"

"No. Can I leave? I mean, sign myself out?"

"No, ma'am," Mahoney said, glancing at me. "You're still in federal custody."

"Oh. Have you read me my rights?"

"We have."

"Then I want a lawyer before I go in the mental ward," she said. "I know what they do to people in mental wards. Dope me up so I'll waive my rights and talk to you."

"Elaine," I said calmly. "For your own safety, you are here for medical care by fine doctors. And a public defender will come talk to you in the morning."

"How do I know you're not lying to me?" she

said, growing agitated and shrinking away when Sampson came around and opened her door.

"You don't know, Elaine," I said, gazing into her eyes. "You have to trust me. Like I said on the beach, I'm just trying to get you back to your daughters."

That got her more wound up. "Where are they? Can I see them?"

"In a few days, I'm sure," I said.

Elaine looked at me, tears welling in her eyes. "I want to see them now."

"I know you do. But unless you cooperate here, it could be weeks before you do."

She got out then. We delivered her to the locked psych ward and left for our respective homes, all of us wondering about her guilt or innocence.

Bree wondered about it too as I ate leftovers and recounted my day.

"You said she was in and out of reality," she said.

"That's how it seemed to me," I agreed. "Which can be caused by all sorts of traumatic states, including killing your cheating husband and his girlfriend."

"The weapons test will tell us one way or the other."

"No doubt," I said, taking my dishes to the sink. "How's Nana Mama?"

"Better. She slept a lot, woke up, ate a lot, then went back to sleep."

After rinsing the dishes, I turned to find Bree about three feet away, studying me.

"Can you be honest with me about something?"

"Of course."

"You knew Kay Willingham before you knew me."

"Back when I was between the FBI and Metro, working freelance."

"Was it professional or personal?"

"She was an acquaintance and almost a client. I drove her home the night we met at a fund-raiser because her car service was late and she'd had too much to drink. I went inside her house."

"You went in her house?"

"She'd broken her heel as well as having too much to drink. She was alone."

"Alone?"

"And I wanted to make sure she was okay," I said, deciding to leave out the Kay-twirling-away-from-me part of the story. "I made sure and left. Two months later, she tried to hire me to investigate an old capital crimes case in Alabama. I declined."

"Why?"

"The kids needed me here," I said. "Nana Mama needed me here. It was no time to be going to Alabama for a month to look into the case of a killer her husband had helped convict and put on death row."

"Wait, what? J. Walter? How long ago was this case?"

"I can't remember. Before they were married."

"So you didn't have an affair with Kay Willingham before we met?"

I laughed. "No affair. I promise you."

Bree chewed on that for a moment, then gave me a grudging smile. "Want to go to bed? Snuggle a little?"

"I'd like that very much."

CHAPTER
24

BREE AND I WERE STILL snuggled up together the next morning and in a deep sleep when my phone rang.

"Don't answer it," Bree grumbled, holding tight to my arm, which was wrapped around her waist. "I want to stay here, just us, just a little while longer."

I ignored the ringing and hugged her tighter. The call went to voice mail, but ten seconds later my cell began to ring again.

Bree groaned.

"Life intervenes." I moaned, kissed her on the cheek, and sat up. It was Sampson calling.

I glanced at the clock and saw it was only six fifteen. "Kind of early, partner," I said.

I got no answer, just a choking sound.

"John?"

"I'm at the hospital," he managed to say in a thick voice. "Billie died ten minutes ago."

"What?" I said, feeling like I'd taken a bat to the gut. "No, John."

My best friend began to sob. "There was nothing they could do. They tried everything but they couldn't save her. She's gone, Alex."

Bree had heard the dismay in my voice and got up on her knees beside me. "What's happened?"

I muted the phone, tears welling in my eyes. "Billie died ten minutes ago."

The shock on her face was complete. She said nothing and started to weep.

I put the phone on speaker. John's anguish filled the room along with our own.

"John, I'm so sorry," Bree said. "My God, what happened?"

He sniffed and choked out, "The damage to her heart from Lyme disease. Her heart just gave out."

"Where are you?" I said. "You shouldn't be alone."

"I'm still with her," he said. "Prince George's Hospital ER."

"Where's Willow?"

"Asleep," he said. "She doesn't get up until seven. Please, Bree, can you go there? And can you not tell her?"

"I'm on my way," Bree said, jumping out of bed.

"I am coming to you, brother," I said, following her.

"Thank you, Alex. I don't know where to go or what I'm supposed to do. About anything."

We put the phone between us as we struggled into our clothes, listening to Sampson tell us that Billie had actually been feeling stronger the day before. She'd walked two miles in the morning and done some yoga in the late afternoon.

"We got up at five this morning, just like she wanted, and she didn't complain about anything. She took her pills, and we went out for our walk," Sampson said. "We were about a mile out, ready to turn around, and she'd been saying how grateful she was that she'd been given a second chance at…life. And I was holding her hand, thinking that we'd finally gotten beyond the Lyme disease, when she said she felt dizzy. I held her up. She looked at me, kind of scared, and she said she loved me and Willow, and Andrew and Kari, and the whole Cross family, and then she just collapsed in my arms."

He kept crying. "She knew, and all she wanted was to give us love before she left us."

Bree and I both had tears streaming down our faces as he described calling 911 and starting CPR on Billie. There was a fire station not far from where they were. The ambulance and EMTs were with her in minutes.

"They worked on her, and she opened her eyes, but they wouldn't focus," he said.

Billie made it to the ER but coded almost immediately.

"Her heart just gave out," he said again. "The Lyme disease did too much damage. The docs at the ER said there was nothing they could do."

Sampson sobbed harder. "How do I do this, Alex?"

"With help," I said, tying my shoes. "I will be there in fifteen minutes."

CHAPTER

25

AS I DROVE TO Prince George's Hospital, I had to fight off waves of grief that crashed over me. Billie Houston had been John Sampson's salvation, the one who set him free, the one who unlocked his heart.

John and I had been friends since the fifth grade. He was the first kid I met on the playground after Nana Mama brought me and my brothers north after my mother died.

Within weeks John was closer to me than my own brothers. We just seemed to understand and support each other reflexively.

But even after we'd known each other for almost three decades, there had been a big part of himself he kept closed off. He'd had a few girlfriends over the years, but the relationships had always ended badly.

He'd declared himself a confirmed bachelor

shortly before we started investigating the deaths of several men who'd fought in Vietnam. One of them was the late husband of Billie Houston.

Before Sampson met Billie Houston, there was Sampson the stoic, Sampson the warrior, Sampson the best friend and partner. But with Billie, it was like John grew in new dimensions, became a whole man, and he was the better for it, happy, confident, and hopelessly in love. I adored Billie for the changes I saw in him.

Which is why I had to keep wiping at my tears on the way to the hospital. If there'd ever been a fine and selfless person on this earth, it was Billie Houston Sampson. She'd been a U.S. Army nurse, then an ER trauma nurse. She'd been part of a helicopter medevac team, too, responding again and again to crises.

It did not seem right for her to die like this. It did not seem right at all.

I pulled into the hospital parking lot, and as I headed toward the ER, I kept thinking, *How do I comfort him? How do I give him the right support?*

A nurse, Juan Castro, waited for me outside the trauma room. He had tears in his eyes. "Billie took shifts here all the time. We loved her too, Dr. Cross, but we've got two gunshots on the way in. John has to leave her now, and I can't bear to tell him."

"I'll do it, Juan," I said. "And thanks for your kindness."

I went in and found Sampson sitting by the side of the bed, holding Billie's lifeless hand, his head bowed, crushed by the weight of his loss.

"John," I said.

He slowly raised his head, then turned to look at me. I saw ruin in his bloodshot eyes and knew his heart was shattered. I went over, put my arm on his shoulder, and looked at Billie's body. "You have to let her go for now, John. There are gunshot victims on the way, and they need the room."

Sampson sniffed hard and nodded. He rubbed her hand, so tiny in his big paw, then kissed the back of it and laid it over her heart. He got up, nodded to Billie, and let me put my hand under his elbow when he faltered as he walked toward the door.

Castro and two other nurses were standing outside.

"We'll take care of her, John," Castro said.

"Thank you, Juan, thanks to all of you," Sampson said, and he didn't look back as we walked away. "I need to be with Willow now. And call Andrew and Kari."

"I'll take you straight home," I said.

Outside, leaden clouds hung low above us, and it was already hotter than it should have been. Sampson kept it together until we reached my car. Then he collapsed over the roof and sobbed while I kept a hand on his back to let him know I was there.

Sampson stayed quiet for the first part of the drive. Finally he said, "I keep seeing her. You know, like, when I saw her the first time?"

"Tell me again," I said.

"I drove out to the Jersey shore on the Ellis Cooper case," he said. "Just wanted to talk to her about her late husband. It was two years after he'd been executed for a crime she said he didn't commit, and she was house-sitting this big place on the beach."

"I remember."

"I'd called ahead, and there she was waiting for me, and I don't know what I expected, but it wasn't her. Little bitty thing."

"What was she wearing?"

"Khaki shorts, T-shirt, and no shoes," he said, smiling. "She made me roll up my pants legs and take off my shoes to go for a walk on the beach." He laughed and shook his head. "I couldn't take my eyes off her because she was so beautiful and so tiny, like a doll, but strong, you know?"

"Fierce," I said.

"Yes."

Although I knew the answer, I asked, "When did you know you loved her?"

Sampson didn't reply for a few moments; his lower lip trembled as he looked into the middle distance and smiled sadly.

"In about an hour, I liked her," he said. "I liked her even more when she invited me to dinner that night. But I knew I loved her, head-over-heels love, when I went up there the second time, and she put on 'One Night with You' and we danced on the porch of that beach house. I could feel her every breath, her every heartbeat, like it was my own."

CHAPTER

26

THE REST OF THAT DARK day came at us in
waves.

Bree had been with Willow, Sampson and
Billie's seven-year-old daughter, since she woke
up. Bree came out on the porch, hugged John,
and told him how much she loved him and how
much she had loved Billie. Then we stayed on
the porch to give him space for the terrible deed
he had to do.

We sat quietly on the glider Billie had
had installed because she loved the one we
had on our front porch. We held hands and
tried not to anticipate the pain that was not
long coming. Willow's crying came in short,
sharp gasps, like the fabric of her heart was
ripping.

"Oh my God," Bree said. She leaned forward
and put her face in her hands.

I rubbed her back. "She's going to need you."

"I know," she said. "I'm wondering if I'm up to it."

"You have to be. We all have to be. They're family."

She got a tissue out and dabbed at her eyes before looking at me. "I adore you," she said. "Desperately. I want you to know."

I kissed her softly as Willow's crying died down. "I can feel it. I hope you can feel my love for you."

Bree nodded. "Always. And now I think we're needed inside."

She squeezed my hand, and we steeled ourselves to take as much of the burden as we could from Sampson. Bree brought Willow out to the porch and got on Billie's glider with her and held her close while John and I went into his home office.

Another wave of pain crashed around us when Sampson got hold of Billie's grown children to tell them their mother had died of a massive heart attack caused by the damage done to it by Lyme disease.

Andrew, an attorney in Boston, was dumbstruck. "I thought…she said she'd beaten it, John."

"We all thought she had, even the doctors. You heard them, Andrew," Sampson said. "We were going for a walk this morning and she collapsed in my arms, but not before telling me how much she loved you and Kari."

Andrew choked up and then cried, "I can't believe this. I mean, why Mom? She had so much left to give."

His younger sister, Kari, had much the same reaction when Sampson reached her at the advertising agency she worked at in New York. She screamed, sobbed, and then demanded to know what had happened.

Sampson was a rock for them, answering every question, then he asked them to come to Washington to help prepare for their mom's funeral. They said they'd come as soon as possible.

Sampson, drained by those two calls, went off to be with Willow. I called the medical examiner's office to request that Billie's body be treated with kindness until the undertakers came for her.

When John returned, he slumped down in an overstuffed chair and closed his eyes. "I've been shot three times in my life. This is worse than all of them combined."

"I wish I could tell you different, but you're going to feel that way off and on for a long time."

Tears seeped out from under Sampson's closed eyelids. "It feels like we were two trees so close that our roots and branches were all combined, and something I can't even explain just grabbed hold of her and tore her right out of the ground."

I listened quietly. This was the aftershock of grief, the phase of trying to find a way to psychologically accept a tragic loss. I'd talked many people through this. It's easier when you don't know the victim. But Billie had been like a sister to me, and I was still struggling to find a way to accept her death in my own heart.

Sampson made his hands into fists and sat upright, shaking his head.

"I'm no good to anyone like this," he said.

"You're allowed time, John. Lots of it."

"There will be time," he said firmly. "But not now. I have to stand up for Billie when she needs standing up for."

"Let's do that," I said, and we called the rectory at St. Anthony's to arrange for a funeral Mass the following Saturday. Then we contacted Billie's favorite restaurant and organized a reception for mourners there after the funeral.

Bree and I stayed until midafternoon, when we knew John's stepchildren were on their way and Willow was taking a nap.

"We are a call away," Bree said. "Always, John."

He hugged her, said, "I'm trying to find the courage to go into our bedroom."

I said, "I know this will seem impossible, but try to go in there with gratitude for all the amazing years you had with her. Go in there thankful for the great experiences you shared and the love you still feel for her before you even think about her being gone."

Sampson said, "I don't know if I'm there yet."

"Try."

"Okay, Alex," he said, and he went back inside.

CHAPTER

27

THE FOLLOWING MORNING AROUND ELEVEN, Ned Mahoney and I listened to the hydraulic locks being thrown behind the bulletproof, Plexiglas doors to the psych unit and saw them slide back under the watchful eye of a redhead in a white lab coat.

Dr. Alice Martel smiled, shook our hands, and led us to a conference room. "Elaine has given me permission to talk to you about her case," she said.

"You've had a chance to evaluate her?" I asked.

"Not a definitive evaluation, but I spent time with her yesterday after she'd had a decent night's sleep," Dr. Martel said. "And another half an hour earlier this morning. I can tell you her current state remains irrational at times, jumps from subject to subject in midsentence, and she tends to focus on certain wrongs that her late husband allegedly perpetrated. And she asks over and over when she can see her daughters."

"Can we talk to her?"

A knock came at the door.

Dr. Martel glanced up and waved in a harried-looking man with a neatly trimmed beard and horn-rim glasses. "You'll have to ask her counsel," Dr. Martel said. "Thomas Bergson. Dr. Alex Cross. FBI Special Agent Mahoney."

Bergson shook our hands. "You brought her in. Prevented the suicide."

"She prevented it herself once she saw the world differently," I said.

"Can we speak with your client?" Mahoney asked.

Bergson appeared torn but said, "I've just spoken with Ms. Paulson and she wants to cooperate if she can. But I want to state clearly and for the record that allowing you to talk with her in no way constitutes a decision on the defense's part as to whether Elaine Paulson is of sound mind. I think the jury's still out, right, Dr. Martel?"

"It is," the psychiatrist said.

"We just want to talk to her," Mahoney said. "Get her perspective."

Bergson said, "Do you know when the ballistics report will come in?"

"Next couple of days," I said. "We sent it to the FBI lab at Quantico, rush."

The public defender paused, then nodded. "Okay. Half an hour. Nothing admissible in court pending Dr. Martel's findings."

"Agreed," Mahoney said.

Ten minutes later, Dr. Martel wheeled a wan Elaine Paulson wearing a hospital gown and robe into the conference room. She had an IV in her arm that Martel said was for fluids to treat her dehydration.

"Thank you," Elaine said as soon as she saw me. "For doing what you did, Dr. Cross. I...I want to live for my girls, just like you said."

"Love is the most powerful force in the universe," I said.

"It can build you up or destroy you," she replied, bobbing her head a little too vigorously. "I can see now that that was my relationship with Randall, build up and destroy...and when can I see Tina and Rachel?"

Mahoney said, "After our talk, I'll see what can be done."

Elaine's story came out in fits and fragments, and it was jumbled and tangential at times. She told us she'd had a crush on Randall Christopher from the first moment she saw him, at a basketball game their sophomore year at Maryland. They met by chance at a party, started talking, and did not stop for hours.

Christopher wasn't like the other athletes she knew. He understood he wasn't good enough to go professional, and his passions were teaching and coaching to make an impact on teens.

They fell in love and got married after

graduation. Christopher became a teacher in an inner-city school in Baltimore and found out what worked and what didn't work when it came to motivating students the way a sports coach might. Elaine worked at a financial firm for the seven years her late husband spent at the school. Her substantial salary enabled him to think long term about establishing a school of his own design based on his own theories.

"Randall liked being a maverick, going against the grain," she said. "It fit with infidelity."

She suspected that he'd had several affairs over the years, all short-term flings that were followed by long periods of monogamy when he was an excellent father and husband. A year ago, as people began urging Christopher to run for office, she recognized signs from earlier affairs and suspected that her husband was once again dallying outside their marriage: He was working late. He had to spend an extra day on the road. He'd shy away from her when she tried to initiate intimacy.

"A woman knows," she said. "I expected the affair to end in a week or a month, as they had before. But this was different. This had a whole other level of stink about it."

She smelled faint whiffs of his affair on his clothing, the scent of perfume.

Two months went by, then three. Christopher seemed more distracted, inventing more reasons to be away from the house. But when she confronted him, he denied everything, said this was just his life getting more complicated, that he was trying to juggle the school and a possible mayoral run.

"I know it was stupid, but I went off my meds around then and started to obsess about the affair," she said. "Pretty soon it was all I could think about."

One day Elaine decided to follow her husband, and she caught him going into Kay Willingham's town house in Georgetown when he'd claimed he was attending a breakfast prayer meeting. Another time, she caught Kay going in the back way to the charter school after hours.

"They'd have sex in his office," she said acidly. "Easy, close to home, and sneaky. I think they liked that. I mean, he knew I suspected, and here he was, throwing it in my face."

"You confront him again?" Mahoney asked.

"I did," she said. "Randall admitted it, said he loved her and that he was sick of my ups and downs. He said he was leaving me."

"When was this?" I said.

"Ten days ago?"

"Did he move out?"

"Into his office at the high school," she said. "That's why I was there that night he was killed. In the schoolyard."

CHAPTER

28

THE FIRST FORTY-EIGHT HOURS after Randall Christopher walked out were the worst. Elaine sent the girls to her mother's in Baltimore and locked herself in her bedroom, weeping, drinking, phone off, everything off.

"I'd think about killing myself. I'd think about killing Randall," she said. "I'd think the problem was me and beat myself up. But then I'd think, *No*, and get angry. Randall was the one who cheated. Not me. Elaine Paulson? She is a good woman, a good mother. But her thoughts, they just kept coming back to Randall and how he left her."

I thought it was odd that she'd started talking about herself in the third person. "Explain why…Elaine—you—were at the murder scene."

"I know who I am and I'm getting to that," she said, suddenly upset with me. "Please, I was trying to think differently at the time, I really was, but it wasn't working. For every good thought, I'd have five bad ones about losing Randall to a woman ten years older than me, and the bad ones became interlocking obsessions, playing over and over in my head."

She said she soon felt compelled to spy on her husband, to find out what he was doing in his new life without her. Four days before her husband's body was found, she said she woke up at three thirty a.m., unable to sleep. She decided to go for a run.

That run led her by the school, where she saw a light on in Randall's office. But on early runs the following morning and the morning after that, the light was off.

"He was staying at her house, I guess," she said. "I mean, I knew he was. But I couldn't help waking up and going for a run the fourth morning."

Elaine claimed she jogged toward the school campus, going past the bodega and the laundromat and crossing the street to Harrison Charter, which puzzled me, because Sampson said he'd watched the footage and didn't see anyone on it.

Before I could press her on that, she said her husband's offices were on the second floor, northeast corner of the building. She said she stopped below the windows, looked up, and to her disappointment saw the lights were off for the third morning in a row.

"But Randall often worked in two adjacent rooms, a formal office where he met parents and a smaller personal space where he liked to get things done," Elaine said. "I went around the north end of the school to the football field so I could look back at the window to the smaller office, but it was dark too."

I remembered the two offices from our search of the school and was following her description in my mind. "What did you do then?"

She hesitated and closed her eyes. "I'd decided to loop back through the rear parking lot and head home when I heard this popping noise, two of them, and then a woman's scream that got cut off with two more pops."

Elaine said she stood there petrified for several minutes and then crept forward. She started to take a peek around the corner of the building when flickers of movement caught her attention.

She opened her eyes. "I can't be sure, but I believe it was a person crouched over and moving in the dark shadows over near the football stands."

"Headed?" Mahoney said. "Direction?"

"North," she said.

"Male? Female?"

Elaine said she didn't know. Her heart was beating so wildly, she was just happy when the person vanished into the dark. Then she looked around the northwest corner of the school and south through the rear parking lots. "There were two of them, males, running away from the dumpsters," she said, motioning with her hands. "Headed south. They wore dark hoodies and went through a hole cut in the fence that gets you into the alley."

I nodded. I knew the hole in the fence. I'd used it.

Elaine said she stood there at the northwest corner of the school, unsure of what to do. Then she figured she'd better see what had happened before she called 911.

She shook her head. "I had no idea it would be…them. No idea I'd find them…like that."

You could see her visibly reliving the horror of the moment, her hand covering her mouth. She had wanted to scream at the sight of her husband and the woman who'd stolen him from her, both of them half naked and dead.

"At first, I was in shock, sensory overload, like it wasn't really happening, and yet it was happening, and I just knew my entire life was shattered. Mine. The girls'. All of it was gone."

"Why did you run?" Mahoney asked. "Why didn't you call the police?"

"Because I knew how it would look. Jilted wife who just happens to be there in the middle of the night, just happens to hear the shots and sees the killers leaving? My mind said, *Look at Randall's face one last time, Elaine, and then get as far away as you can as fast as you can.*"

"Did you have the pistol with you at that time?" I asked. "The one you had in the sand dunes?"

Elaine looked confused. "The gun? That night? No."

"But you had it with you another night at the school?"

Elaine peered into the distance, frowning. "I wasn't going to shoot them with it. I swear. Scare them. It's all I wanted to—"

Bergson, her attorney, threw his arm in front of her. "And that will be all for today, thank you, Detectives. We're done here and anxiously await the results of the ballistics report on Ms. Paulson's pistol."

CHAPTER

29

MAHONEY AND I BOTH LEFT the hospital with Elaine Paulson's final words about her pistol and her confusion as to whether she'd had it at the scene the night of the crime echoing in our heads: *I wasn't going to shoot them with it. I swear. Scare them. It's all I wanted to—*

"She certainly had the gun with her on another night," Mahoney said out on the sidewalk. "And she meant to threaten her husband and Kay with it."

"Definitely," I said. "And Sampson says she wasn't on the bodega security footage, so she didn't enter the campus the way she says she did. Can you make some calls to Quantico to get the ballistics report speeded up?"

"They were swamped and irritated when I called there yesterday," he said, then he cocked his head as if he had an idea. "We're supposed to sit down with the vice president tomorrow morning. I'll call his office, see if they can get things moving."

"I'd try Breit or Price first," I said. "You'll get straight to Willingham."

Mahoney did, talking to Agent Price and giving him the pertinent numbers to call.

At that point, Ned had to return to FBI headquarters to brief his bosses on the case and I decided to check in with Sampson to see if he needed help or a friendly ear. But my calls just kept going to voice mail.

"Call me, brother," I said after leaving three earlier messages. "Love you and I have your back one hundred percent and always."

I decided to return to Harrison Charter School and the crime scene to see if the layout jibed with Elaine Paulson's description of the night of the murders. I found a parking space south of the main school entrance and across the street from the apartment building where workers in respirators were sandblasting the brick face.

I got out and tasted dust on the breeze. Burying my nose and mouth in the crook of my elbow, I squinted as I hurried north out of the dust plume, then brushed it off my shirt. I gazed around, reorienting myself, imagining Elaine with a pistol in her fanny pack coming here.

She said she'd run by the bodega but we knew

that wasn't true from the security footage. So how had she come here? Did it matter?

Elaine Paulson claimed she'd gotten to the northeast corner of the school building, looked up at her husband's formal office, and saw the light off. From that point forward, I walked the path Elaine Paulson had described to us that morning.

At the northwest corner of the school building, I stopped. The rear of the stands about fifty yards across the parking lot blocked my view of the football field beyond. But I could see how someone could have been moving there along the back of the stands in the shadows heading north. And the three dumpsters across the parking to the south would certainly have blocked Elaine's view of Kay's Bentley.

My eyes followed the route Elaine said the two hooded males had taken, going south from behind the dumpsters to that hole in the fence. So who had gone north in a crouch? And who were the two hooded males running south? Were the three people she said were on the campus grounds working together? Were they part of a conspiracy?

Given that someone had tampered with most of the security cameras in the area, I decided the whole thing absolutely reeked of a conspiracy to assassinate Kay and Christopher. The fact that their jewelry and money had been taken could easily be explained as a diversion to suggest a robbery gone lethal.

But when I stood outside the police tape looking at where the Bentley with Kay's lifeless corpse and her lover's had been, I recalled the position of their bodies. Her right leg had been crossed over her left, toward Christopher. Her shoulders were turned slightly from him and down, but that could have been from the bullet impacts turning her. Christopher's body position in death suggested his torso had been turned toward Kay when he was shot. What about it?

I stood there for a long time, trying to see what it all suggested, before I realized we had it wrong. Given the position of the shooter, fifteen feet back from the center of the front bumper, and given their body positions in death, I decided that the killer had not put two successive rounds in Kay and then Christopher. Or vice versa.

No, they were each shot once within a moment of each other, little time for the second victim to move at all. Maybe as much as Kay's shoulders had turned?

It looked that way to me. Christopher was shot first, then Kay. Not the other way around. Then they were shot a second time, impacts within four inches of the first hits, Kay, then Christopher.

It's hard to shoot a pistol accurately like that, even at targets less than twenty feet away. In the heat of the moment, as I can attest, bullets tend to go far wide of the mark.

Looked at through this filter, I was seeing a highly skilled shooter who'd aimed first at Christopher, then at Kay. That suggested the charter school's principal was the primary target.

Was Elaine Paulson an accomplished shot? Was she a member of one of those combat-shooting leagues around the country?

If so, given what she'd said to us earlier in the day, it was not out of the realm of possibility that she had shot her husband and then his lover.

I doubted it, but I intended to find out one way or another before—

My cell rang. Sampson. "How are you, John?"

He cleared his throat, said, "Unable to write Billie's eulogy. I just can't do it, and someone needs to speak for her on Saturday."

"I'll speak for her," I said.

"You will?" he said, shocked.

"If you can't do it, I'd be honored. Billie was an amazing person."

CHAPTER

30

THE FOLLOWING MORNING, THURSDAY, Ned Mahoney and I presented passports, driver's licenses, and official FBI identifications to Marines at the front gate of the U.S. Naval Observatory north of Georgetown.

Donald Breit and Lloyd Price, the two Secret Service agents who'd shown up at the murder scene of Kay Willingham and Randall Christopher, met us on the other side of the gate. Agent Breit, the lanky, buzz-cut agent, shook our hands.

"I know the VP appreciates you coming, Dr. Cross, Special Agent in Charge Mahoney."

Agent Price, the short, stocky one, gestured to a black Suburban. "We'll drive you up to the house. He's just finishing his workout."

"Thanks," I said.

"We heard about your partner's wife," said

Price, opening one rear door. "Please offer our condolences, Dr. Cross."

"I'll do that," I said, climbing in. "Thank you."

From the other side, Breit said, "And I know the boss made a call out to Quantico, Agent Mahoney."

"Did he get anywhere?" Ned said, sliding in next to me.

Breit laughed. "I guess whoever answered didn't believe it was him at first, but yeah. They're on it."

The Suburban's rear doors sounded heavily armored when they were shut on us and the agents climbed up front.

"Bulletproof?" I said.

Breit said, "It'll take an anti-tank round and shrug it off."

We drove through the grounds to One Observatory Circle, a hundred-and-twenty-year-old white Queen Anne–style mansion that is known as the "temporary official residence" of the vice president of the United States of America.

"Why is it the *temporary* official residence?" Mahoney asked.

Price shrugged. "Congress was supposed to authorize the construction of a permanent residence for the VP. But that was decades ago."

"Government in action," Mahoney said.

Breit nodded. "Like Darwinism, only we seem to be regressing."

"Don't tell Willingham that," Price said.

"Never," Breit said. "Not a chance."

I was half listening to the conversation. A bigger part of my attention lingered on the ripples of grief that had continued to roll out from Billie's death.

The rest of our family had taken it hard, Nana Mama especially. She and Billie had shared a special relationship through their mutual interest in cooking.

"We just saw her recently," my grandmother had said, shaking her head. "I gave Willow cookies."

Jannie and Ali both cried and wondered about Sampson and Willow. Damon, my oldest, was working as a counselor at a basketball camp, but he said he was coming home for the funeral.

"Can a tick kill me?" Ali had asked as I put him to bed.

"I guess so, but we live in a city."

"So, no ticks?"

"Nope," I said, and I shut off his light.

Ali's question was on my mind when Breit pulled up in front of the vice president's residence because I had Googled it after talking to him and found cases where hikers deep in Rock Creek Park had been bitten by ticks and contracted Lyme disease.

"Okay," Price said after listening to someone talk in his earbud. "He'll be sitting down to breakfast in two minutes and expecting you. Let's move, gentlemen."

He got out of the Suburban and opened my door. Breit opened Ned's.

"Any advice?" I asked Price.

"Don't BS him. He has a BS detector like no one I've ever known."

CHAPTER

31

I'D NEVER MET J. WALTER WILLINGHAM in person, but I'd observed him enough on various media formats to know the Secret Service agents were right. We would be dealing with a formidable mind.

The late Kay Willingham's ex-husband did not disappoint, arriving in the dining room fifteen seconds after a server set his breakfast tray at the head of the table. Dressed in navy-blue suit pants and a starched white shirt open at the collar, Willingham was of medium height and very fit, with brushed-back silver hair and piercing green-gray eyes that immediately went not to Mahoney but me.

The vice president started my way but then paused to look over his shoulder at the server. "Thank you, Graciela."

She grinned, half bowed, and said, "Thank you, Mr. Vice President!"

Graciela ducked back into the kitchen, and Willingham's focus returned to me. He stuck out his hand, studied me, and said in a slight Southern drawl, "Walter Willingham. I'm pleased to meet you, Dr. Cross. I've actually read a lot about you."

"Mr. Vice President," I said, shaking his hand while those green-gray eyes danced over me. "I wish we were meeting under different circumstances."

"I do too," he said and clapped his other hand over the back of mine. "I can't tell you how much I wish that."

With a nod, Willingham moved on to Mahoney, and I felt like I was coming out of a mild trance. I understood then what Kay had always said about being in her ex-husband's presence. The VP had the uncanny ability to make each and every person he spoke to feel like he or she was the only other person on the planet.

As Willingham was shaking Ned's hand, a very attractive woman in a red sheath dress entered the room. In her mid-forties, by my guess, she had dark hair cut elegantly short, flattering makeup, and flawless pale skin. She was carrying several files and a yellow legal pad in her arms.

"This is my chief of staff, Claudette Barnes," Willingham said. "She'll also act as my counsel for the purposes of this informal meeting."

Barnes set down the files, shook our hands, thanked us for coming.

"Well, then," Willingham said, taking his seat. "Please, gentlemen," he said to us and the Secret Service men, "make yourself comfortable. And give me a moment to get a little in my stomach. I went long on the treadmill this morning and feel like I'm crashing."

Graciela appeared with coffee and poured for the six of us while the vice president dug into three eggs sunny-side up, three strips of thick bacon, an English muffin, half an avocado, and a small cup of fruit. After several bites of each and a long drink of orange juice, Willingham asked the server for privacy, then sat back in his chair and looked at Mahoney and me in turn. "So where does the investigation stand? And how can we help you besides calling Quantico?"

Mahoney and I had talked on the way over about how best to handle the vice president. It had seemed reasonable to give him an update on the investigation so far, but Willingham had not been married to the deceased for nearly two years. Did he really have any right to know? Especially given the apparent acrimony of their divorce?

Mahoney said, "Sir, I'm glad to share the fact that the case is ongoing and receiving the attention of a four-agency task force—"

"Stop," Willingham said, and held up his hands.

"Special Agent Mahoney, with all due respect, you know my background as a prosecutor?"

"I do, sir."

"Then cut the stall. I want to know what you know about Kay's death." His shoulders sagged, his eyes got watery, and he gestured toward his chief of staff. "Despite what counsel tells me, I think I have some right to know, even if Kay was no longer my wife. I mean, I still loved her even if she didn't love me. I still do. And there has to be some perk to being vice president of this damned country."

Claudette Barnes shifted in her chair.

"Well," I said, retreating to our fallback position, "we came prepared to give you the facts as we know them in return for answers to questions that we have."

"What kind of questions?" Willingham's chief of staff asked.

The vice president smiled appreciatively and held up his hand to silence Barnes. "Of course, Dr. Cross. Anything. Ask away."

Barnes wasn't happy but sat back.

"Agents Price and Breit say you were here at the residence the night of the murders."

Willingham cocked his head at Mahoney. "That sounds right, but we can check the security logs to give you confirmation. I believe I gave a speech at the Hilton that night and returned here around eleven?"

"Ten fifty-eight, sir," Price said, pushing papers at me and Mahoney. "Those are the time-stamped entries at the front gate and here at the residence."

"And then you went to bed, sir?" Mahoney asked.

"No, then I had a piece of blueberry pie and a glass of white wine in the kitchen before going upstairs to read."

"What are you reading, sir?"

"*The Gathering Storm*, by Winston Churchill," he said. "About the rise of nationalism and un-checked belligerence in Europe before World War Two."

I smiled. "A nice light read, then."

"Nice and light has never been my long suit, Dr. Cross."

Mahoney said, "Mr. Vice President, did you feel ill will toward your ex-wife?"

"You don't have to answer that, sir," Barnes said.

Willingham ignored his chief of staff. "Once upon a time I did. I suppose I wouldn't be human if I had not hated being publicly spurned during the run-up to a national election."

I said, "But not enough to have two, maybe three people conspire to shoot her in the midst of a sexual tryst with her lover, an African-American with his eye on political office?"

Willingham gazed at me levelly. "No, Dr. Cross. It has been almost two years since Kay left me.

I've dealt with it. But as I said, even though her life was her own, I still loved her."

"How do you know there were two or three assassins?" Barnes asked.

"An eyewitness claims it," Mahoney said.

The vice president sat forward. His chief of staff did as well.

"Someone saw them shot?" Willingham said.

"Who was that, exactly?" Barnes asked.

CHAPTER

32

WE HAD AGREED BEFOREHAND TO share this information, but Mahoney still appeared uncomfortable as he said, "The eyewitness didn't see the actual shots, but she heard them and claims to have seen two figures, males with hoods, escaping. She's less sure on the other, saw a crouched figure moving in the shadows."

"You believe this witness?"

"Not entirely," Mahoney said. "She's also a suspect."

"Name?"

"Elaine Paulson. Randall Christopher's widow."

Willingham blinked, took a steadying breath, and said, "Let me get this straight. Christopher's wife was there?"

"Admits being there, and she has a weapon," I said. "A thirty-eight."

"The gun you wanted tested?" he said.

"Correct."

The vice president thought about that. "I take it she was unhappy with her husband's fling with Kay? She knew, didn't she?"

Mahoney nodded. "She did, sir."

"Upset about it?"

"Very," I said.

"I found in my years as a prosecutor that most often the simple explanations in life are the correct ones," the vice president said. "She went there to scare them, but when she saw them, she went into a jealous rage and shot them both."

"We're certainly considering that possibility," Mahoney said.

"What else?" Willingham said.

I said, "The killers took jewelry, watches, and wallets from the bodies."

Willingham sat forward. "Anything on their clouds?"

Mahoney nodded. "We have specialists getting access to Mr. Christopher's cloud, thanks to his widow's consent. But we're having trouble finding anyone who has access to your ex-wife's accounts and passwords."

"Good luck with that," he said. "I know she changed every single account and password after the divorce. Who's the executor of her will?"

"Good point," Mahoney said.

"I'm sure it's someone at Carson and Knight, right, Claudette?"

"I would assume, sir," Barnes said. "The family's longtime law firm," she told us.

"Where are they located?" Ned asked.

"Montgomery, Alabama," Willingham said.

"Sir, with all due respect, why did Kay suddenly come out and smear you the way she did?" I asked. "Calling you unfit for office and of low moral character right before the election?"

Willingham got a strange, sad expression on his face. "If I fully understood that, Dr. Cross, I might still be married and Kay might still be alive."

CHAPTER

33

VICE PRESIDENT WILLINGHAM RETURNED TO his breakfast while his chief of staff continued to scribble. After a moment, she looked up at us.

"So we're done, Detectives?" Barnes said. "The vice president has a busy schedule today and a meeting starting in about five minutes."

I cleared my throat. "Just a couple more questions. You never retaliated after Kay's attacks, Mr. Vice President. Never responded."

Willingham chewed, swallowed, and said, "I was in no position to respond. I'd like to leave it at that."

"Okay," I said. "But are you saying, sir, that you have no idea what Kay was talking about when she leveled those accusations at you?"

He was soaking up egg yolk with an English muffin but stopped to gaze at me. "No," he said. "I don't. And if you go back and watch the videos where she made those claims, you'll see there were never any specifics. It was just rage against me."

"But what triggered it?" I asked.

Willingham pressed his hands as if in prayer, then sighed. "I'd hoped it would not come to this. Show them, Claudette."

"Are you sure, sir?" Barnes said. "They have no legal right to it."

"They could subpoena it, and I'd rather not be that public about Kay's...issues."

"Yes, sir."

Barnes selected several documents from the files she'd brought in. "These are medical records that ordinarily would be covered by HIPAA, but Kay signed a release allowing her ex-husband to access them."

Barnes slid them across the table at me. "I think you'd be the best person to review them first, Dr. Cross."

I turned the documents around and saw I was looking at medical records from West Briar, a psychiatric inpatient facility in Hedges, Alabama, where Kay Willingham spent three months in the middle of her two-year hiatus from Washington, DC, following the death of her mother. I scanned the medical narrative, cringing at times, then I closed the file and pushed it to Mahoney. "But the meds helped her?"

"They always helped until she decided not to

take them," Willingham said, nodding. "Which led to her delusional outbursts the last week of the campaign and her sudden decision to divorce me and denounce me in the press."

"Why didn't you reveal her history?"

"Kay didn't like the stigma attached to being mentally ill," Willingham said. "She was old-school old South. Being committed to the psych ward again and again, well, revealing that would have been life-shattering. It's why I never responded to her taunts and smears. I knew she was off her meds, having an episode, and I wanted to spare her the public pain of having her darkest secret revealed."

I sat there, feeling like Kay Willingham was a stranger, not the socialite queen of the nation's capital, not the woman I'd thought her to be.

Barnes said, "The vice president would prefer it if this part of Kay's life did not become public unless absolutely necessary."

Willingham laughed bitterly and shook his head. "Here I am, trying to protect Kay even on her way to the grave. How do you explain that, Dr. Cross?"

"Love," I said.

His eyes welled up with tears, and he patted his chest. "I suppose you're right."

Barnes got to her feet, said, "We really must be going, Mr. Vice President. You're expected at nine."

Willingham threw his hands up in surrender and stood. "I wish I could help more, but duty calls."

"One more thing, sir," Mahoney said, also standing up.

"Yes?"

"No one's come forward to claim your ex-wife's body."

He appeared nonplussed by the comment for a moment. He glanced at his chief of staff, then said, "Of course I'll claim her and contact the executor of Kay's—"

His chief of staff's cell phone rang. She answered it, listened, held up one finger, then said, "You're sure? Yes, please send a copy to my e-mail."

She hung up, looked at Willingham. "There it is, then, Walter. That was the Quantico lab. The gun's a match for the bullets that killed Kay and Mr. Christopher."

CHAPTER

34

LATER THAT DAY, BREE LEANED back in her chair in her office inside Metro Police headquarters downtown. "Did you expect it?"

"That it was as simple as jealous rage and a love triangle?" I said. "No, actually. But the ballistics are a match and, as Willingham's aide said, 'There it is.'"

"She fit to stand trial?"

"That I do not know," I said.

After a moment, Bree said, "Kay Willingham was in a psychiatric institution?"

"Committed to multiple three-month stays over the course of almost thirty years. Considered a danger to herself and others."

"What happened, exactly?"

I gave her the CliffsNotes version of the medical file I'd read that included only the details of her most recent stay at West Briar and references to earlier stays at the facility. In the wake of her mother's death, Kay Willingham had sunk into a depression, which concerned her husband, as she'd already endured severe bouts with the illness, the first one at age seventeen. During the three breakdowns that followed, Kay bottomed out and had psychiatric breaks; she had to be hospitalized for her own safety.

"Did Willingham bring her to the psychiatric facility?" Bree asked.

"The first two times," I said. "The most recent stay, she was evidently brought in by a childhood friend in Alabama. Kay was in a dissociative state after attempting suicide by trying to cut her femoral artery with a pair of kitchen shears. It explains the scars we saw in the autopsy report."

Bree looked appalled. "She tried to commit suicide by stabbing herself in the leg?"

"Repeatedly," I said.

"That's a harsh way to try to kill yourself."

"The wrists are easier," I said.

"Punishing herself," Bree said.

"Yes. But for what, I don't know. And given the chemical imbalances she was experiencing, who knows whether her reasons mattered."

"It's all just gossip fodder now," she said. "Elaine Paulson is the killer, so you can spend more time now on the Maya Parker and Elizabeth Hernandez cases."

"You've got it," I said. "Anyplace specific you want me to start?"

Bree said she'd been looking at the old files regarding the earlier rapes and murders. A year before Elizabeth Hernandez disappeared, there was a woman named Peggy Dixon who claimed she was attacked and got away from the rapist. "She was a druggie and I think the detectives who talked to her might have discounted what she said. She evidently called here again a few days ago, wanting to talk to someone about Hernandez and Parker."

"Contact information?" I asked.

"Right here," Bree said and slid a piece of paper across the desk to me. She glanced at the desk clock. Quarter to six. She made a sour face. "I'm fifteen minutes from yet another update meeting with the chief and Commissioner Dennison. See you at home afterward?"

"Yes. By the way, Willingham said he'd prefer to keep Kay's psychiatric history quiet."

"Of course. Have you heard from John?"

"No," I said. "Maybe I should stop by before dinner?"

"I think he'd like that."

CHAPTER

35

WHEN I REACHED SAMPSON'S HOME, the front door was ajar. I knocked but got no answer, so I pushed open the door and called out, "John?"

"Kitchen," he called back.

I found him drying pots and pans. "I was going to invite you to our house to eat."

He shrugged, kept drying. "Andrew and Kari came in hungry, so we ate early."

"They here?"

"With Willow. They took her out for ice cream."

"How are you doing?"

"I have the feeling I'm going to get sick of that question awful fast."

"Understandable," I said. "Take a walk?"

Sampson thought about that for a moment and then nodded.

It was a warm night, perfect for walking, which we did in silence for ten minutes, moving side by side, me trying to keep up, trying to subtly mirror his every motion so he felt comfortable enough to open up.

"This was a good idea," Sampson said at last. "Before you suggested it, my chest hurt and it felt like I wasn't breathing right."

"You've probably been breathing shallow because of everything," I said. "And when your breathing deviated from its natural depth and rhythm, you got out of what neuropsychologists call heart coherence. Because of that, you felt the pain."

John stopped, looked at me. "Heart coherence? For real, Alex?"

"For real what?"

"Nothing," he said and started walking again.

I jogged to catch up. "What was that about?"

Sampson shook his head, got teary. "It was like she was preparing me, man." Over the next ten minutes, John reminded me of Billie's long-standing interest in meditation, a practice she'd begun after her first husband was unjustly executed. Billie's interest had led to a retreat in the Poconos, which was most likely where she'd been bitten by the tick.

"Anyway," Sampson said. "That's what the entire retreat was about—heart coherence— using your breath to get your heart, I don't know, beating in sync with its natural rhythm or something? Honestly, I thought it was a bunch of woo-woo—heart coherence—but it made her happy to think it was real. I'll say this—even though she was sick, she wasn't beat down by it."

"That's because heart coherence *is* real," I said. "It's scientifically measurable. I've seen it achieved. On the screen of a sensitive electronic-monitoring system, anyway. But if you can learn to find it, there are all sorts of health benefits, mental as well as physical."

I explained that neuropsychologists at Michigan State had developed a way to measure a person's depth and pattern of breathing at the same time they were tracking the heart through a finger sensor that monitored not only the pulse but the quality of the pulse.

Sampson frowned. "I didn't know pulse had a quality."

"Well, it's the quality of the electrical impulse given off by the heart beating, but the point is that when people start out, especially when they're under stress, their breathing is usually shallow and ragged. And their hearts react in kind, throwing off the sharp spikes you see on cardiac monitors on medical dramas on TV."

Sampson's jaw tightened, and I realized that in his mind he might be seeing the monitor in the room where Billie died.

"John," I said, touching him on the elbow. "Stay with me."

He blinked, looked at me oddly, said, "I'm with you."

I said that the scientists taught their subjects first how to breathe deeply from the abdomen in order to create a pattern on a monitor that looked like one perfect bell curve after another. Within minutes, the heart responds to this breathing pattern by sending out a different electrical signal.

"The tracing on the cardiac monitor looks entirely different," I said. "Not jagged at all. More like a series of curves that stack up to a peak and then step down, forming a soft pyramid of sorts. But what's remarkable is when you see people who are good at it. On the monitors, their heartbeats shift and get inside their breath curves and they, as Billie told you, sync up."

"And that's good, huh?"

"Supposedly the best thing you can do for yourself."

"Billie was onto something, then."

"From a different angle, but yes."

"She was trying to teach me something, like she could sense it."

"I'm not going to deny it."

We'd come by a roundabout route back to his house. His stepchildren and his daughter were already home. We could hear a television droning inside.

"Maybe I'll have to look into it," Sampson said. "Heart coherence, I mean."

I nodded. "It will help. And it will honor Billie."

He nodded sadly, then gestured with his head toward the house. "I just wish I understood it well enough right now so I could go in and teach it to three other people with busted hearts."

CHAPTER
36

WHEN I GOT HOME ABOUT an hour later, I felt wrung out.

Jannie was stretching on the floor in the front room watching *Ozark* on Netflix, the latest binge-watch series in the family.

"Hello, darling," I said.

She hit Pause, looked up, and smiled quizzically at me. "Hi, Dad. You look tired."

"A long day that ended at Sampson's house," I said.

Her face fell. "How are they?"

Nana Mama came out from the kitchen and called to us, "No use repeating it three or four times, Alex. Dinner's on, so come tell us there so we can all hear you at once."

With that, my grandmother barreled back in the direction she'd come from. I looked at Jannie and we both started laughing.

Jannie whispered, "Sometimes I wonder whether Nana's got every room in the house bugged. Ali thinks she does."

I snickered at the idea. "No."

"Ali thinks she has this panel hidden up in her room and she can listen in on——"

My grandmother appeared again, sterner now. "Dinner's on. We're waiting."

We exchanged smiles and headed to the kitchen, where Bree was already sitting at the table. Two whole chickens slow-roasted in a mustard sauce lay carved on a serving tray next to boiled root vegetables and sautéed greens, garlic, and onions.

"If I knew it smelled like this in here, I would have run in," I said, kissing Bree on the cheek and then taking a seat next to my youngest child, who was staring into space while playing with the lobe of his right ear.

"Hey, kiddo," I said. "What's buzzing around up there?"

He looked at me in surprise. "Oh, hi, Dad. When did you get here?"

"Like five seconds ago," Jannie said, waving her hand in front of his face. "Hello? Earth to Ali. Earth to Ali. Too much radio silence."

He scrunched up his face. "Bill Gates's mom used to say that kind of thing to him when he was a kid down in the basement."

"What? She did not."

"She did so. If Gates was there and she hadn't heard from him in a while, she'd yell down to ask what he was doing. And he'd yell back, like, 'Thinking, Mom. You've heard of that, right? Thinking?'"

"He did not."

"Look it up," Ali said.

"That's enough," Nana Mama said, taking her seat. "We're here to eat as a family, which, as we know from Billie's passing, is a blessed but fragile thing."

"Amen," Bree said.

"Amen," I said, and we all bowed our heads and gave thanks and praise for the miracle of our lives and our food.

After we'd eaten much of the delicious meal, Nana Mama sat back. "How are they?"

"I asked John the same thing and he said he was going to get sick of that question, but he's fixated on making sure Billie's funeral befits her and trying to be a rock for his children."

Bree said, "It gives him a purpose to get through the initial loss."

"What's that mean?" Ali asked.

I said, "After someone dies, people go through the same stages of grief, but they work through them in different ways and in different sequences, sometimes over and over."

"But John's going through grief by making sure her funeral's beautiful?"

"Yes. But that lasts only until the funeral is over. Then the tough part begins."

Jannie said, "It's so sad. After Billie's kids go home, Sampson will be alone with Willow. How's he going to do that?"

"With our help," Nana Mama said. "Once he's ready to accept it, we'll offer it."

"We already have," I said.

"We keep offering it, then."

"Anything John or Willow needs," Bree said, nodding and looking around. "The Sampsons *are* as much part of this family as any of us."

We all nodded and there were more than a few watery eyes at the table.

I couldn't have been prouder of Bree and Nana Mama for getting the sentiment just right or more in love with my family for opening up their lives and their hearts. Sampson was already my best friend, but in shared grief and out of sheer goodness, they'd just made John and Willow so much more.

CHAPTER
37

BOTH OF OUR CELL PHONES started buzzing and ringing at five forty-five a.m.

"Not good," Bree said, accepting her call.

I did the same and we both learned that a congresswoman from Michigan had just been shot mere blocks from our house. Officers and ambulances were racing to the scene and a commander was requested. Bree said we'd be there in ten minutes.

We dressed fast and didn't bother with a car; we just ran toward Pennsylvania Avenue, Seward Park, and the flashing blue and red lights. Before we got there, the ambulance had already raced away. The uniformed Metro and Capitol Hill Police officers on the scene recognized Bree immediately.

"You got here fast, Chief Stone," one of them said.

"We don't live five blocks from here," she said, gasping. "What happened?"

"Someone shot Congresswoman Elise McKenna while she was out jogging. Bullet hit the flank of the right buttocks, exited the left. She said she didn't hear the shot. That's all she said before we left."

"Witnesses?" Bree asked.

"One so far," he said. "Lady she was running with. Another congresswoman. Tracey Williams. From Arkansas. She's over there."

He gestured with his chin across the crime scene toward a woman in running gear, her arms crossed, talking to a female uniformed officer.

Bree looked at me. "Can you call in FBI forensics? I don't want any conflict on jurisdiction between Metro and Capitol Police to screw up the evidence."

"Smart," I said and made the call to Ned Mahoney as we walked around the crime scene, seeing a sizable smeared pool of blood on the brick sidewalk and growing crowds of onlookers across the street by the park.

A satellite news van rolled by with a cameraman hanging out the window.

"Keep them moving!" Bree yelled at the uniforms.

The female Capitol Police officer saw us coming and walked to meet us. "You can hear it from her, Chief," she said, and she kept going.

Representative Williams, who was in her late thirties, was extremely agitated. We introduced ourselves and shook her trembling hand.

"I feel like I need a cigarette and I quit smoking ten years ago," she said in a soft Southern accent. "Maybe a carton of cigarettes." She tried to laugh before looking over at the bloody sidewalk in a daze. "That could have been me, and I left my phone at the apartment so I can't call my husband and kids back home and tell them I'm all right, and I gave Elise's phone to the EMTs...Jesus, why would someone do such a thing?"

Bree handed over her cell phone. "Call your husband, Congresswoman, and then we'll talk."

Williams hesitated but then took the phone and called her husband.

"I'm okay, but something's happened," she said. "I'm fine, really. I'll call after I talk to the police and I'll tell you everything. I love you. Kiss the kids."

She smiled at us, her eyes glassy, and thanked Bree before describing how she, Elise McKenna, and a third freshman congresswoman lived together in a small apartment east of the Capitol. Four mornings a week, she and McKenna went for an early run.

They had taken their normal four-mile route and were roughly three miles into it when

McKenna, who was leading, suddenly screamed and then sprawled on the sidewalk.

"I had no idea what had happened," Williams said, tearing up again. "I ran to her, she was grabbing at her…butt cheeks and screaming she'd been shot. I saw the blood, used her phone, and called 911, and here we are."

"You never saw the shooter?"

"I never heard the gun," she said. "We were running and then she was down."

"Traffic?"

Williams nodded, but looked puzzled. "Yes. I mean, I think so." She turned to orient herself so she was facing east, then waved her left hand. "Yes, there was traffic, but I couldn't tell you what cars they were or how many because I don't think the shot came from Pennsylvania Avenue." The congresswoman pivoted clockwise and gestured back across the intersection with Fifth Street toward a line of cars parked against the far sidewalk by the Capitol Hill United Methodist Church. "You ask me, it came from back there."

"Why do you think that?" Bree asked.

Williams thought about that before she faced east again, shifted her torso and hip to her left and forward, northeast.

"Because Elise kind of did that before she screamed and went down," the congresswoman said. "Am I free to go?"

"We can arrange a car if you don't want to face the media horde," Bree said.

"Kind of you, Chief, thank you, I'll take you up on that offer," she said. "I'm going to shower and head straight to the hospital to see Elise."

Bree and I walked over to where the congresswoman thought the shooter must have stood, behind that line of cars parked by the church. Low on the church wall was newly painted graffiti that said *Shoot the Rich!*

My phone rang. I saw a number I didn't recognize but answered anyway. "Cross."

"The good doctor himself. This is Clive Sparkman."

"How did you get this number?"

"A triviality," Sparkman said. "I want to meet for breakfast. Now."

"Forget it. Never," I said.

"Suit yourself, then, Cross. Blow up your life when I'm giving you the opportunity to put out the fuse."

CHAPTER

38

AN HOUR LATER, I WALKED into Ted's Bulletin, a restaurant on Eighth Street in Southeast DC, four blocks from my home. I was sure Clive Sparkman was aware of that and was letting me know that he'd studied up on me, which only added to my general surliness at having to meet him to see what he planned to write about me.

Sparkman sat in the back booth on the left, facing the door. His face lit up when he saw me, and he stood to shake my hand.

"Dr. Cross," Sparkman said. "I appreciate you coming on such short notice."

"You didn't give me much of a choice," I said, but I shook his hand anyway.

Sparkman gestured at the booth. "Shall we?"

I slid into the booth, watching him the way I would a sleeping snake. He held my gaze. Was that amusement on his lips?

"Coffee?" he said. "Breakfast? It's on me."

"I've got things to do, Mr. Sparkman," I said. "A congresswoman was shot this morning, or hadn't you heard?"

"You're on that already? You do get around, don't you?"

"Out with it. And by the way, I am talking to you off the record, and if you don't like that, I'm walking, and you can write whatever you want. Which you'll probably do anyway."

Sparkman sat back, irritated. "You don't think much of me, do you, Dr. Cross?"

"I rarely think of you at all."

"I'm not who you think I am."

"Is that right?"

"I'm not sleazy and I'm not second rate," he said. I didn't reply.

Sparkman said, "I went to Yale, Dr. Cross."

"Bully for you."

"I have a master's in economic and political journalism from Northwestern. I graduated at the top of my class."

"And yet you peddle gossip."

"I write about gossip with facts. Which is about as close as anyone can get to the heart of the matter these days. Don't you feel it? Like everything is malleable, even the truth? In many cases, gossip is the story; how it moves and grows and influences the facts."

"I believe you can find the truth if you dig hard enough."

"And what is the truth to you, Doctor?" he said.

"An unassailable argument built on facts. The rest is conjecture or clickbait."

Sparkman seemed to be enjoying himself. "Yes, in your world, you're right. In your world, Dr. Cross, every action is designed to get the bad guys into court where just such an argument supported by facts will determine their fate."

I thought about that. "Not every action I take, but the majority, I'll grant you."

"And never—not once—has some snippet of gossip you've heard from a witness along the way turned out to be material, a seriously strong fact to be used?"

"I didn't say that."

"You're an honest man. Good. So, when you think about it, we're kind of in the same line of business, Dr. Cross. You employ your investigative skills for various exalted government agencies, and I employ mine for the site and the blog."

"Except I don't throw around wild accusations and bogus innuendo in public to juice up a story."

The enthusiasm drained out of Sparkman's eyes and he put on what I took to be his game face. "Like I said, Dr. Cross, I don't do that. I'm trained. I check things out, which is what I'm doing here."

Before I could reply, the blogger reached into

a leather messenger bag and pulled out a manila envelope. He opened the clasp, drew out a piece of glossy white paper, and turned it over, revealing a photograph. He slid it across the table to me.

It was upside down, so I spun it around and felt almost immediately nauseated, like I'd been caught in a carefully laid trap.

CHAPTER

39

THE PHOTOGRAPH HAD BEEN TAKEN years ago and through a long lens. It was a night scene, a diagonal view across a street toward a brick sidewalk, a low iron gate, and the green front door of Kay Willingham's home. Just outside the gate, Kay and I were embracing; her right foot was raised behind her and her eyes were on mine. It looked like we'd just kissed.

"You told me you never had an affair with Kay Willingham," Sparkman said.

For a long moment, I didn't reply, just studied the picture and Kay. I remembered that moment, how she'd laughed.

"Cross. The affair."

I looked at the blogger, who'd taken out a pencil and a notebook. "There was no affair."

"The picture says otherwise."

"No, the picture says that I was taking Kay

Willingham home from a fundraiser because her ride was a no-show and she'd had a little too much champagne."

"Uh-huh," he said, sounding skeptical as he scribbled a note.

"Hey, Mr. Yale and Northwestern, Mr. Legit Journalist," I said, spinning the picture toward him and tapping on it. "Take a closer look at her raised foot."

The blogger blinked, set down his pen, and bent over to study the foot. "No shoe."

"Because Mrs. Willingham's heel went into a crack in the brick sidewalk and her shoe slipped off a moment before that picture was taken. I caught her before she could fall, and her shoe dropped into that puddle you can see there behind her. I was a helping hand. No affair."

Sparkman studied the photograph and then me. I could see gears grinding in his head. "When was this taken?"

I thought about that. "It had to be April early in Willingham's term as governor of Alabama."

"Eight years ago?"

"Sounds right."

"When she was estranged from her husband."

"I don't know about that."

"She was. They spent nearly ten months apart that year. Her call."

"If you say so."

Sparkman flipped his pencil neatly between

his fingers, studying his notes. "Did you go inside?"

"Yes," I said. "She asked me to check the house, which is what her driver usually did before she set the alarm and went to bed."

"How long did that take?"

"I don't know, fifteen minutes?"

He looked disappointed. "You didn't try to get an after-dinner drink out of her? A woman like that?"

Some things are worth lying about, and I wanted this guy off the story of the photograph. "I did not ask for an after-dinner drink. Would I have liked to? Sure. Kay Willingham was beautiful, smart, and a little out there—in a good way. But I have a rule about imposing on women who have had too much to drink."

"How sensitive-male of you," Sparkman sniffed.

I shrugged. "You've been asking all the questions, Sparkman. I'd like a few of my own answered."

"Okay?"

"Where'd you get the photograph?"

He stiffened. "You know I can't reveal my sources."

"Who took the photograph?"

"I have no idea."

"It just came to you."

"In a manner of speaking, yes. I am known. People in power do send me things."

I paused, seeing his obvious hunger to be thought significant. I decided to feed that, change my whole attitude and approach. I sat back, showed him my open palms. "Mr. Sparkman, I don't doubt it. I've been unfair to you. I came in here with a set idea about you, but I have to say, you've impressed me with your intelligence and your willingness to be fair and impartial in listening to my side of the story behind that photograph."

The blogger sat up taller, nodded. "Okay, well, I appreciate that."

Then I leaned across the table and in a low threatening voice said, "But don't think for a second I won't use the full force of the FBI against you if you do not tell me where the hell you got that photograph and right now."

Sparkman retreated, pressing his head against the back of the booth. "You can't do that."

"Watch me," I said. "I'm an investigative consultant to the FBI. I'm working with the FBI on the deaths of Kay Willingham and Randall Christopher. And I want to know who wants me off the investigation."

"Well, you are compromised, don't you think?"

"By a broken shoe? I don't think so. Listen hard, Mr. Sparkman. If I tell Special Agent in Charge Mahoney that you have evidence concerning the killing of the vice president's ex-wife and that you're not cooperating, he will seize everything you've got and shut you down until you've spent tens of thousands of dollars to hire lawyers to get your stuff back. By then you'll be bankrupt."

He looked sickened. "He can't do that."

"Actually, he can."

The blogger lost some of his confidence then. I could see the growing confusion in his expression. His brain was spinning, trying to find a way out.

I gave him one. "So maybe we can help each other, Mr. Sparkman. You sit on that photograph, you do not publish, and you wait while we do our work. When we are done, we will grant you an exclusive on the story, and you can use the picture or not. I won't care at that point because I'll have found Mrs. Willingham's killer, and you can print whatever you'd like, although I'd prefer you to base it wholly on facts."

I'd had his entire attention at the word *exclusive*, but he said nothing.

I said, "This is one of those rare moments, Mr. Sparkman, where the decision you make might just determine the course of the rest of your life. Do you want to be arrested for obstructing justice in a high-profile federal investigation? Or do you want to patiently lay the foundation for a blockbuster story of real journalism that's all your own?"

Sparkman's eyes darted left and right as if he were looking at lists of pros and cons. Then his shoulders relaxed. "I'll take the story," he said at last. "Put the exclusive in writing."

"As long as we get what you know. Deal?"

"Deal."

I smiled and reached over to shake his hand.

He grinned now. "We're like partners, me and you."

"No," I said firmly. "But we both benefit here. Now tell me where that picture came from."

CHAPTER

40

CHARLIE PALMER STEAK ON Constitution Avenue is as close to an off-site congressional dining hall as you can get in the nation's capital. The restaurant is a few minutes' walk from the U.S. Senate office buildings, the food's excellent, and politicians and power brokers of all persuasions are drawn to the eatery.

According to Clive Sparkman, the politicians and the power brokers were why I might find a woman named Kelli Ann Higgins eating lunch there. Probably alone. Sure enough, when I arrived at the restaurant, showed the maître d' my identification, and asked after Ms. Higgins, I was told she had just been seated.

"She's at a table for two, I imagine."

He looked down at his seating chart. "No, just her."

"She's an old friend," I said. "I'll join her."

Before he could reply, I dodged around his station and strode through the main room to the back, where Higgins liked to sit so she could track the comings and goings in the room. Or at least, that's what Sparkman had said.

I spotted her almost immediately, mid-forties, rail-thin, stylish dark hair, pale, almost translucent skin, and wearing her signature red dress and pearls. She was entranced by something on her cell phone and didn't glance my way until I sat down opposite her.

Higgins looked at me with disdain. "Who are you?"

"My name is Alex Cross."

She was good, I'll give her that. At my name, she barely took a breath before shaking her head. "Am I supposed to know you?"

I smiled, showed her my FBI contractor's ID. "I'm a consultant to the investigation into the deaths of Kay Willingham and Randall Christopher."

"And?"

Before I could answer, a waiter came over and asked what I wanted to drink.

"Oh, he won't be staying," Higgins said.

I smiled at her. "We can do it here, Ms. Higgins, or I can make some calls and you'll be hauled out of here for questioning."

Her nostrils flared, but she said, "Get him what he wants."

"A Coke," I said. "And I heard the steak sandwich is good."

When the waiter was gone, she said, "I don't know why we're even having this conversation. I was looking forward to a nice lunch, maybe seeing some old—"

"Stop," I said. "You have a law degree and run a PR business, Ms. Higgins. That's what it says on your office door, anyway, although I understand your real game is something entirely different."

Indignant now, she said, "I don't know what you're talking about."

"Blackmail," I said.

"Would you like to be sued?"

"Oh, I don't mean you do the blackmailing yourself, though I suspect you've strayed close to that line more than a few times doing what you do."

Higgins crossed her arms. "And what is it that you allege I do?"

"You deal in dirt, Ms. Higgins. Damaging information, the kind of leverage you need in a blackmail scheme or a plot to tear down or build up some politician. It's why you're here or in one of the other power-lunch venues around town every day, Monday through Friday. You're trolling for business."

"Wherever did you get the idea that I deal in dirt?"

"A dirty little bird told me."

"You'll have to do better than that or I'm going to ask you to leave, FBI or no FBI."

"Clive Sparkman," I said.

"That worm," she said. "Don't believe a thing he says."

"Ordinarily, I don't," I said. "But he told me he was talking to you in the hours after the murders of Kay Willingham and Randall Christopher, and you said that you had so much on those two you could light up Sparkman's site like 'the *Drudge Report* on a down day for Democrats.' Is that correct?"

Higgins's focus drifted into the middle distance for a moment before she squinted and laughed. "Yes, I said something like that. I did! But I was doing what my little brother would call 'yanking his chain.'"

"Sparkman's chain?" I said.

"He's easily played. I like to play with him. It makes him eager to please when I really need him."

"To do what?"

She shrugged. "Float a theory. Roll out a hidden fact or two that might sway public opinion."

"So you have nothing on Kay Willingham or Randall Christopher?"

She smiled sweetly at me. "Wish I did, but I'm afraid not."

"Did you know her? Kay?"

"We met several times. I liked her, but we weren't friends."

"Really? Kay was friends with everyone."

"I suppose she thought I knew things she did not want out in the open."

"Did you?"

"Not really. I mean, not things that I would consider cause for scandal."

"What about beneath your scandal threshold?"

"She liked men *and* women and often strayed outside her marriage, but that's been reported. She may have had a nervous breakdown or two. That's a persistent but unconfirmed rumor."

"Did you send Clive Sparkman a photo of me and Kay Willingham?"

She ducked her chin and then laughed in wonder. "There's a photograph of you and Kay Willingham?"

"It's not like that."

"It never is, Dr. Cross."

I studied her. Higgins was practiced and polished in her gaze, but I was still picking up something that said I wasn't getting the entire story. "Did you send the picture?"

"I have no idea what you're talking about."

"I'm going to go, then."

"Not staying for the steak sandwich?"

"You take it—you look like you could use

the iron," I said, standing. "But in the meantime, whatever game it is that you're playing, Ms. Higgins? Be very, very careful. I suspect there are forces involved you have not even begun to consider."

CHAPTER

41

LATER THAT SAME AFTERNOON, Metro Chief of Police Bryan Michaels and Chief of Detectives Bree Stone were on the receiving end of a titanic venting from Commissioner of Police Wayne Dennison.

"I told you both time and again that my friend getting shot in the ass was part of something bigger, something sinister," he said. "The *Washington Post* put it together before we did; rich people and politicians were getting shot at in the streets of DC before Phil and the congresswoman were actually hit. Where were we, Chief Michaels? Chief Stone? Where was Metro?"

Bree's boss glanced at her. She threw back her shoulders and said, "With all due respect, Commissioner Dennison, Metro was there. We knew about the shootings. Dr. Cross interviewed Mr.

Peggliazo at length. We couldn't anticipate an escalation away from wealthy targets to shooting a sitting congresswoman."

"No?" Dennison said. "Isn't that the job of a leader, Chief Stone? To anticipate what might happen and take appropriate action so it does not?"

"What exactly did you want me to do, Commissioner? Take over congressional security? That's the Capitol Hill Police's job."

"That's true, sir," Chief Michaels said. "And even so, Chief Stone was on the scene of that shooting this morning before any other agency with primary jurisdiction."

Dennison fumed a moment. "I do not want the people in this department looking like fools. I will not have Metro be the third-stringer in this town. Metro leads. Metro anticipates."

"Yes, sir," Chief Michaels said.

"Yes, sir," Bree said, though she wasn't sure what she was agreeing to.

"Show me," he said, sitting down in his office chair and leaning back. "Show me how we anticipate and get out in front of these shootings. I want plans for review tomorrow morning at seven thirty sharp. All top brass on deck."

Bree felt a tightness in her chest. "Sorry, Commissioner, I can't be here until at least two tomorrow afternoon."

That ticked Dennison off all over again. "Can't or won't, Chief Stone?"

"Can't, sir, and won't."

"I can order you here, Chief."

"Not tomorrow morning, sir. I am attending the funeral of a dear friend, the late wife of Metro Detective First Class John Sampson, one of my men and my husband's best friend. So order away. I'll be paying my respects to a woman I loved."

Chief Michaels said, "I was going to attend the funeral as well, Commissioner. John Sampson is an eighteen-year veteran of the force. It's the least we can do."

Dennison struggled, then nodded grudgingly. "Of course. Can we have a three p.m. meeting with contingencies on paper to anticipate and thwart any more shootings?"

"I'll be here at three, sir," Bree said.

"We both will," Michaels said.

"Thank you," the commissioner said and he turned his chair away. "Carry on."

Out in the hall, Bree said, "Chief Michaels, permission to speak freely?"

"If you won't, I will."

"He's making everything that happens in the District his personal problem."

"Which means our personal problem," Michaels said. "But he's right about one thing. These shootings aren't stopping anytime soon. We do need to anticipate."

"I agree, but honestly, I think we need to

understand why these shootings are happening. If we can figure that out, we can anticipate and stop any future shootings."

"We just have to figure it out by three tomorrow afternoon," Chief Michaels said, sounding dubious.

"Better than half past seven tomorrow morning."

CHAPTER

42

WE WERE ALL UP EARLY, Nana Mama made sure of that, and she also made sure we were turned out in our somber finest. There would be nothing but the best for Billie Sampson.

My grandmother made us breakfast wearing her funeral dress beneath an apron. She frequently seemed lost in thought. I wasn't the only one who noticed.

"Are you all right, Nana?" asked Damon, my oldest, who'd come home from basketball camp the night before.

"No," she said. "There are many blessings that go with reaching my age, Damon, but outliving a beautiful, vital soul like Billie is not one of them." Nana Mama fell silent a moment, then said, "It feels like something's out of balance, like God made a mistake."

With a glance at me, Bree said, "Things are unbalanced, Nana. I feel it too."

I nodded at them in understanding, then said, "But if we're walking to the church, we need to go."

After helping Ali into his navy blazer, adjusting Damon's tie and seeing him guide Nana Mama to the sidewalk, I led the way to St. Anthony's Catholic Church. We could hear the organ music from down the street, which got to all of us, because Billie had often played the same organ over the years.

John Sampson waited at the entrance along with Billie's son, Andrew. Sampson was as stoic as I'd seen him. "Thank you, Alex, for agreeing to do this."

Andrew said, "Neither of us is up to it."

"I'll try to do her proud," I said, and we went inside.

Damon led Nana Mama to her seat. Bree and I followed and sat beside them with Ali and Jannie behind us.

Bree leaned over and whispered in my ear, "I love you. And I trust you."

I whispered, "Same here."

We squeezed each other's hands, and the mild friction between us from the night before was gone. Bree had been stressed to begin with after her run-in with Commissioner Dennison, and she had not been prepared to hear that there was a photograph of me and Kay Willingham and that it might soon hit the internet.

I'd done my best to calm her down enough to have a dispassionate discussion about the picture. Who had taken it? Any number of people, we supposed. But why? And for whom?

Kay and Governor Willingham had been estranged when the picture was taken, so her husband might have hired a private eye to follow her. But why would Vice President Willingham have wanted to discredit me and get me thrown off the case if he knew he'd be a logical source of the picture?

"He's too smart," Bree had said. "He'd never do that. And besides, it's a moot point. Elaine Paulson did the deed."

I agreed with her, so we'd spent the rest of the evening discussing other possible sources of the photo, from a jilted lover of Kay's to a fixer to paparazzi. We discounted the last because the picture had never made its way into the tabloids.

I was pondering those and other possibilities when the funeral procession began. We all stood. The church behind us was full. A packed house for Billie.

CHAPTER

43

ANDREW AND HIS SISTER, KARI, walked behind the priest following Billie's casket. John and Willow followed them.

Billie's young daughter was trying not to cry but couldn't help it, which really tore open the emotions in the room. You could literally feel the collective grief in the church in a way I had rarely encountered before, and I wondered if I had the strength to deliver Billie's eulogy.

During the Mass I thought of her constantly, however, and that helped when the priest at last invited me up to speak. For a moment after I'd gotten to the lectern, I let my eyes wander over the people in the pews and the ones standing in the back, all of them looking at me expectantly. I glanced down at Billie's casket and felt strangely calm.

"I thought this would be hard," I began and

smiled sadly. "I thought getting up here and seeing all of you gathered to mourn the loss of someone who was truly beautiful, inside and out…I guess I feared that my own grief might prevent me from talking about Billie Houston Sampson in a way that celebrated who she was and what she meant to all of us."

I gazed at Sampson and his family. "But John, Willow, Andrew, and Kari, I am here to tell you that Billie's spirit would not let me be afraid. I was sitting over there thinking about her, and suddenly I was no longer fearful about doing her justice. Though her body lies in a casket, her spirit is here. Billie—your wife, your mom, my friend—her spirit lingers in me and in each of you, and it always will."

I lifted my head, pointed a finger at the mourners in the back, and smiled. "And I'm guessing Billie's spirit lingers in all of you or you would never have come to say goodbye like this in such numbers."

I could make out people all over the church nodding and dabbing their eyes.

I said, "It takes an extraordinary person to touch this many hearts, but Billie Sampson was an extraordinary person by every measure. She grew up in poverty and went to nursing school on scholarship before joining the United States Army and working her way up to head nurse at a trauma and burn hospital.

"During that time, Billie met the first love of her life, Andrew and Kari's father, a decorated Green Beret who was framed for murder by fellow officers and unjustly executed before evidence exonerating him could be found. During the entire ordeal, Billie stood by her husband and believed in his innocence. To my knowledge that never wavered, not even after his passing."

Her daughter, Kari, shook her head, said, "Never."

I struck my chest lightly with my fist. "That takes heart, and Billie had heart. John felt it the first time he met her, told me he could not get over how much energy that little woman had."

Sampson smiled.

"My son Ali used to call her the Energizer Bunny," I said. "My grandmother called her Billie Whirlwind."

Laughter rippled through the audience and there was a long low murmur and the sound of folks adjusting in their seats.

"I'll bet every one of you has a Billie story to share, a testament to various aspects of her life. Her skills as a nurse. Her love of cooking. Her fitness. Her ability to connect almost instantly with people. The genuine warmness she projected at all times."

I struck my chest again. "That warmness? That ability to connect? The discipline to stay in shape and constantly learn as a nurse? They all take heart, and Billie Sampson had heart in spades.

"In fact, one of the things I admired about her most was that she always led with her heart, and in times of conflict she always responded from her heart. It was what made her so genuine and special.

"Heart was what lit Billie up and heart is what lit up John and Willow and Andrew and Kari and I suspect every person in this church at one time or another. Heart was what allowed Billie to forgive the men who conspired to kill her husband. Heart was what allowed her to move on and find love again. And weakened as it was, heart was what made Billie, in her dying words, speak of her love for family and friends."

I got choked up then and had to wipe my eyes and compose myself.

"She was remarkable that way," I said, putting my right hand on my chest. "I hope we can all honor her by thinking less with our heads and more with our hearts in the coming days. If we do that, each and every one of us, there will be more love, more Billie Sampson in our lives, not less. And the world will undoubtedly be better for it."

CHAPTER

44

BREE LEFT WITH THE CHIEF for a meeting with the commissioner. Damon took Nana Mama, Jannie, and Ali home. But Mahoney and I hung with Sampson after Billie's funeral until the end of the reception, then saw him to his car with Willow and Billie's children.

John hugged me weakly before he got in the car. "Thank you for what you said about her, Alex. So many of her friends told me you got her just right."

"It was a privilege to talk about Billie," I said.

After they drove off, Ned said, "I've never seen John look like that."

"Broken," I said, grieving for him now as well as his wife. "And it's going to take him a long time to put himself back together, to start believing again."

"I have the feeling it will start with Willow," Mahoney said.

I glanced over at Ned, reappraising him. I'd known the FBI agent for almost twenty years and he continued to surprise me with his instincts. "I think you're right," I said.

"Are you going to Randall Christopher's funeral this afternoon?"

"With Jannie," I said. "She's friends with the daughters."

His phone rang. He answered, listened, said, "Reconnect us on a conference call with Dr. Cross."

Mahoney hung up, said, "Rawlins says he has something for us."

Our phones rang at the same time and we answered.

Keith Karl Rawlins, the brilliant computer scientist under contract to the FBI's cybercrimes unit, said, "Dr. Cross?"

"Right here," I said. "What have you got?"

"I know the wife is being charged, but the executor of Kay Willingham's estate gave me access to her known iCloud accounts and passwords and files. And Randall Christopher's attorney got me into his iCloud accounts and files as well. I'll be sending you each a link and a password that will give you access to both if you think it's necessary."

"That would be a big help," Mahoney said.

I said, "Anything jump out at you, Keith?"

"As a matter of fact, yeah," he said. "I ran

histories and searched in both clouds, and neither one mentions the other in any of their computer files, e-mails, or web accounts. I believe they were both using VPN services and a software system called Tor to give themselves a cloak of anonymity in most of their interpersonal communications."

"I thought anonymity on the internet was impossible."

"That's what we like to tell people," Rawlins said. "But Tor is a heavily encrypted privacy system that uses onion technology to send any message or e-mail or internet command through multiple servers around the world, which makes tracking virtually impossible. Tor had noble beginnings. It was designed for activists and internet users to avoid surveillance and get around censorship. It has also been used by women to escape violent relationships. But at the same time, it has become a notorious way to access the dark web without leaving a trace."

"And you think Kay Willingham and Randall Christopher were communicating through this Tor system?" Mahoney said.

"I strongly suspect that, yes, but not always," Rawlins said. "A few times they broke the silence and communicated by text, the most recent one from Christopher to Kay the day before they died. Quote: 'You won't believe what I'm onto. If

I'm right, big, big boost in profile. Can't wait to see you tonight.'"

"A big boost in profile," Mahoney said. "Did she reply?"

"Yes, with an emoji blowing him a kiss."

You won't believe what I'm onto.

Though I wondered about what Christopher had been onto, I couldn't let go of the fact they both seemed to have been using the dark web. I asked, "What was the motivation for them to use Tor? I mean, there had to be a reason that they would want to use heavily encrypted methods of communicating in the first place."

The computer scientist was quiet, then said, "I see where you're going. One or both of them might have believed that they were under electronic surveillance."

"Were they?" Mahoney asked.

"I was going to ask you the same thing," Rawlins replied.

"Not that I'm aware of. But who knows? I'll have to contact the NSA."

I said, "Can't you tell from the cloud accounts, Keith? Wouldn't there be digital markers somewhere that would suggest they were under surveillance and, if so, by who?"

Rawlins said, "I can look, but if there is, don't be surprised if I set off some alarms."

"I look forward to that, actually. It's about time we shake some trees, see what falls out."

CHAPTER

45

BREE HAD WORN HER DRESS blues for Billie's funeral and did not have a chance to change before she followed Chief Michaels into Commissioner Dennison's office.

Dennison sipped from a cup of coffee and then stood to greet them. "I appreciate this," he said, gesturing to the chairs. "How was Detective Sampson's wife's memorial?"

"Touching," Bree said. "Thank you for asking, Commissioner."

Chief Michaels nodded. "Billie was an exceptional person."

"Again, I am sorry to hear that she passed," the commissioner said, sitting back down and then looking at Bree. "So, Chief Stone, how do we anticipate the next shooting?"

Bree had spent the better part of the prior evening going over the investigative files and the news reports about the "Shoot the Rich shoot-ings," as they were being called in the local media. She'd given the matter a lot of thought before and after Billie's funeral. "The shootings do appear to be escalating," she said. "They started almost as a scare tactic and then ramped up from there to Mr. Peggliazo's wounding to the shooting of Congresswoman McKenna. I think we can anticipate the shooter or shooters will try to up their game again, raise the stakes."

"Makes sense," Dennison said. "How?"

"I think there are two possible ways. Incre-mentally, in which case one of a hundred U.S. senators could become the likely target. Or a big jump if the shooter is looking for someone even more high profile. The Speaker of the House, say. Or the Senate majority leader. Or one of the nine Supreme Court justices. Or the president."

The commissioner sat forward. "So how do we handle this?"

Bree looked at Chief Michaels, who said, "We don't, sir."

"What?" Dennison snapped.

Bree said, "Again, Commissioner, with all due respect, protection of members of Congress is the job of the Capitol Hill Police. The Secret Service guards the president, the vice president, and the members of the cabinet except for the secretary of state, who is protected by the Diplo-matic Security Service. And invariably, once there's been a shooting of a member of Congress, the FBI swarms the case."

"It's simply not our job, sir," Chief Michaels said.

"Not our job?" Dennison roared. "What the hell is wrong with this city? In Boston, the PD had clout. We worked hand in hand with the Feds on the marathon bombing. I simply do not understand why we are not functioning at the same level here."

Bree said, "We do function at that level."

"When we're called upon to do so," Chief Michaels said.

The commissioner chewed on that for several moments, and Bree could see he was having trouble swallowing what they'd just told him. In fact, he was angered by it.

With that realization came another. When Dennison was deputy police commissioner in Boston, he'd been able to throw his weight around, get noticed as a serious player. And now she understood why he'd been pressuring her from the get-go. He was the new commissioner. He wanted a big arrest to stake his claim on the job.

"Anything new on the Maya Parker case?" Dennison asked.

"Dr. Cross is going back to interview some people we think were overlooked during the Elizabeth Hernandez part of the investigation."

"The Willingham case? Something? Anything?"

"Other than Elaine Paulson being charged, I have nothing of consequence to report, sir."

"It's all everyone's talking about. Tell me something I don't know about the case. Something I might find surprising that the ordinary citizen wouldn't know."

Bree felt uncomfortable. She glanced at Chief Michaels, who was no help, then returned her attention to Dennison. "After her mother died a few years back, Kay Willingham evidently spent three months in a psychiatric facility," she said.

The commissioner's eyebrows arched up. "Well, that is interesting," he said, leaning forward. "Who's the source?"

"My husband."

"Who's his source?"

"Her ex-husband. Who has asked that that information not be made public."

"Is that a fact?" Dennison said, twiddling his thumbs. "I can't imagine why Vice President Willingham would want to keep something like that a secret now that she's dead."

CHAPTER

46

DESPITE THE SCANDAL SURROUNDING RANDALL CHRISTOPHER'S death, the memorial service for him at Harrison Charter High was well attended. Jannie and I followed a crowd past two satellite television trucks and into the school's gym.

As we looked for seats, I saw parents and local community members I recognized, including Ronald Peters, Dee Nathaniel, and her mother, Gina. Then I spotted Clive Sparkman in the bleachers. Our eyes met and we nodded to each other.

Jannie and I sat down in folding chairs arranged on the gym floor off to one side, five or six rows back. My daughter pointed out Christopher's unidentical twin daughters, Tina and Rachel, when they came in wearing dark dresses and supporting their paternal grandmother.

I was not surprised to see them followed by

their next-door neighbor Barbara Taylor, who sat with them.

A reverend from their church presided. He gave a quick, rather bland homily and seemed about to wind down the service when Rachel and Tina suddenly got up and went forward.

This flustered the minister. He got even more flustered when they asked for the microphone, but he handed it to them.

"Thank you all for coming," Rachel said with great emotion. "It means a lot to us, given everything."

"Thank you," Tina said, her hand on her chest. "To have your support as we get ready to bury our father is something we'll never forget. Despite the way he died and the circumstances, our father was a good man."

"A decent man," Rachel said loudly. "He built this school and changed so many lives. I don't want that to be lost in this story. And he loved us and made us who we are. We don't want that lost either. And our father had a crazy-bright future ahead of him. He didn't deserve to die this way and we are left…we want…"

She couldn't go on. Tina took the microphone. "We want to tell you one thing from the bottom of our hearts: We love our mother as much as we loved our father. We love her and we know—in our souls—that she did not kill Dad. We know what it looks like to people. We know about the gun matching the bullets. And we know Mom can get wound up at times, real wound up, but she would never kill our father. Never."

I realized both of Elaine Paulson's girls were looking directly at me and I nodded.

When it was over, I stood and looked up into the bleachers again. Sparkman was already gone. Ronald Peters was on his way out. Dee and Gina Nathaniel were climbing down together, and they came over to me.

"Hello, Dr. Cross," Gina Nathaniel said.

Dee smiled weakly. "Sad, confusing day."

"In too many ways," I said.

"Did she do it?"

"Ballistics don't lie," I said.

Jannie and I waited until the crowd thinned before approaching the twins, who were standing to one side of their grandmother and Barbara Taylor. Rachel saw me and went stone-faced. Tina gave Jannie a hug and shook my hand.

"We know you kept Mom from killing herself," Tina said. "Thank you. And we know absolutely that Mom did not do this. I don't care what the report said about that old gun and the bullets."

"Mom never shot that gun but once or twice," Rachel said. "And it scared her. I know that for a fact. Dad was the only one who ever shot that gun."

Tina said, "And Mom and Dad used to watch

Twenty/Twenty, you know, the one where the husband or the wife is always the killer?"

I shrugged. "Yes, I've seen it once or twice."

Rachel said, "Mom and Dad used to laugh about that. They'd throw up their hands, say, 'Why didn't they just get a divorce? Why did they have to kill each other?'"

Tina said, "Every time they watched *Twenty/Twenty*, they'd make each other promise that if they weren't in love anymore, they'd get divorced and not try to kill each other."

"But the gun," I said. "She had it with her on the beach when I found her, girls."

"There's got to be more to it," Rachel insisted. "Please, Dr. Cross, you are our only hope here."

There was such desperation in their expressions, I finally nodded. "I'll go over the ballistics report again and look at my notes."

Tina burst into tears, and a moment later Rachel did the same.

CHAPTER

47

BREE AND I GOT UP before dawn and went for a run. We'd been separated quite a bit by work obligations the past few months and it felt good to get out together, even if we were huffing, puffing, and sweating.

"I think I've got Commissioner Dennison figured out," Bree said about a mile into our normal route.

"Okay?"

"He was a player in Boston. He wants to be a player in DC. He wants Metro to be taken seriously so he'll be taken seriously."

"And that's a bad thing?"

"I haven't decided. Though I have to admit, he was less irrational than usual in my meeting with him yesterday. Almost reasonable."

"There you go. He's new to the job. He doesn't

know you or Chief Michaels all that well. There's bound to be some tension at first, and I don't think his wife's friendship with Mrs. Peggliazo helped you."

"True. And I think his instincts are spot-on. These shootings are not over, and when you look at the targets in a string, they are escalating."

"I agree. But if the next target is a bigger public figure in this town…"

"We can't compete with the FBI or the Secret Service or the Capitol Hill Police."

"Exactly, so don't. Stay in your lane. Play to your strengths. The new commissioner will figure you out."

When we were almost home, a block away, we slowed to a walk to cool down.

"You're good at this," she said. "Helping people talk through their problems."

"Thanks."

"No," she said, and she smiled at me over her shoulder. "I mean, you should really think about doing it professionally."

"Funny, funny," I said. I came up behind her and tickled her under the ribs.

She softly shrieked with laughter, ran up the stairs to our porch, and turned to wait for me with both arms open.

"Happy lady?" I said, stepping into her arms.

"Very," she said. "I don't think it would be possible for me to be unhappy today."

"Especially after a run and a kiss with your husband."

"Exactly my thoughts," Bree said and kissed me deeply. "I love you."

I kissed her back. "I adore you. Especially when you're like this."

"Like what?"

"Relaxed. Less preoccupied."

"Oh, well, it helps not to have something to be preoccupied with, and I feel like I turned the corner with Dennison yesterday."

"Good for you," I said, glancing at my watch. "I'm going to take a shower and then spend the morning studying the digital files of Kay Willingham and Randall Christopher before I see clients in the afternoon."

"Sounds more interesting than a personnel records review," she said. She pecked me on the cheek and put her key in the door.

I noticed that morning's *Washington Post* on our porch slider, unfolded the paper, and found myself looking at a picture of Kay Willingham.

"Damn it!" I groaned as I scanned the story that went with it. "I can't believe this."

"What?" Bree asked, halfway through the door.

I turned the paper around and showed her the front page and the headline:

KAY WILLINGHAM SPENT TIME IN MENTAL HOSPITAL

"It quotes anonymous law enforcement sources as saying that Kay's past history of mental illness has become quote 'part of the investigation,'" I said angrily. "A part of the investigation? That is not true. What the hell does that mean? And how the hell did the *Post* get this? Willingham was adamant about us not—"

"Alex," Bree said, sounding stunned. "I think I know."

"You know?" I said, almost shouting.

"Lower your voice and come upstairs, please."

We could hear Nana Mama bustling around in the kitchen when we climbed the stairs and went into our bedroom. Bree closed the door and looked me straight in the eye.

"Yesterday I told Dennison about Kay spending time in a psychiatric facility."

"What? Why? I told you Willingham wanted—"

"I know. I just felt under pressure to give him something. And here he goes and tells some journalist! Why would he do that?"

"I don't know," I said.

"I'm at fault, but he did it to help himself, I'm sure."

That made me think about Kelli Ann Higgins, the PR flack, and something she'd said about Clive Sparkman. "He's grooming that reporter. Feeding him a story like this so he'll get a flattering profile down the road."

"That's it exactly," Bree said, disgusted. "That's Dennison one hundred percent. Alex, again, I'm sorry, I should have known better."

"Water under the bridge. Although I can't imagine the vice president being very happy with me or Ned this morning."

"Why is that?"

"Besides Willingham's chief of staff and his Secret Service agents, I believe we were the only others who knew."

Before she could reply, I heard the doorbell ring twice. I glanced at our bedside clock.

"Quarter to seven?" I said, going to the window over Fifth Street. A black Suburban was double-parked in front of our home.

I scrambled down the stairs before Nana Mama could get to the front door. I opened it and knew I was about to have a bad morning.

U.S. Secret Service Special Agent Lloyd Price was standing there. He grimaced as he looked me up and down. I was still drenched from my run.

"Take a shower and get dressed, Dr. Cross," Price said. "My boss would like a word with you."

CHAPTER

48

THIRTY MINUTES LATER, AFTER AN awkward car ride during which Special Agent Price refused to answer any of my questions, the Suburban turned into an alley in Alexandria, Virginia. Two Secret Service agents guarding the alley waved us through. We parked behind two other black Suburbans.

I followed Agent Price through a pair of unmarked industrial steel doors and down a hallway that smelled of flowers. Ned Mahoney was waiting there with Agent Donald Breit, who appeared as thrilled with us as his partner was.

"Inside, both of you," Breit said, motioning to a door next to Ned.

Mahoney took a deep breath and went through it. I followed him into a well-appointed viewing room in a mortuary. The six rows of white chairs were empty. Beyond the chairs, bouquets of lilies and other funereal flowers surrounded the open casket in which the body of Kay Willingham lay in repose.

I stood there gaping for several moments. I had had no idea where Price was taking me, but I certainly didn't expect this. But I recovered and walked toward the casket.

The last time I'd seen Kay, she was lying in the back seat of her convertible, shot to death. The luridness of that scene flickered deep in my brain, but it was soon gone because the socialite was as lovely in death as she had been in life.

Kay looked so natural, she could have been taking a nap, merely resting before the first doorbell chime of one of her legendary parties. And her dress? Was it the one she wore the night she'd broken her heel in front of her house? The night we were photographed?

My mind returned to that night, to when we'd gone inside her home and she'd spun away from me, a little tipsy on champagne and freer than any woman I'd ever known.

And now here you are, I thought as I knelt before her casket. *I promise I will find out who did this to you.*

Then I said a prayer for Kay's soul, made the sign of the cross, got up, and turned around to find J. Walter Willingham walking down the aisle between the empty seats toward me and Mahoney.

"They've made her look quite beautiful, have they not, Dr. Cross? Agent Mahoney?"

"Yes, Mr. Vice President," Mahoney said.

"Remarkable, sir," I said.

"That's because they are the best here," Willingham said. "If a president dies in office, this is where they bring him. Since Lincoln."

He paused to gaze at Kay in her casket, then his expression hardened and he fixed his angry attention on us. "I asked for her privacy and you leaked it to the press."

"I most certainly did not, sir," Mahoney said. "I hate the press."

"I believe I am responsible, Mr. Vice President," I said and explained that I'd relayed the information to my wife, Metro's chief of detectives, who was pressured into revealing the information by the new commissioner of police.

"I deeply apologize for this, Mr. Vice President. My wife does too. We never wanted to disrespect your wishes. I guess we expected more out of Commissioner Dennison, but ultimately I shoulder the blame."

I thought I'd get a harsh response, but Willingham just studied me a long moment and then reached out to shake my hand. "Thank you, Dr. Cross. I respect a man who accepts the consequences of his actions."

Then he walked past me and stood at his ex-wife's casket, his eyes roaming over her. He touched the back of her hand with two fingers, raised his fingers to his lips, then touched her lips.

"Bye, Kay," he whispered, and he reached up to shut the lid.

When he turned, his eyes were watery, and he had to clear his throat. "She'll be sent south in an hour."

"And from there?"

"Her second cousin and her executor will meet the casket at the plane and see to her burial in the family plot on the old family plantation."

"No funeral or memorial, sir?" Mahoney asked.

Willingham shook his head. "In her recently revised will, she specifically requested no remembrance of her other than a headstone. Cruel, really, to those of us who loved her."

I found that puzzling but didn't comment. "Again, I apologize for what happened," I said.

"Apology accepted, Dr. Cross, and I appreciate you finding Kay's murderer."

"Thank you, sir. I know it's not the time or the place, but could I ask you a question?"

His chief of staff, Claudette Barnes, appeared and walked toward us. "Mr. Vice President?"

Willingham held up a finger. "One second, Claudette. Go ahead, Dr. Cross."

"When you and Kay were estranged, back when you were governor, did you hire someone to follow her?"

"Follow Kay?" He smiled and shook his head. "No. Never. What's this about?"

"There appear to be photographs of her from that time taken with a long lens."

His expression narrowed. "What kind of photographs?"

"Just of Kay out and about in DC, sir," I said. "In one of them she was with me. It was taken the night I drove her home from a fundraiser. The picture was shot in front of her place in Georgetown."

Barnes said, "Mr. Vice President, we really need to be going."

He held up his palms. "I'm sorry, Dr. Cross. It upsets me to hear she was being followed, but I have absolutely no clue who was behind that. I can tell you that Kay was ramping up to one of her episodes about that time, which was why we were separated. I had Alabama to run while I waited for her to come crashing down again."

With that, he turned, moved fast past his chief of staff, and said, "Air Force Two is not going to fly without me, Claudette. I am the vice president. It's got to count for something, for God's sake!"

"Yes, sir," Barnes said. She glanced at us, threw up her arms, then followed Willingham out of the room.

CHAPTER

49

I TOOK AN UBER HOME. On the ride, my thoughts drifted to Elaine Paulson and her daughters at the funeral the day before, to Tina saying, *We know absolutely that Mom did not do this. I don't care what the report said about that old gun and the bullets.* And Rachel saying, *Mom never shot that gun but once or twice. And it scared her.*

I didn't have to reread the ballistics report to know for certain that the gun that killed Kay and Christopher was the same gun I took from Elaine Paulson. Sometimes you hear about lab tests being contaminated. But comparing the grooves in a gun barrel with the markings made on a bullet fired through it is an exact science. There's no mistaking it.

Still, could someone lost in a fit of jealousy who had fired the gun only a few times and was supposedly scared of guns have displayed the kind of cold-blooded marksmanship shown in the tight grouping of the bullet wounds? Unless Paulson had secretly trained herself to shoot, I couldn't see it.

I supposed it was possible that she had not had the gun the night of the killing and that the real shooter had used it and then brought it back to her house, but that was so unlikely, I set it aside. I got out of the Uber and thanked the driver.

It was after ten a.m. when I walked into the kitchen and found Nana Mama having coffee with John Sampson. He was dressed in jeans and a dark polo shirt with his service weapon in a shoulder holster. His badge was visible on his left hip. His jacket hung on the back of his chair.

"What are you doing here, John? Where's Willow?"

"With her brother and sister," he said. "They decided to take Ned up on his offer and bring her out to his place on the Delaware shore."

"Great spot," I said. "Don't you think you should be with them?"

"At the moment? No. At the moment, I need to work."

"I think you should be with your family. Billie's funeral was yesterday, John."

"Alex, I'll join them in a day or two, but right now I need to work. Okay?"

There was such desperation in his eyes. I glanced at Nana Mama, who nodded sadly.

Sampson was looking for a case to get lost in so he could forget his grief, and I realized it was more merciful to let him.

"I have to cancel a few appointments, but I agree, let's go to work, John."

He acted like I'd just thrown him a life preserver. "Thank you. Where are we going? What case?"

"The rapes and killings," I said.

Sampson jumped up, said, "I got a car parked down the street."

"Why don't you go get it and I'll make my calls," I said.

He nodded, hugged Nana Mama, thanked her for the coffee, and left. When the front door banged shut, my grandmother came over and took my hand.

"You're a good friend as well as his best friend," she said.

"I know."

"You'll be doing two jobs out there with him."

"I get that. You're right. It could be a good thing."

She gave my hand a little shake and said, "Cancel your appointments."

Ten minutes later we were rolling, John at the wheel, driving to an address in Landover, Maryland. It was just like old times except for the ghost of Billie. I did not bring her up or ask how he was doing. Instead, I was quiet, present with him, waiting for him to talk. When we got close to the address, he finally asked, "Who are we speaking to here?"

"Peggy Dixon," I said. "Several months before Elizabeth Hernandez was taken, Dixon claimed she was attacked by and escaped from a man trying to rape her after a party in Southeast DC. But she was evidently under the influence of an illegal substance at the time and unable to describe her assailant."

He looked over at me. "Kind of a long shot going back to her, don't you think?"

"You never know. There's the address."

We pulled over in front of a sign reading PATROL, A UNISEX HAIR SALON, parked, and got out. There was a line of ten people waiting to get in.

"Feel like a trim?" I asked, running my hand over my hair.

"I already keep mine high and tight," Sampson said. "She work here?"

"That's what I'm guessing," I said. We cut to the front of the line, held up our IDs, and entered a small waiting area.

A receptionist with blue fingernails and long blue bangs like the rock star Sia's sat behind the counter and said in a high nasal whine, "Wait your turn. No reservation, no cutting the line."

Sampson held up his ID and badge, said, "Hey, Sia, do me a favor? Please tell Peggy Dixon we're here and would like to talk to her."

Fingers flew to the bangs and pushed them aside, revealing an Asian guy. "I'm not Sia," he said. "I don't do derivative. And Ms. Dixon is with clients. All day."

I said, "Whatever your name is, have you heard of the Maya Parker case?"

"Who hasn't?"

"We're here about that."

"Oh," he said, perking up. "Oh, oh, okay, then, let me see what I can do."

CHAPTER

50

WITH THAT, THE RECEPTIONIST JUMPED up and scurried through the salon, which seemed to be doing a bustling business; there were patrons in all ten chairs.

"Gold mine," Sampson said.

Before I could answer, Sia, or whatever his name was, motioned for us to come through the salon. We ignored the looks of indignation from patrons and stylists alike and went to Sia.

"Peg's upstairs," he said. "With a client, but the old thing's half deaf and under the dryer already, so she says go on up."

We climbed narrow steps into an airy loft space with a single chair, sink, and dryer. There was an older woman under the dryer reading *People* magazine.

A plump woman in her late twenties with a wild hairdo—purple roots rising to frosted spikes—

peasant clothes, and lots of piercings got up from behind a glass-and-steel desk. "I'm Peg Dixon. I thought someone might come months ago when she disappeared. Maya, I mean. It's him, right? The guy who took Elizabeth Hernandez and who tried to take me?"

"You tell us," I said after we showed her our credentials. "According to the report we saw, you were under the influence of an illegal substance at the time of the attack?"

She cackled with laughter. "Is that what it said? That dweeb. Sorry. Well, I suppose I was. A little, anyway. I mean, how long does a good dose of molly last? Eight, ten hours? And I was like twelve out from dropping, on the downward slide of the trip for sure, so I was like, you know, in that dreamy and unaware but, like, totally-there state you get into sometimes. That's when he grabbed me."

She cackled again. "He didn't expect *me*. That's for sure."

I could see why the original detective had found Peggy Dixon frustrating, but I decided to relax and listen to her tell the story in her own way and at her own pace. Over the next fifteen minutes, until her client under the dryer was done, we listened to her ramble and spin and double-back in her narrative multiple times before we got a clear sense of what had happened.

She'd been at an underground rave at a

condemned factory building in Southeast. There were four or five hundred people partying in the building, lots of people of all ages in rave-wear staples like bunny and raccoon suits.

"I was there from four in the afternoon, real early, dosed at five, and lasted until four in the morning," she said. "I just hit that point where I was done and I couldn't find my friend so I put it on autopilot and headed home."

"On foot?"

"Correcto-mundo," she said. She made her fingers into a pistol and set it to her head. "Peg here was not too bright. But to this day I don't know why I noticed this, like, weird smooth black rock in the weeds near the building. I picked the rock up. It was maybe five inches long, thick, and kind of cylinder-shaped in the middle, too big to go in my pocket, but I thought my little brother would like it, so I decided to carry it home."

A block and a half from the rave, as she was going by another factory, she was attacked from behind.

"He was quiet, never heard him. He came up behind me and got his arm around my neck," she said. "Next thing I knew he was dragging me into an alley, and I could feel he was big because he kept lifting me off my feet, and I'm not exactly a lightweight." She cackled again. "But anyway, I could feel this crazy kind of dark energy coming off the dude and I'm thinking, *Peg, you have one chance to live here. Make it count.*"

Halfway down the alley, her assailant slowed, brought out a strip of duct tape with his free hand, and covered her mouth with it. She whined, stiffened, and then intentionally went limp, as if she'd lost consciousness.

He relaxed his hold and she sagged to the ground and went over onto her side.

"I was looking up at him sideways then, my eyes barely open," she said. "And the light in the alley was weird, but I believe he wore a ski mask and had a big zip tie in his mouth. I swear, he had the darkest, deadest eyes I've ever seen."

"And then?" Sampson said.

"I waited until he crouched over me and reached for my arm, then I swung that rock sticking out the bottom of my fist like it was my daddy's ball-peen hammer. I can't tell you where I hit him, only that I did. Hard. I mean, that sucker went back on his heels, tripped, and sprawled on the ground, and this gal was up and moving."

Dixon said she ran screaming down the alley, got to a road, and ran the full fourteen blocks home. Scared, wired, she called the attack in and a police officer came and took her report.

"He was more concerned about the drugs I'd been on."

Sampson said, "Anything you might have

remembered about him later? I mean, after you made that report?"

She thought about that. "You know, yes. I had terrible nightmares after the attack. For almost a year. And really the only thing that kept coming up in those nightmares was his smell."

"What did he smell like?"

"Like this men's cologne I'd smelled before. And I didn't know what it was until just a few weeks ago when I smelled it in a bar and almost had this, like, freak-out, but I kept cool enough to ask the guy wearing it what it was."

"What'd he say?"

"Versace Eros for Men," she said and cackled. "Isn't that, like, ironic and dark in a twisted kind of way? A rapist and killer who wants to smell like Versace Eros?"

CHAPTER

51

TWO HOURS LATER, BREE STONE stared at a spot a few inches over the police commissioner's head as Dennison ranted.

"Your goddamn husband told the vice president of the United States that I leaked Kay Willingham's stay in a loony bin?"

Bree lowered her gaze and glared at Dennison, who was behind his desk in his office with Chief Michaels to one side. "Are you denying it, Commissioner?"

"Denying it? Who the hell do you think you are?"

"I am goddamn Alex Cross's wife," Bree shot back. "And his confidante and his colleague. You took information that you were warned was sensitive and you decided to give it to that reporter for your own reasons. Whatever the hell they were."

Dennison looked ready to blow his stack. "Well, then, I guess you have to decide whether your allegiance is to Alex Cross or Metro PD."

"You're making this too easy, Commissioner," she said. She took out her badge and slammed it on his desk, then followed it with her weapon. "I don't know what your angle is or what you are trying to be, but I am no longer part of it. I have better ways to spend my life, and I intend to pursue them."

She turned to Chief Michaels. "It's been an honor to serve with you, sir, but some things just aren't worth it. I'll have my letter of resignation on your desk and my office cleaned out by tomorrow noon."

"You can't just walk out!" Dennison shouted.

"Watch me," Bree said, heading for the door.

"Chief Stone, stop, and that is a direct order!"

"What is it about the term *letter of resignation* that you don't understand, you self-serving ass?" she said, opening the office door. "I don't work for you anymore."

Bree slammed the door behind her because it made her feel good. So did making a face at Dennison's personal assistant and heading for the elevator without the weight of her job and whether she was good enough at it hanging around her neck. She'd quit barely a minute before and already the stress of it was gone.

I can do anything, she thought giddily. *Anything I want!*

Bree returned to her office thinking about travel and exotic beach vacations and graduate school. But seeing the mementos of a long career in law enforcement all around her dampened her enthusiasm.

Part of her wanted to take it all right then and there and clear out. But she didn't have her car with her, and she wanted to have boxes and packing material to do it right.

She took her purse, briefcase, and laptop and left Metro headquarters. Seeing other officers and detectives coming and going, Bree felt surprisingly removed from their concerns.

I'm free to be me, she thought, calling an Uber. *Free to be Bree!*

She was on Fifth Street by four and got out of the car trying to remember the last time she'd been home this early. It didn't matter; she'd have an even shorter workday tomorrow.

She laughed, walked across the porch, and went inside feeling more alive than she had since she'd taken the job as chief of detectives. Hearing steel bowls clanking in the kitchen, Bree went in and found Nana Mama just starting to prepare dinner.

"Why don't you sit?" Bree said. "I'll cook dinner tonight."

"What?" Nana Mama said. "But you don't know what I had planned."

"Then let me help you."

Alex's grandmother gave her an odd look. "No offense, and I love you, Bree, but you've never offered to help before. You told me you don't like cooking."

"I actually meant I didn't have time for cooking. And honestly, I saw how it connected you and Billie, and I guess I'd like some of that same connection while I still have the chance. If that's okay?"

Nana Mama softened, shuffled over to Bree, and hugged her. "It's more than okay, dear. It's wonderful. Thank you. And you can start by slicing those onions."

Bree grinned, kissed the old woman on the forehead, and said, "Done." She got a knife and sliced the onions and chopped up everything else Alex's grandmother wanted chopped, then they poured the sauce over short ribs, covered them in foil, and put them in the oven on low heat.

"There," Nana Mama said. "We'll eat around seven thirty."

"Perfect," Bree said. "What else can I do?"

"This old lady is going to lie down for twenty minutes before Ali comes home."

"Oh, okay, then," Bree said. "Sweet dreams."

Nana left the kitchen and Bree realized that she had no idea what to do next.

Then she heard footsteps and the basement door opened. Alex came into the kitchen with two coffee mugs.

"Nana Mama said you and Sampson went off this morning," she said. "Canceled your clients to work with him."

"That's right," Alex said, going to pour coffee from Nana Mama's bottomless pot. "We're downstairs trying to see if there's an overlap or pattern to where Maya Parker, Elizabeth Hernandez, and the others vanished beyond Southeast DC. By the way, why are you home so early?"

Bree had barely been keeping her emotions in check. Now she blurted out, "I quit my job because the commissioner made the thought of spending one more day working for him totally unacceptable. He also called you my 'goddamn husband,' and I called him a 'self-serving ass.'"

She felt tears flowing and could barely see Alex when he set down the coffee cups and came to embrace her. Bree held tight to him and let loose her frustration.

"Are those tears of relief or regret?" he asked when her crying had slowed.

"Relief," she said, snuggling into his chest. "No regrets. Yet."

"Well, then," he said, rubbing her back, "I support your decision one hundred percent."

CHAPTER

52

I HATE PHONE CALLS AT two fifteen in the morning, especially when I've fallen asleep past midnight after hours of grief therapy with Sampson (in the form of work) and listening to Bree as she dealt with the emotional upheaval of quitting a seventeen-year career in law enforcement.

So I was not happy when I heard my phone ringing and even less happy when I peered groggily at the caller ID and saw SPARKMAN.

"Not a chance, Clive," I grumbled. I sent the call to voice mail, put the phone on vibrate, and tried to go back to sleep.

He called twice more. I could hear the phone buzzing. I was about to turn it off altogether when he texted me: Damn it, Cross, pick up! Higgins was attacked!

Higgins? I thought. *Kelli Ann Higgins? The dirt-monger?*

I got up without waking Bree, went into the bathroom, and shut the door. My phone started buzzing in my hand. I answered, said, "Tell me."

"She was beaten and her apartment ransacked," Sparkman said, a tremor in his voice. "I...I found her."

"Where is she?"

"The back of an ambulance headed to Georgetown Medical," he said.

"She conscious?"

"In and out," he said. "I must have just missed whoever did it. Thank God."

"Where are you?"

"Outside her place in Foggy Bottom. I'll text the address."

"Police there?"

"A patrol officer."

"Tell him to seal her apartment. Move nothing and stay where you are."

Before he could reply, I cut the connection, slipped out of the bathroom, went into the walk-in closet, and dressed as quietly as I could. But when I came out, Bree sat up in bed and asked me what was going on.

I told her and she flipped on the light. "I'm coming with you."

"You resigned."

"It's not official until noon and I want to see this."

I knew better than to argue and waited while

she got dressed. The city's streets were virtually empty, and by a quarter to three we were parked and hustling up the sidewalk past a patrol car to a swank townhome in Foggy Bottom.

Sparkman was outside the front door, smoking a cigarette, his hands shaking, speaking to the uniformed officer on the scene. "I'm a wreck," he said when he noticed us. "Look at me." He broke down crying. "She always said I was so naive, that I didn't begin to understand how cruel and ruthless DC could be. She told me she feared for her life, and I didn't believe her. Is she still alive?"

"We don't know," Bree said. "Explain how you came to find her, Mr. Sparkman."

He looked at me. I said, "Answer Chief of Detectives Stone, Clive."

Sparkman got himself together and told her that what had started as a purely professional relationship with Higgins had changed in the past few weeks. It had been one-way up to then, Higgins teasing him, leading him on, and, when it suited her, feeding him informed dirt for his blog.

But then there'd been this one drunken night.

"She seemed embarrassed when she woke up, and she asked me to leave as discreetly as possible. I figured that was the end of it, you know, a mistake on both our parts. But she called me a few nights later. She sounded a little drunk. I went over. And, I don't know, it became a secret thing between us. Pretty regular too."

I said, "You don't think you should have mentioned that when you told me to talk to her a few days ago?"

"It's not like we were in love. It's just…you know."

"I don't know, but I assume she called you earlier tonight?"

"Texted me. Around nine. Said she wouldn't be done with work until after midnight, but she'd appreciate the company and to come in from the alley like I always do. Here, I have the text."

Bree took the phone, looked at it, and nodded. "So you got here at what time?"

"Twenty to one?" he said. "The back door was unlocked. I went inside, expecting the place to be lit by candles and some music going. But there'd been one hell of a fight. She was in the kitchen, on her side, bleeding. I called 911 and held her while I waited for the EMTs."

"She say anything?"

"Like I said, she was in and out. Made perfect sense and then no sense. But she knew me one time. Said my name and seemed like she wanted to tell me something, but she couldn't get it out. Just kept saying, like, 'Ahh-sigh. Ahh-sigh.'"

Bree wrote that down, said, "I know you said the place is trashed. Did you notice anything obviously missing that had been there on your previous visits?"

He frowned. "I don't think so."

"What about her computers?"

"Oh, I'm sure those are still there," he said. "She keeps her laptops and backups in her safe at night, said there were all sorts of people who'd love to have a look at them, and even if they managed to get them, they wouldn't find anything."

"Encrypted?"

"Yeah, she used this privacy system called Thor or something."

"Tor," I said.

"That's it. She said Tor was the only safe way for her to do business without getting...without getting killed." He started to cry again. "Jesus, she looked awful. I just want to go home."

"Not until you've been processed," Bree said. "We need your clothes. We need you photographed."

"Why?"

"So we can prove you weren't part of it," I said.

"I wasn't."

"You were the only one who knew the rear door was going to be unlocked."

"But I'm not the only one who knew about the rear door. Everyone who's ever bought or sold dirt with Kelli had to come in from the alley. Discreet."

"Duly noted," Bree said. "I have a forensics crew on its way. It shouldn't take too long, Mr. Sparkman."

He started to argue, but then surrendered.

Bree looked at me. "Go inside?"

"I think I'll leave that to you, Chief," I said. "Your last official act. I'm going to the hospital."

CHAPTER

53

I REACHED THE EMERGENCY ROOM at Georgetown Medical Center at three thirty and learned that doctors were still trying to stabilize Kelli Ann Higgins and determine the extent of her injuries.

I waited outside the trauma room until a doctor exited talking to a med student. "That woman is lucky to be alive," the doctor said. "Skull fracture. Broken jaw. Several busted ribs. Probably a ruptured spleen."

"Blunt-force wounds?" the med student asked.

"Yes, all of them."

I stepped up and identified myself. "She conscious?"

"For a few minutes at a time."

"Did she say anything about the attack?"

"Yes. She said, 'Hit me.'"

The door to the trauma room opened and

Higgins was wheeled out on a gurney. Her face was badly swollen on the right side, and she was being given a blood transfusion.

"Where'm I?" Higgins said, the words slurred.

"Georgetown Medical Center, Kelli Ann," one of the nurses said.

"She headed to surgery?" I asked the doctor.

"CT first," she said. "The neurosurgeon's on her way."

"Mind if I tag along with her to CT?"

"Be my guest."

I hurried down the hallway following Higgins's gurney. I showed the nurses my badge, said, "FBI."

"B? I?" Higgins said, blinking.

They stopped outside the radiology department.

I got down low to where I thought Higgins could see me. "That's right. FBI. You remember me?"

She looked like she was having trouble focusing, but then she said, "Craw."

"That's right, Cross," I said.

The nurses started wheeling the gurney again, and I had to wait until they'd gotten her inside the CT room.

One nurse said, "You've got two minutes while the techs set up, and then you're going to have to leave the area, Dr. Cross."

I went around to where Higgins could see me again.

"Hit me," she said.

"Who hit you?"

She swallowed. "Craw…bar."

"They hit you with a crowbar. Did you know your attacker?"

She blinked. "Claw…bar."

"Why did this person attack you?"

Higgins looked puzzled, squinted at me. "Claw? Craw?"

"Yes. I'm Dr. Cross. Why do you think you were attacked?"

Her eyelids drifted shut.

"Kelli Ann?" I said and touched her lightly. "Stay with me."

"Uh?" she said, opening her eyes.

"Do you know why you were attacked?"

"Na."

"Were you selling or buying something that could get you attacked?"

Higgins didn't move, and I thought she hadn't heard. Then she licked her lips and croaked out, "Why cuh-ay?"

Why cuh-ay? My heart started slamming against my chest. "Why Kay? Why Kay Willingham?"

Higgins relaxed and nodded.

"What about Kay?" I said.

"Why Kay kill."

I stared at her. *Why Kay kill.* "You were beaten because of why Kay was killed?"

Her jaw slackened, her eyes closed, and she nodded slightly.

"You know why she was killed?" I said, knowing the techs were coming.

She nodded slightly again. "Ahh-sigh."

"Ahh-sigh?" I said.

She made a humming noise in her throat.

"I don't understand. Ahh-sigh?"

The radiology tech came over. "We need her now."

"Lum," Higgins said. "Lum." She saw I didn't understand and got agitated. "Ahh-sigh. Lum."

"You can tell him afterward, dear," the nurse said, rolling her away from me. "We just need you to be still while the machine tells us exactly where you're hurt."

I stared after Higgins and suddenly understood what she had been trying to say: *asylum*.

She had been beaten for knowing that Kay was killed because of the asylum.

What asylum? That psychiatric facility Kay went to in Alabama?

Was that what she was trying to tell me?

CHAPTER
54

Alabama
Two days later

NED MAHONEY WAS AT THE wheel as we drove north of Montgomery in stifling heat and humidity that would have made a DC summer day feel fall-like by comparison. It was August. The crops were tall. The foliage between the fields was a dark gray-green, pines, oaks, and creeping vines alike.

"You think Bree's changing her mind?" Mahoney asked.

I shrugged. After the Higgins attack, Chief Michaels showed up at our house and convinced her to take two weeks to cool off and see if quitting was really in her long-term best interests. Evidently, the idea for him to come had been Commissioner Dennison's.

"Dennison was a man about it," I said. "He admitted he was wrong and said he recognized her clear value once it was no longer there, that he wished to apologize and move on. He also apologized to me for sharing the information about Kay."

"Odds of her going back?"

I shrugged again. "Fifty-fifty?"

"That's about what I'm giving this trip of yours not being a wild-goose chase. I mean, we have Elaine Paulson dead to rights."

This was ground we'd covered before, but I replied, "But we don't know the truth. Do I wish Higgins had said more before she died on the operating table? Of course. But we have a dying statement from a known peddler of scandal who told me she was beaten and Kay and Christopher were shot to death because of Kay's time in the asylum. We have to chase this."

My phone buzzed with a text. I read it, then told Ned, "Rawlins says Higgins's computers have one of the most sophisticated encryption systems he's ever seen. He's days from being inside them."

"Kay's asylum it is, then," Mahoney said, surrendering. "And again, I wish I could have justified bringing Sampson down with us."

"He figured out he needed to be with his family," I said.

"I love that guy."

"Me too."

We got off the highway and drove six miles on a county road to the entrance of West Briar, the private psychiatric facility where Kay had stayed on several different occasions over the years. A winding drive climbed up through thick woods, and then the trees thinned and ended, revealing an open, campus-like setting dominated by a large white, rambling structure—more like a country inn than an asylum—with well-kept lawns and gardens.

Arriving unannounced can often result in an initial strikeout for investigators, but sometimes when people are shown FBI credentials with no warning, there's a valuable window of candor before their guards go up and they start posturing and lying to you. The more hardened the criminal or the smarter the sociopath, the narrower the window of candor. The opposite is also true; the more honest the person, the wider the window.

We got out of the car and were met by a temperature of over one hundred degrees and air that was thick with moisture.

"I'm going to need a shower by the time we get inside," Mahoney grumbled.

"Two showers," I said, wiping at the sweat rolling off my forehead.

Inside the building, the air was so cold, we shivered. The receptionist, an older woman with half-glasses, gave us such a frigid stare that I shivered again as Mahoney and I showed her our credentials.

"FBI?" she said. "What's this about?"

"Please notify the administrator that we wish to speak to him or her as part of a federal investigation," Mahoney said, ignoring her stare. "We also want to speak to whoever was medically in charge of the late Kay Willingham during her most recent stay."

The receptionist's eyes widened. She placed a murmured call.

Five minutes later, we were sent to see the psychiatrist who ran West Briar. He stood up behind his spotless desk as we entered his office. He was surrounded by dozens of leather books that looked like they had never been read, generic sailing photographs, and framed degrees from Rice and Baylor. He smiled unhappily as we approached. I couldn't help suspecting we were about to see the smallest possible window of candor.

"I am Dr. Nathan Tolliver," he said, reaching out to shake our hands limply. "To what do I owe the pleasure of a visit from the FBI?"

"We'd like to see any and all files regarding the late Kay Willingham's stays here," Mahoney said. "And we want to talk with everyone who interacted with her, especially her primary doctor, during her most recent stay."

"That would be me," said a woman entering behind us. "I'm Dr. Jeanne Hicks, and I'm sure we would both like to be of help, but our hands are tied under Alabama law. Kay opted, in writing, to keep her psychiatric files secret."

"This is a federal murder investigation," I said. "A federal murder investigation into Kay's death."

"We understand and we support what you are doing," Dr. Tolliver said. "Kay was a special person. But legally there's nothing we can do. To have access to those files, you'll need a court order or the signature of the executor of Ms. Willingham's estate."

"Who is in Montgomery, where we just came from," Mahoney said.

"Unfortunately, that is correct," Dr. Hicks said.

CHAPTER

55

THE LAW OFFICES OF Carson and Knight were housed in a venerable Southern mansion on a side street not far from the Alabama state capitol. For the second time that day, we showed up unannounced. We presented our credentials to Reggie, the young man at the front desk of the busy legal enterprise.

The lobby was paneled in Alabama black oak and up high on one wall were two large paintings of the firm's founders, Robert Carson and Claude Knight. Below them in rows were photographs of the various attorneys who'd been made partner since the firm's inception nearly fifty years before.

While we waited, I studied the pictures and was surprised to see a photograph of a younger Claudette Barnes, the vice president's chief of staff; her late husband, Kevin, who'd died in a biking accident; and, higher up on the wall, a picture of J. Walter Willingham himself.

"Willingham and Barnes both worked here?" I said to Mahoney.

"The VP for about six months after he left the prosecutor's office," boomed a man in a gray linen suit, a white shirt, and a bow tie coming down the staircase. "A great man, and his picture helps the firm's image."

He grinned and stuck out his hand to shake ours. "Robert Carson Jr. People call me Bobby. I understand you have a question about Kay Willingham's estate."

"Are you the executor, Mr. Carson?"

"I am not," he said. "I am the son of one of the founders. I manage the firm and oversee the executor of her estate, Nina Larch, who is unfortunately away for the day taking a deposition in Valdosta. However, I am also Kay's second cousin and am familiar with her estate, so I am hoping I can help. Let's go into this conference room, gentlemen. It's not in use, Reggie?"

The man at the front desk said, "No, Bobby."

"Do not disturb, then," he said and gestured us inside.

When the door shut, Mahoney said, "To avoid having to get a federal court order, we need the executor to sign a release allowing us to review Kay Willingham's medical files from her time at West Briar psychiatric."

The hail-fellow-well-met expression melted from Carson's face. "I am afraid I cannot help you there," he said. "I know for a fact that Kay feared being ripped apart and dissected after her death. She stipulated that—"

"Hold on," Mahoney said. "'Ripped apart and dissected'? How do you know that?"

"She told me so herself," he said. "She worried about what the media might do with her mental illness and got a judge to agree to seal her medical and probate files."

Mahoney said, "Local judge?"

"State level."

"We'll have to see a federal judge, then," I said.

We started to go, but Carson said, sounding pained, "Kay's not going to get her wish, is she? Since it's a murder case, once the files become part of the chain of evidence, they're fair game, I suppose."

"We're not out to destroy Kay's reputation if that's what you mean," I said.

"No, no," he said. "My poor sweet cousin did a lot of that on her own, long before she inherited her grandma's money and land."

Before we could reply to that, there was a knock at the door, and Reggie gingerly put his head in. "Your four-thirty is waiting, Bobby."

Carson looked at us. "Can't put this one off, gentlemen. Can you let me know what the judge decides? I feel very protective of Kay and just want to make sure her wishes are taken into consideration."

"Of course," Mahoney said.

He shook our hands and we went out into the inferno of an Alabama August day. The rental car felt like the inside of a blast furnace until the AC kicked in.

"I'm not going to bother with the local judges," Mahoney said, picking up his phone. "I'm going straight to the U.S. Attorney General's office to get them to file for it in federal court here in Montgomery."

He spent several minutes on the phone with an assistant U.S. attorney, and when he hung up, he said, "She says we'll probably get it in the morning. Hotel? Shower?"

"Tempting, but we've got daylight left," I said. "Let's go find that plantation. Kay was always conflicted when she talked about her grand-mother's place. She'd light up about its beauty and then express remorse at the history of it. I think she told me she was giving the property to the state for a park when she died. I'd like to see it."

"It's also where she's buried, isn't it?"

"That too."

CHAPTER

56

THE ROAD GOING OUT TO the Sutter family's plantation was badly in need of repair after a spring of flooding. After the car bottomed out several times, we finally found the entrance to the property some seven miles east of the highway on the south side of the road. Crumbling brick pillars supported an iron gate with peeling paint.

The Sutter name was still discernible in the rusted ironwork, as was a faded No Trespassing sign on one pillar. The gate was chained and padlocked. Beyond it, a gravel road disappeared into the woods.

"Feel like a walk?" I said.

"In this heat?"

"I think we can lose the coats, ties, and starched white shirts this once, don't you, Agent Mahoney?"

He gave me a glum gaze for several seconds,

then sighed. "J. Edgar will be rolling over in his grave."

"I think that's already happened a few times for a lot of different reasons."

We both stripped down to our undershirts, suit pants, and shoes before getting out. It was past six and the heat had ebbed a little, but it was still ungodly hot and humid as we went to the gate. I was about to start climbing when Mahoney gave the padlock a shake.

It opened.

"See?" he said. "We don't need to bother J. Edgar."

We pushed open the gate. Mahoney drove through and I shut it, wrapped the chain and lock the way we'd found it.

"I hope no one decides to close that lock," Mahoney said as I got in the rental. "We don't have bolt cutters."

We drove down the gravel road, raising dust, then crossed a low spot that had flooded during the rain. There was mud splashed out on both sides.

"Other trucks have been in here recently," I said.

"More than the burial detail?"

I stuck my head out the window, saw water glistening on tire tracks. "More recent."

We drove through the woods into fields that must once have been full of cotton plants but were now overgrown with bramble and thistle.

It was a deeply disturbing feeling to imagine the backbreaking hours that enslaved people had spent in those fields.

The plantation house appeared. In its day, from the way Kay had described it to me, her paternal grandmother's mansion must have been breathtaking, a sprawling antebellum manor finished in alabaster white and forest-green trim with a covered porch that wrapped around the entire house and a well-tended flower garden on the front lawn.

Now, however, the neglect showed everywhere. The alabaster finish was speckled and splashed with mold and peeling away in big strips. Parts of the porch roof had caved in. Kudzu choked the front columns and the entire porch railing. Tentacles and shrouds of the creeping vine had already reached the upper floors, where birds were flashing in and out of dark windows with broken, jagged glass.

"This is where Kay Willingham, queen of the DC socialites, is buried?" I said.

CHAPTER

57

WE DROVE TOWARD THE DECREPIT plantation house and saw that a road had been cleared and maintained beyond it. Mahoney continued down the road through more overgrown fields and pine thickets. We were well out of sight of the mansion when I spotted headstones up on a knoll ahead.

"Stop there," I said.

Mahoney pulled over by a stone path leading up to the knoll. I got out, felt a breeze for the first time all day, and began to climb, Mahoney right behind me.

I don't know what I expected, but with each step higher, I was surprised to see more and more headstones on the knoll and more and more of the remarkable scenery spread out below and beyond the Sutter family cemetery. There had to be at least three hundred and fifty headstones there. Below them, at the bottom of a gentle slope, a mature oak forest grew on a flat that ran out to several arms jutting into a large lake. The sun was behind us, throwing golden light on the timbered points and the water.

"Beautiful spot," Mahoney said.

"Spectacular," I said. "No wonder Kay wanted to be buried here."

I tore my attention from the lake and looked around at the headstones nearby. I found the graves of Kay's parents, Beth and Roy Sutter, her paternal grandparents, and various other Sutter relatives.

But there was no immediate sign of Kay's grave. Finally I looked way to the back of the family cemetery and spotted freshly disturbed earth.

I walked in that direction, scanning the older headstones as I passed, seeing earlier generations of the Sutter family and their kin, people who'd died in the late 1800s.

Eight rows from the back of the cemetery, something changed. Every other headstone I'd looked at so far had the person's name, his or her relationship to a Sutter if the individual had married into the clan, and the birth and death dates.

But then I saw a worn headstone that said simply DAPHNE, 1799–1857.

Beside Daphne was BIG GEORGE, 1802–1861. There were more one-named headstones in that

row and all the others behind it. LADY BIRD, 1772–
1821. LUCAS, 1706–1794. MIRIAM, 1698–1766.

"What's with the single names?" Mahoney said
behind me.

I looked around and felt a turbulence of emotions. "They're the plantation's slaves. Almost
two hundred years of them."

As I said, my emotions were all over the place,
but they swiftly moved toward reverence as I
walked through the last of the headstones to the
mound of overturned earth and the polished-
granite headstone behind the slaves' graveyard.

KAY SUTTER WILLINGHAM
1968–2020
I'LL SLEEP HERE, THANK YOU. THEY'RE MORE
MY KIND.

CHAPTER

58

CLIMBING BACK DOWN TO THE vehicle, Mahoney and I veered between smiling at the first part of the inscription—*I'll sleep here, thank you*—and trying to understand what she meant by *They're more my kind.*

"Slaves?" Mahoney said as we got in the car.

"Certainly one interpretation."

"Any others come to mind?"

"African-Americans? The road keeps going, doesn't it? Let's go to the end and turn around."

"I've got nowhere to be. Except in a shower and then a rib joint. There has to be a stellar rib joint in Montgomery."

"Humor me," I said. "The road ahead looks newer than the one behind us."

"Fine," he said. "But if I get this thing stuck, you're hiking back to the highway."

"Deal. It looks freshly graded to me."

Mahoney put the car in gear and drove past the cemetery down into the oak forest. The road was smooth and newly graveled. I looked out through big mature trees, catching sight of what looked like the mossy ruins of stacked stone foundations scattered here and there through the forest. More than a few of the oaks had been girdled with fluorescent surveyors' tape.

"Someone's been marking trees for cutting," I said.

"Look at them all ahead of us!"

Indeed, for two hundred yards and as far as we could see to our left and right, the majority of the trees were marked with fluorescent tape. This part of the old-growth forest was about to be leveled.

"I can't see a state park authority doing this," I said.

"Unless Kay decided to take timber off it before giving it to the state."

Beyond the grove of trees marked for the saw-mill, the road ended in a turnaround by the rocky shores of a large, empty, and pristine cove cradled in those big timbered arms of land jutting out into the larger lake. We got out of the car to get a better look.

"I never knew places like this existed in Alabama," I said. "And the water makes me want to take off my clothes and dive in."

"You see anyone around to stop you?"

"That's true. And I think Kay would actually approve."

"I'm sure she skinny-dipped here a time or two in her life," Mahoney said, kicking off his shoes and unbuckling his trousers.

A few moments later we waded out and shallow-dived into water that was a good ten degrees cooler than the air. I felt the entire day of travel and work and sweat wash away and surfaced in about twelve feet of clear water feeling thoroughly refreshed.

"That was great," Mahoney said when he came to the surface. "I think there are springs in this lake. I felt a cold spot back there."

"And there's no one here," I said. "I mean, I haven't heard a boat, have you?"

"Not one," he said, rolling onto his back to take in the entire cove. "I could live in a place like this. I could live in a place like this forever."

"I think a lot of people could," I said, treading water. "The road. The logging. I think this place is being developed, and not as a park."

"Could be," Ned said. "But we can't look at any of it until we get the order."

Before I could reply, I caught a flicker of movement out of the corner of my eye and twisted to look along the far side of the cove. A lean, muscular African-American man in faded green military gear was crouched at the edge of the forest where it met the rocky shore. He held a scoped hunting rifle that was aimed in our direction.

"Duck!" I yelled a split second before the gun went off.

CHAPTER

59

I HEARD THE BULLET CRACK by me as I dived. I swam deep and went as far as I could toward shore before surfacing for one quick breath. When I dived again, I could see rocks in the shallows ahead of me. I needed to get to my clothes and my gun.

When I surfaced the second time and scanned the shore, the shooter was gone. I swam behind a rock and made sure I could not see him before quickstepping from the water to my clothes.

Mahoney was right behind me, sputtering. "Who took that shot?"

"African-American with a hunting rifle," I said, snatching up my pile of clothes and pushing my bare feet into my shoes. I trotted back toward the car and out of sight of the north side of the cove.

"Dress," Mahoney said. "I'll cover you." He had his back to me and held his service weapon two-handed as he swept it back and forth across the cove.

I threw my pants on, got my gun out, and told Ned to dress while I covered him. We threw everything else in the vehicle and got out of there as the sun began to set and the golden light turned to shadows.

"Who the hell was he?" Mahoney said.

"Got me," I said. "He was there. He shot. He was gone."

"If he's security, he just shot at two federal officers in the course of an investigation."

"Buck-naked in the water where we weren't supposed to be."

Ned glanced at me. "Whose side are you on?"

"The side of my reputation and good standing with the Bureau."

Ned considered that, then said, "I see your point."

It was a fifteen-minute drive back to the gate. But it wasn't until we were almost there that I got enough bars of cell service to download a satellite view of where we'd just been.

"That was Lake Martin we were swimming in," I said. "If I'm right, this property is one of the largest undeveloped tracts of land on the lake. It could be worth a fortune."

"Maybe we had it all wrong," Mahoney said, putting the car in park at the gate and turning on his headlights so I could see.

I nodded, climbed out to open the gate, and said, "Maybe Kay wasn't killed for political reasons. Maybe she was killed for something much more mundane, like a huge pile of cash."

Darkness had fallen by the time Mahoney drove through the gate and I rewrapped the chain and hung the lock the way we'd found it. The road was worse going back than coming in.

We were bouncing around and trying to avoid potholes and ruts when a brilliant light flared behind us, filling the car, showing the road ahead like it was broad daylight. I turned and saw a fast-approaching truck with its headlamps on high beam and a big, powerful spotlight array on the roof that threw blinding light. I caught a glimpse of a heavy-duty bumper and grille guard that looked like it belonged on an army tank.

"He's going to ram us!" I yelled.

The truck engine roared. The bumper smashed into our rear, throwing us sideways onto a slick patch. Mahoney clawed at the wheel, squinting at the glare, and almost righted us before the truck hit us again.

We went sideways to the left. Our rear quarter panel hit an embankment, and we were thrown back across the road and right in front of the truck with the lights and that bumper. I thought for sure we were going to be rammed broadside and flipped end over end into the trees.

But the truck hit a huge cross-road rut where

a culvert had washed out, which bounced the rig to the right, and the left corner of the bumper just missed us as we spun out and off the road. I expected a massive crash and tried to brace myself, but we just sort of bumped and slithered to a stop in a pasture.

The truck did not slow and did not shut down the lights as it went on toward the highway. We both sat there a few minutes, rattled and gasping at the adrenaline coursing through our bloodstreams.

Mahoney finally put his hands back on the steering wheel and touched the gas. The front end pulled hard right, but he was able to get the rental out of the field and onto the road. We had to pry the front fender off one of the wheels, but, traveling at about forty-five miles an hour, we managed to get all the way back to Montgomery without the car shaking apart.

When we pulled up in front of our hotel, I said, "We've been given the runaround, shot at, and forced off the road, and we've been here less than twelve hours. I'd say that was a pretty strong first day."

"And you know what's even better?" Ned asked as he parked the rental, the front tires rubbing and squealing.

"We get to take a shower?"

"Nah," he said, gesturing across the street at a garish red neon sign. "Rib joint."

CHAPTER

60

AFTER A SHOWER, AN OUTSTANDING baby-back-rib dinner, and a fitful night of sleep, Mahoney and I were at the door of the state court clerk in Montgomery ten minutes before the office opened, drinking coffee.

"No word on the federal order?" I asked as he checked his phone.

"It's all been filed," Ned said. "Just has to get under Judge Adams's nose."

I wondered what we'd find in Kay's medical files, what other dark secrets the socialite might have been hiding. She'd led multiple lives, I decided. That was certain. And within each life, she wore many, many masks.

"I made the right call not reporting that we were shot at and almost run down by a truck," Mahoney said.

I nodded. "At least until we know the lay of the land and who's on our side."

A worker opened the doors at precisely 8:30 a.m. We went to Leroy Wolf, the clerk himself, presented our credentials, and asked to see the probate files on Kay Sutter Willingham.

He peered at us through reading glasses for a moment and then typed on his keyboard and hit Enter. "Sealed twelve days ago," he said, turning the screen in our direction.

I leaned forward. "Is there a time stamp on that? What exact time was it sealed?"

Wolf frowned and typed again. "Four thirty p.m."

"Eight and a half hours after I was on the scene in the schoolyard," I said to Ned.

"At whose request was probate sealed?" he asked.

Wolf studied his screen and then smiled. "The late Justice Richard Fortier of the Alabama Supreme Court."

"A state supreme court justice sealed it and then died?" Mahoney said.

"No, Justice Fortier was elevated to the high court early last year," Wolf said. "He wrote this order six years ago to go into effect upon notice of Kay Willingham's death. He had a heart attack March of last year, not six weeks into his term on the bench. But his seal stands."

I thought we were at an impasse until Mahoney said, "That seal includes the latest documents, right? As in the most recent last will and testament?"

"That's correct."

"But not old wills. They're considered null and void and therefore not sealed."

"That's true," Wolf said. "But as a policy, we discard and expunge legal documents that are no longer in effect."

"But as a practice, people are lazy," Mahoney said. "Especially state employees."

Wolf slowly turned his head to look at him. "I'm trying to be nice and helpful here."

"And I appreciate it, and I would be even more appreciative if you'd look for earlier filings of Kay Willingham's last will and testament. And any other file with her name on it."

Wolf sighed, typed, looked at the screen, and said, "Well, lazy or not, there are too many filings here to be easily printed out."

"Give us an index," I said. "We'll be selective."

Within thirty seconds we were looking at a three-page list of documents filed in Alabama's state court with Kay's name on them. The first and latest was her sealed probate file. Others had to do with the death and burial of her mother.

The eighth on the list was a revised will filed twenty months ago, which we asked Wolf to print. As those pages piled up, we continued down the index list and found a land title transfer of eighty acres from Kay Willingham to Althea Lincoln. It was dated five years ago.

"Althea," I said, remembering the framed photograph in Kay's house of the two young girls embracing after a swim. "That was her childhood friend."

"Check this, Alex," Mahoney said, looking up from the pages of the old will. "Kay's got elaborate plans for her funeral here. Bible readings. Music. A letter to be read. Reference to an obituary already being written."

"That goes against what Vice President Willingham told us about not wanting a ceremony or memorial."

"Unless she changed her plans for her funeral along with her plans for the plantation," Mahoney said, reading on. "Okay, here's the language regarding the land in the twenty-month-old will: 'Upon my death, the lands of Sutter plantation will be sold to the highest bidder and the proceeds distributed to charities listed in appendix A.'"

"But again, that will is null and void," Wolf said.

"Here's another from five years ago," Mahoney said, looking at the index.

To the clerk's annoyance, it too had not been expunged, and he printed it.

Ned went straight to the disposition of the land and found, as I'd remembered, that it was to be given to the state as a park and the grounds restored so people would understand the entire story of the Sutter plantation.

The clerk said, "And the three wills prior to that one have indeed been expunged."

"Do you have appendix A from the twenty-month-old will?" I asked Mahoney. "The list of charities that were supposed to get the money?"

Ned flipped ahead through the document and nodded. He pulled it out and showed it to me. I scanned the list and saw a variety of nonprofits that would have benefited from the property, including Georgetown University and groups fighting for crime victims' rights, women's issues, and civil rights. It was not until the bottom that I saw the catch, a big one.

Tapping the page, I read, "'Monies shall be distributed and disbursed after the deduction of all costs associated with the legal appeals of Napoleon Howard.'"

"Who's Napoleon Howard?" Mahoney asked.

I was about to say I had no idea, but then I remembered something. "I can't be sure, but I think he might be the guy on death row Kay wanted me to investigate years ago. The one who might have been wrongly convicted."

"Okay?"

"Vice President Willingham was the prosecutor on that case."

CHAPTER

61

WE WALKED FROM THE COURTHOUSE over to the law firm of Carson and Knight. The humidity had abated by a percentage point or two, but even at nine a.m., the heat was headed toward blistering. We climbed the front steps and went into the chill air.

"Hello, Reggie," I said.

He looked up at us, adjusted his glasses. "Don't you guys make appointments?"

"Not as a rule," Mahoney said.

He sighed. "Bobby's not around. He's at a hearing until eleven."

"That's okay, we're here to see Nina Larch," I said.

"Oh," he said, brightening. "She just came in."

A few minutes later, a woman in her mid-forties with a bad slouch came down the circular staircase. She looked very unsure of herself.

"Ms. Larch?"

"Yes?"

"We're with the FBI," Mahoney said, and we showed her our credentials.

"Bobby said you stopped by yesterday. How can I help?"

I gestured toward the conference room. "Is it empty?"

"Until ten," Reggie said.

We went in and Larch shut the door. "If it's about the will or any of the probate, I can't talk about it unless there's a court order rescinding the seal."

"We're working on that," Ned said. "But for the moment, we're interested in what you *can* talk about. Kay's earlier wills and testaments."

"I don't follow."

"They're considered null and void and therefore not subject to the seal," I said. "So you can talk about them."

She thought about that for a few moments. "That's correct."

Mahoney showed her the twenty-month-old will that had the land being sold to charities and then the five-year-old will that had the plantation going to the state for a park.

"Can you say which option is in the actual will?" Ned asked.

She shook her head. "Sealed."

"Okay, why did she change her will from giving the land to the state to selling it for charity?"

The lawyer looked blankly at the table and frowned. "I can't say that Mrs. Willingham ever mentioned specifically why she made that decision. I received a formal letter from her announcing her intentions, and I followed them."

"And the same thing happened when she changed the will more recently? You received a formal letter?"

"Duly notarized."

"I'm sure," I said. "Was she still paying for all of Napoleon Howard's legal bills in the most recent will?"

"That I can answer: No. Mr. Howard had a heart attack and died in prison shortly before it was revised the final time."

The door opened, and Bobby Carson stepped inside with a shark smile on his face.

"You're back!" he said with feigned enthusiasm. "And I see you've met Ms. Larch. I hope she's filled you in."

"Only on what I was allowed to discuss outside the sealed material."

"We were talking about Kay's wills," Mahoney said. "How they changed so often."

Carson glanced at Larch and then sat down, looking uncomfortable. He stared at his phone and said, "Yes, my cousin could be impetuous and mercurial."

I said, "We went up to the Sutter plantation yesterday and took a look around. Seems like whoever inherited it is going to take out most of the timber."

"You went in without a search warrant?" Carson said. "Are you kidding me?"

Mahoney said, "Gate was open and we wanted to see the most important remaining asset our victim had when she was murdered."

"Who controls it now?" I asked. "And when did they get it?"

Both attorneys looked at each other. Carson closed his eyes and said, "You see the bind we are in—*I* am in—because of the…oh, the hell with it."

He opened his eyes, looked at Larch, and said, "If it comes to an ethics violation, I'll take the heat for breaking the seal, Nina."

Then he gazed at us each in turn and said, "I had no idea."

"That is correct," Larch said. "He absolutely did not."

"Out with it," Mahoney said.

Larch said, "Shortly after the twenty-month-old will was filed—I can get you the exact date—Mrs. Willingham wrote me a notarized letter authorizing me to change the will yet again. This time the beneficiary of the plantation was Mr. Carson."

He held his hands up. "I had zero idea until I saw the new will. I thought it was going to the state."

"That is true, he did not know!" Larch said. "Kay—Mrs. Willingham—she swore me to secrecy in the letter. She said she'd had another change of heart about the land and thought her only living relative should decide what to do with the plantation, with the bulk of her estate going to charity."

Carson said, "Gentlemen, I know this has to look funky."

"In the extreme," I said. "How long ago was this?"

"Eighteen months?" Larch said.

"And you never told Mr. Carson?" Mahoney asked her, sounding skeptical.

"I take my job seriously. I said nothing to anyone about any of the changes."

"Until when?"

"Excuse me?"

"When did you tell Mr. Carson about his inheritance?"

"Later on the day I heard she died, after I notified the court clerk and confirmed that probate was duly sealed per her wishes. I walked into Rob's office to express my condolences. He was shaken by her death. I mean, his last living relative. Then I told him about the inheritance."

I said, "And what was Mr. Carson's response?"

"He was so shocked he almost missed his chair sitting down, and then he kept looking at the will to make sure I was right."

"I told you I didn't believe it," Carson said. "I still don't."

"Uh-huh," I said. "You move pretty fast, then."

"How's that?"

"We saw all the timber up there already marked for logging."

He held up his hands. "That was Kay's decision over a year ago."

"Also true," Larch said. "She needed to raise cash for reasons that were not made clear to me. I have the documents authorizing the timber sale with her signature notarized on all of them."

"Where will the proceeds of that sale go now?" I asked.

"To the charities stipulated in the will, I suppose," Carson said. "Someone smarter than me will have to figure that out."

"We'd like to see those documents," Mahoney said.

"You don't believe us?" Carson said.

"Trust but verify, Counselor. Especially since someone took a shot at us near that cove last evening and a truck ran us off the road from the plantation. The government frowns on people trying to kill federal agents twice in one day."

"Whoa, wait a second there, Special Agent Mahoney," Carson said, hardening. "I have no idea who the truck belonged to, but that was probably crazy Althea taking a potshot at you."

"It looked like an African-American male," I said. "Lean. Bald. Hunting rifle."

He nodded. "That's Althea Lincoln. Nutcase artist who's taken a vow of silence for…anyway, she thinks she owns the north point of that cove, but she does not. She got Kay to sign some shaky title-transfer document when Kay was at West Briar the last time. There isn't even an address on the document for her, which is illegal. I predict it won't hold up in court."

"Was Kay aware of this?"

"I doubt it. She was totally out of it on anti-psychotics when she signed that thing."

Larch said, "I found out about Ms. Lincoln's transfer filing only last week, when probate began."

"We'd like copies of all the documents you've mentioned," Mahoney said. "It saves us all the hassle of a court order."

Before they could answer, Mahoney's phone began to ring and buzz with an alert. He pulled it out, stared at the screen, and said, "We've got the go-ahead to look at her medical files."

Sounding discouraged, Carson said, "What-ever you find in there, please be kind to Kay. She deserves that much in death."

CHAPTER

62

WE RENTED A NEW CAR, and as Mahoney drove us north to West Briar, I went through my notes on the conversation.

"You believe them?" Mahoney asked.

I looked up from my notes about Napoleon Howard. "Like you said, trust but verify. Kay could be fickle, and she did suffer from mental illness, but something about it just seems a little off."

"I hear you."

I did an internet search on the dead prison inmate and read out loud what I'd found to Mahoney while he drove. Howard was forty-nine when he died at the state penitentiary at Huntsville after spending more than half his life on death row. He had made multiple appeals. All were denied.

Almost thirty years prior to his death, Howard

was arrested, tried, and condemned for the savage murder of twenty-three-year-old Jefferson Ward in what the state said was a drug-fueled dispute over profits. Howard had steadfastly maintained his innocence, said Ward was his best friend, his idol, and that he would never have killed him. He claimed he was being framed.

But eyewitnesses put Howard at the scene the evening of the murder, and police found blood and fingerprint evidence that put his hand on the murder weapon, a nine-inch buck knife that was used to decapitate Ward after his death.

I read out loud: "'Due to the viciousness of the crime, J. Walter Willingham, the prosecutor assigned to the case, filed for special circumstances and sought the death penalty, which he got.' And then after sentencing, Willingham said, 'This punishment fits the crime. That's the way it should be with animals like Mr. Howard.'"

Mahoney turned the car into the winding drive that led up to the psychiatric facility. He said, "And yet Willingham's ex-wife came to believe that Howard did not commit the crime. How did that happen?"

"And why did she even care in the first place?" I said. "Who got her on Howard's side? She told me he wrote her letters. Did we ever find any in her house?"

"Letters from death row? No, I don't remember

seeing anything like that on the evidence manifest."

We went inside the building, found Abigail, the same cheery receptionist with the ice daggers for eyes, and told her we wanted to see Drs. Nathan Tolliver and Jeanne Hicks.

"I'm afraid that's impossible," Abigail sniffed. "They're making rounds."

Mahoney said, "You like your computer, Abigail?"

She craned her head around at the monitor. "I do. Brand-new."

He held up a piece of paper and pressed it to the glass that separated us. "This is a federal order. We want to see Tolliver and Hicks and all documents pertaining to Kay Sutter Willingham now or I will bring in an army of FBI agents and they will take your brand-new computer and every other computer in this place along with all the records."

Abigail pulled back. "You can't do that. We have patients."

"Watch me," Mahoney said. "I'm giving them five minutes."

Four minutes later, a flushed Nathan Tolliver ran to the security door and motioned us in, breathing hard. "Do you have to threaten people like that?"

"If I'm not getting what I want when I want it, yes."

"The files are being gathered, and Dr. Hicks is just finishing up," he said. "May I see the court order?"

Mahoney handed it to him. He studied it, his lips moving, while we walked.

"Everything look right?" I asked when we arrived at his office.

"Appears so," he said, handing the order to Ned. He gestured toward the office. "Please."

We entered. A few moments later, his secretary came in holding several files. She was followed by Dr. Hicks.

"There's a lot to digest," Tolliver said. "We're here to help."

"And we appreciate it," I said.

The secretary put two files down in front of us. I flipped one open. Ned opened the other. I scanned the first few pages, recognizing them as much the same as the file the vice president had shown us. I said, "You believed Kay Willingham's problem was largely chemical."

Dr. Hicks nodded. "She'd go off her meds and within weeks, she'd have a crash."

"What were the triggers for her going off the meds?"

"Usually a traumatic incident."

"Such as the death of her mother?"

"That occurred shortly before she checked in last time, yes."

Ned said, "Big mom issues?"

Hicks glanced at Tolliver, who was listening intently. She said, "She had all sorts of issues, some of which included her mother. But then again, I'd hear about them when she was fragmented mentally. One day her mother was a saint and her father her best friend. The next she'd claim her father was a racist who killed black people and that her mother was a willing accomplice and so was half of Montgomery and on and on, all the way to the White House and back. It was incredibly paranoid, delusional, and hard to follow."

"And the parents?" Mahoney asked.

Tolliver said, "Both her mother and father had deep local roots, money, and land going back generations. The dad was a city father in Montgomery. Her mother hosted charity balls."

"When Kay was here, even in her fragmented state, did she ever talk about Napoleon Howard?"

CHAPTER

63

DR. HICKS HESITATED, THEN SAID, "She believed he was innocent, framed for murder, but she couldn't prove it. She obsessed on his case, as a matter of fact."

"Any reason for her interest and belief in his innocence?"

Tolliver said, "He wrote her. I think they carried on a correspondence."

"That's right," Dr. Hicks said.

I said, "In the file, there's not a lot of narrative about her state of mind and not a lot of history about her earlier stays here."

Dr. Hicks smiled. "There's not a lot of narrative because we are psychiatrists, not psychologists, Dr. Cross. Whatever Kay's issues were, as far as we could tell, her psychiatric challenges were largely chemical. It's the population we serve."

"And earlier files we have to shred after seven years," Tolliver said. "That's the law."

"Of course," I said, because I had to do the same with my client files. I began wondering if this had been a wild-goose chase, coming down to Alabama, sticking our noses in Kay's past because of Higgins's dying words.

While Mahoney determined how Kay paid for her stays at West Briar, I went back to her medical file and started going through the pages again, deeper this time. I found the intake form for her most recent stay at the facility. Near the bottom, I saw a scrawled notation I must have missed in the vice president's copy of the file.

Patient friend AL says patient state deteriorating rapidly since she went off meds while dealing with two deaths, mother and close friend.

Two deaths? I thought. *Who's the close friend?*

Mahoney said, "We can keep this copy of the file?"

"Federal judge says you can," Tolliver said. "I hope we've been of some help."

I was going to ask them about the two deaths and then decided not to. In the same way I'd felt something off about Bobby Carson and Nina Larch, there was something a little shifty about the doctors. Or at least Tolliver. He struck me as a man who was hiding something.

Outside, I tore off my jacket and told Mahoney my feelings about Tolliver.

"Could be," Mahoney said, opening the front door of the car to let the heat out. "There was nothing in that file we haven't seen before."

"Not true. There was something I didn't notice in Willingham's copy," I said and I told him about the notation on Kay's intake form. "I think AL is Althea Lincoln. She brought Kay to West Briar the last time."

Ned started the car and fired up the AC. "The same one who shot at us?"

I nodded. "She told the admitting nurse that Kay had been deteriorating after going off her meds as the result of *two* deaths, her mother and a close friend."

"You have an address for Ms. Lincoln?"

"I do not, and she's not listed anywhere online."

"Then how do you propose to find her?"

"Go for a swim later?"

CHAPTER
64

AT ROUGHLY THE SAME TIME in Washington, Bree Stone was close to losing her mind with boredom after just a handful of days away from the chief of detectives job.

She had gotten a deeper appreciation for just how creative a cook Nana Mama was by working with her in the kitchen every day. And she enjoyed being home when Ali and Jannie returned from school, which had just started up again.

But most of the time she felt caged. She'd talked to Alex about it after he'd told her about being shot at and run off a road in rural Alabama. He said the caged sense was her feeling anxious about what came next.

That was true. Bree had been trying to envision a different life for herself during her daily runs but had not come up with one that excited her deep in her gut. And at this stage of the game, she'd decided that was the minimum she was willing to settle for.

"You're thinking about going back, aren't you?" Nana Mama said as the midday news played on the screen on the counter.

"Not if it's more of the same," Bree said. "I do love certain aspects of my job, but I despise others. If I could stay with the roles I love and delegate the others, I'd consider it. But only if I got that in writing."

"Smart lady. I don't count on much if I don't see it spelled out and signed."

Both of them heard a crash in the basement.

The kids were at school. Alex was still in Alabama. Bree went to the hall closet to retrieve her backup weapon.

Nana Mama had an iron skillet in one hand when Bree returned.

"Hear anything?" Bree whispered.

"No, you want me to call 911?" Nana Mama said.

Bree toed off her sandals. "I want you to turn down the television as I open the door. When I start to close it, raise the volume back to normal."

The old woman's eyes widened at the sight of the pistol, but she lowered the skillet and picked up the remote with her other hand. Bree nodded and eased open the door as the volume dropped on the news.

She took a step down the carpeted stairs,

nodded again, and as the volume increased, she slipped the door shut and released the knob. Both hands on the gun, she padded down the stairs.

The door that led outside was dead-bolted shut. What had made that crash?

Bree heard a keyboard clacking in Alex's office. After a deep breath, she took three soft strides and then stepped to the side of the doorway, gun up. "John?"

Sampson jumped and spun away from Alex's desktop, saw the gun, and cried, "Whoa! Jesus, Bree, you scared the hell out of me!"

"And you terrified Nana Mama," she said, lowering her weapon. "What are you doing here? Alex said you went to the Delaware shore to be with Willow and Billie's kids."

"The older kids decided it was time to go back to work and Willow got stung by a jellyfish and didn't want to stay any longer," he said. "We came back this morning."

"Where is she?"

"With her friend Lana and Lana's mom. And Jannie, her favorite babysitter, is picking her up before dinner. I'm sorry, I should have knocked and told you I was coming down here to work, but I had this crazy idea about the rapes and murders and wanted to look at the files in Alex's computer and I just used my key."

"Hold that thought. I have to go take a skillet out of Nana Mama's hand."

CHAPTER

65

SAMPSON LAUGHED, SAID, "THAT'S A scary thought."

"Isn't it?" Bree said. She went up, calmed Nana Mama, and came back with a plate of cookies and a cup of coffee for John, who was typing again on the computer. "So what's the crazy idea?" Bree asked.

Sampson rubbed his temples and said, "Okay, so Alex and I were looking at the last known locations of each of the eight victims, including Maya Parker and Elizabeth Hernandez, and marking where their bodies were found. We got this."

He hit Return and the screen jumped to show a map of the greater DC area with the last known locations of the girls flagged in green and where their bodies were found in red.

"They're being taken in and around Southeast and dumped randomly," Bree said.

"I know, but are they random? That's what I'm trying to figure out. I had this idea that if we could put on the map the location of everyone who'd been interviewed about these crimes, we might see a pattern, or a focus, anyway, by connecting them all."

Sampson hit Return again and the map morphed to show a web of lines connecting all the red and green flags along with yellow ones, which indicated people who had been interviewed. Bree tried to see something significant in the clusters and weavings, but if it was there, she wasn't seeing it.

"Now watch," he said. "I'm going to add where the young women lived and take out where they vanished."

Bree cocked her head as blue dots began to appear and connect. Something was different about the result. There were visible intersections where dozens of unflagged lines met.

"Can you show me what's under those lines here and here?" she asked.

Sampson typed something into the computer. A satellite image of the DC area appeared. He zoomed in on the first of those intersections, which was in the Douglas neighborhood south of the Suitland Parkway, roughly five blocks from the rave party where Peggy Dixon said she was attacked.

"Looks like a warehouse," he said. "I'll flag the address and go look."

"What are these other intersecting lines?" Bree asked.

Sampson zoomed in on an apartment building in Marshall Heights and made a note of the address. Then he looked at the third area, which was north of the Suitland Parkway between Garfield Heights and Naylor Park.

"Look at Harrison Charter High School," Bree said. "There's a yellow dot by it. Who was interviewed there?"

Sampson highlighted the yellow dot and hit Enter. A report came up detailing an interview a detective had with Randall Christopher eighteen months before.

"Why did they talk to him?" she said, looking over Sampson's shoulder.

"He was concerned about his female students after Elizabeth Hernandez was taken. Elizabeth didn't go to the school, but evidently, she lived nearby. After Maya was taken, he asked to help organize searches."

"Show me where Maya and Elizabeth lived again," Bree said. "All the girls, for that matter."

Sampson typed. Up came the blue dots.

Elizabeth Hernandez and Maya Parker both lived within seven blocks of Harrison Charter, Peggy Dixon within ten blocks.

To Bree's surprise, three of the other girls lived within six blocks of that apartment building in Marshall Heights and the three early victims lived within five blocks of that building in Douglas.

"My God, look at that, John," Bree said, clapping him on the shoulder. "Do you know what this means?"

Sampson nodded. "We know his favorite hunting ground now."

CHAPTER
66

Alabama

AFTER A BRIEF THUNDERSTORM, THE afternoon turned sultry and buggy. Mosquitoes whined at my ears and multiple times I wanted to scratch at something crawling up my leg, but I had not moved a muscle in nearly two hours in my hiding spot in the woods along the north shore of the cove.

Mahoney was waiting farther out on the timbered point, beyond where I'd seen the shooter crouching. At five thirty, as we'd planned, I hit the panic button on our second rental, an SUV, parked deep in the woods. I counted to three and then shut it off.

Soon after, Mahoney started throwing rocks into the water. I tugged on a fishing line that ran out to a cheap, blow-up kid's raft that held a cooler and a mannequin wearing a bathing suit, sunglasses, and a wig.

We'd put a Bud Light can in the mannequin's hands. From fifty yards away, you'd have sworn it was some slob out for a swim and a drink.

Althea Lincoln must have thought so too because there was a twig snap, a rustle of leaves, and there she was, sliding out of the forest, the hunting rifle already rising.

"FBI!" Mahoney shouted, leaping out on the shore with his pistol up. "Put the gun down, Ms. Lincoln! Now!"

She looked toward the road as her escape but saw me stepping out with my weapon drawn. Then it was as if she became more deer than human. In one fluid motion Althea Lincoln turned and vanished into the woods.

"Flank her!" Mahoney yelled and ran into the trees as well.

I charged and jumped and broke through branches and vines, trying to stay roughly parallel to what I figured was her line of travel. Every thirty or forty yards, I'd stop, listen for breaking branches, adjust my direction, and charge off again.

The ground climbed and the vegetation got thicker. When I'd gone three hundred yards, I stopped to listen once more.

I heard branches breaking but farther away. Rather than run toward the noise, I got out my phone and called Ned. He answered and I whispered for him to stop moving.

The noise I'd heard in the distance stopped.

"Where are you?" I asked quietly.

"Near the cove on the north side of the point."

I couldn't see water from where I was, but I didn't have to. "I think she doubled back on us," I said. "She's out on that point somewhere."

I had Mahoney caw like a crow and moved quietly to him. We backtracked the way he'd come through the woods until I found what I was looking for: a well-used game path heading out to the timbered point.

I started to sneak out the path, but Ned asked if she could have been going for a boat or a canoe. I threw caution to the wind then and ran down the path, ducking under broken branches and leaping over logs. Ned stayed right beside me.

A rooster crowed and hens squabbled. The woods thinned into an opening with a majestic view of Lake Martin, golden in the late-day sun.

In the clearing, surrounded by blooming wildflowers, stood a small cabin built of hand-hewn logs with red-trimmed windows and a roof that looked like it was made of moss.

Beyond the cabin on the rocky point, there were two heavy chairs and a table crafted of logs and bent branches near a firepit. Everything, from the chicken coop to the gardens to the stacked firewood, was neat and cared for. Ned circled to one side of the cabin and I went to the other.

"Althea Lincoln?" he called out. "I'm FBI

Special Agent in Charge Edward Mahoney. Please, ma'am, we mean you no harm. We just want to talk about Kay Willingham."

There was no answer.

"My name is Dr. Alex Cross," I called. "I was a friend of Kay's. She told me you were the best friend she ever had, Althea. I saw her favorite picture of you as young girls in her house in Georgetown. I am grieving for Kay too, and we're here investigating her murder, Althea. Please, we need your help to find who killed her."

After several beats, Althea stepped out onto the cabin porch with her hands raised.

"Thank you, Althea," I said.

Althea stared past me a moment, her eyes watering, then licked her lips and ran her hand over her bald head. She cleared her throat and said in a scratchy, hoarse voice, "She talked about you too, Dr. Cross. Said you were a good and honest man." She cleared her throat again. "Sorry, I don't talk much. And I still can't believe my sweet Kay's gone."

"Neither can I. She was a force of nature."

Althea smiled sadly, said, "That she was and always will be."

"You'll help us get justice for Kay?" Ned said.

"Justice?" she said with a bitter sigh. "I don't believe in your form of justice, Special Agent Mahoney. But which hornet's nest do you feel like kicking first?"

CHAPTER
67

"**HOW FAR FROM HERE WAS** Peggy Dixon attacked?" Bree asked Sampson.

It was about six in the evening, and they were standing in front of the building in the Douglas neighborhood of Southeast Washington, DC. It had been a warehouse once upon a time but now served as an incubator for start-up businesses, including the current tenants: an SAT tutoring firm, a data-mining venture, and a children's-clothing designer.

"According to the landlord, the place was converted seventeen years ago and has been busy ever since," Sampson said. "Forty people work here now. Could have been anyone who ever worked here."

"Or in one of these buildings around us," Bree said.

Sampson pulled out his phone, oriented

himself, and pointed east. "The attack must have been about five blocks from here."

She thought about that. "We don't have to look at everyone who ever worked here, just the men who did around the time of the attacks."

Sampson nodded. "Difficult, labor-intensive, but not impossible."

That sentiment changed after they'd driven north of the Suitland Parkway and gotten out in front of the large apartment building in Marshall Heights. It was seven stories high and had two wings, one on either side of a central courtyard.

"Must be three hundred people here," Sampson said. "Turnover's probably constant."

"Again, we just need to look at the residents and workers who were here when the girls vanished," Bree said.

Sampson gestured across the street at another apartment building and then another beside it. "We're going to need manpower."

"I know," she said.

"You coming back to work, Chief?"

"I don't know yet," she said. "Let's go to the charter school and then to the Hernandez and Parker residences. I need to see this straight in my head."

He glanced at his watch. "That'll work. Jannie's with Willow until eight."

They drove past Harrison Charter to the Parkers' apartment building and went from there to where the Hernandez family had lived. "We're not talking a big area to select victims from, are we?" Bree said.

"No," Sampson said. "Just three distinct small ones."

"But it's not like he focused on one area exclusively and then moved on to the next," she said. "He returned to each locale. Fifteen years ago, Audrey Nyman, the first victim in the series, lived about a mile north of that apartment building. Victim two lived within nine blocks of the business incubator thirteen years ago. Victim three lived south of the apartment building eleven years ago. Number four was taken north of the incubator nine years ago and victims five and six were south and west of the incubator eight and six years ago."

Sampson nodded. "He hunted every two years for quite a while. But then Dixon was attacked near the incubator two years ago. Elizabeth Hernandez vanished six months later when she was living near but not attending Harrison Charter. Eight months later, Maya Parker, also living close to but not attending Harrison, was taken."

"It's not just the proximity to those three places. It's the timing again. Shorter and shorter between the attacks."

"I see it," Sampson said. "He's escalating."

"He is. And it's been almost five months since Maya Parker. He's going to hunt again, and sooner rather than later."

"I agree. But I need to go home, read to Willow before bed. That's always been our daddy time."

Seeing Sampson's eyes glisten, Bree said, "Keep it that way, John."

"I'm trying," he said. "Everything I've read says continuity is the best thing I can give her. I know how to be a good father. What I'm scared to death about is how to be a good mother to Willow, how to be what Billie was to her. You know?"

Bree heard and felt the turmoil in his voice. "You will figure out how to be what Willow needs, John. The same way Nana Mama became the person Alex needed after his own mom died. And the same way Alex had to adapt after his first wife was murdered. You will grow into who you have to be for her. And we will help you every step of the way. Jannie told me just this morning that she can babysit Willow anytime you need. And Ali says he'll tutor her in math."

Sampson smiled, tears welling in his eyes as he pulled up in front of Bree's home. "Thank you. I needed to hear that."

"We'll talk in the morning? By phone? No sneaking into the basement?"

"I promise," he said, laughing.

"Kiss Willow good night for us," she said, climbing out of the car.

"Will do. And give my best to Alex when you talk to him, wherever he is."

CHAPTER
68

NED MAHONEY AND I SAT around Althea Lincoln's firepit for almost four hours as night came on and the flames danced and roiled, as mesmerizing as the disturbing stories she told us.

"You're a brave woman, Althea," I said after she'd finished talking. "Kay was blessed to have you as a friend."

Althea burst into tears. "Kay was my sister in every sense. My mom worked for her grandmother. We played together in diapers. What else could I have done?"

"You did the right thing," Mahoney said. "From where I'm sitting, you're the only one who always looked out for her interests."

I nodded. "You never manipulated her. You never took advantage of her."

"Well," she said, wiping her tears with her

sleeve. "I asked her for this land and she gave it to me. And I asked her to help Napoleon."

"He was your half brother," I said. "And besides, you know Kay loved him."

"And Napoleon loved Kay to the day he died. The whole mess was just so sad, unjust, evil, you know? What some men will do to others for money and power."

"And what some women will do for love," I said and smiled at her across the dying fire, still trying to wrap my head around everything she'd told us.

It began to sprinkle rain.

Ned stood. "We're going to need to get out of here so we can set about proving all this in the morning, get the U.S. Attorney in Birmingham involved."

"Thanks for the food, Althea," I said. "The fish was excellent."

"Fresh-caught this morning," she said, gesturing toward the lake in the darkness. "The fish like it off the point there for some reason, the way it's shallow and then drops deep. I think—"

A flat, suppressed crack came from the woods behind the cabin; the bullet hit Althea, spun her around, and dropped her. The second shot missed me but came so close, I heard the high zip-whine of it ripping past my ear.

"Get to cover!" Mahoney shouted before diving

to his right, away from the fire, and going over the bank.

I threw the table on its side, grabbed Althea by the collar, and dragged her behind it just before a volley of shots rang out from multiple guns fitted with suppressors, sounding almost like a paintball war. Bullets splintered the wood above me as I glanced around the table and caught the muzzle flash of the last two shots coming from the direction of the chicken coop.

I returned fire, three quick shots, then ducked back down. Althea groaned. "They shot me."

Two unsuppressed shots rang out from Mahoney's last position. He's flanking them, I thought.

"We're going to get you out of here and to a hospital," I told Althea. "Is there any way off this point besides swimming?"

Before she could reply, the shooting started again, closer now, hitting the stout table and the chairs beside it. I jumped up and fired four rounds, left to right, and ducked down, expecting another volley, but there was silence.

"My skiff," Althea gasped. "It's off the right side of the point, pulled up onshore."

"Outboard?"

"Yes."

It began to rain harder. Even so, I heard a movement to our left and emptied the gun in that direction, dropped the clip, and rammed my second one home. "Can you walk?" I asked.

"I'm having trouble breathing. It hit me left of my right shoulder."

Her lung could be damaged, I thought. The shooting started up again, this time in the direction Mahoney had gone, which was also roughly where Althea said the boat was.

"You trust me?" I said.

"I do."

"I'm putting you across my shoulders, fireman's carry. We're getting out of here."

"Ohhh," she moaned. "That's gonna hurt."

"Better than dying." I grabbed her, hoisted her up over my left shoulder, staggered to my feet, and bolted down the path in the dark, bullets clipping the ground behind me.

CHAPTER

69

I STEPPED OFF THE BANK. With Althea's weight across my shoulders, I landed awkwardly on the slippery, rocky shore. My knee twisted, but I stayed on my feet and moved left.

The night was near pitch-dark with the rain clouds, which did not help. My knee burned as I gingerly took one step after another up the shoreline. I kept my eyes wide open, blinking against the rain, because in low light, we see better peripherally than straight ahead.

My knowing that fact probably saved both our lives.

"Not far now," Althea said in a gurgling voice that made my fears real. I could hear that her lung was filling with blood.

Out of the corner of my left eye I caught movement between the side of her cabin and the bank. I pivoted and tried to raise my pistol and aim at the movement, but Althea's weight threw me off balance. I staggered right. The shot just missed me and went into the lake behind us.

He won't miss twice, I thought. *Not at this range.*

My instinct was to put Althea down and get on her to protect her. But before I could, Mahoney turned on his Maglite from thirty yards up the shore, revealing a pro in black with an AR rifle equipped with a banana clip, a night-vision scope, and a silencer about to shoot me and Althea.

The light blinded the guy. Mahoney touched off twice. Both rounds punched him in the throat. He fell and the light went off.

I moved fast toward Mahoney. He was taking cover behind a blown-down tree.

"She's hit," I whispered. "Chest wound. There's a boat somewhere here."

"Boat's right behind us, pulled up on the rocks. Go to it. Get her in. I'll cover you."

"They'll shoot at us going out of here."

"I'll get that guy's gun with the night scope. Even things up."

"How you doing, Althea?"

"Can't breathe good," she rasped.

"One more pull, okay?" I said and didn't wait for an answer. I brought her toward the lake, trying not to kick any rocks, knowing the sound would carry back into the woods.

I toed the side of the metal johnboat, then

eased her off my shoulders and onto the floor of the skiff. She moaned and shifted.

There was nothing I could do for her until we were safe, so I felt my way to the outboard engine, found it cocked up out of the water. I heard footsteps coming.

"Ready?" Mahoney whispered.

"Can you see with that thing?"

"Plain as day, pretty amazing."

"We slide it into the water, you get up front and cover the shore. This engine is going to draw them."

"Let's do it," he said and went around to the bow of the skiff.

Together we slid the metal, flat-bottomed boat, scraping and squealing, into the water. I went up to my knees, felt Mahoney get in, and was about to climb in after him when the shooting started once more. The first rounds hit the bow right in front of Ned, who shot back as I scrambled aboard, found the starter cord, and pulled. It coughed but did not catch.

"Prime it," Althea gasped. "The bulb on the gas line. Then choke."

Another bullet pinged off the hull of the boat. Others knifed into the water around us and Mahoney unleashed a firestorm on them, ten, twenty, thirty straight rounds.

During that time, I found the priming bulb, squeezed it three times, then groped for the choke lever and shifted it. I grabbed the starter cord again and yanked.

The engine coughed, sputtered. I eased the choke until it caught, put it in reverse, and gunned the outboard just as Mahoney ran out of bullets with the pro's weapon and shifted back to his pistol.

I spun us broadside to shore, wincing at every shot coming at us, shifted out of reverse and buried the throttle. The outboard engine roared. We blew out of there, away from the point toward the big lake and open water.

CHAPTER
70

TWO DAYS LATER, MAHONEY AND I sat in our SUV, looked at each other, nodded, and then, carrying manila files, climbed out of the car and into stultifying heat and humidity. But given what we had to do that morning, I'd have walked through an inferno and been grateful for the experience.

We entered the august firm of Carson and Knight and smiled at Reggie the receptionist as if we were old friends. He looked at us as if we were ghosts, then jumped to his feet, waving.

"Bobby's not here," he said. "He's gone to—"

"He's here," Mahoney said. "We saw him go in the front door ten minutes ago, so if you don't want to be charged with obstructing justice, Reggie, I suggest you sit down and shut up. Where is he?"

The receptionist glumly pointed at the closed door of the conference room.

Mahoney led the way, and we entered without knocking to find four people around the conference table: Nina Larch, the executor of Kay Willingham's will; Bobby Carson, Kay's second cousin; and Dr. Nathan Tolliver and Dr. Jeanne Hicks, Kay's shrinks from West Briar.

"Well," Mahoney said, breaking into a smile. "The gang's all here, aren't they?"

"This is a private meeting," Carson sputtered. "You can't just barge in like this. You could have the decency to—"

"Save it for your closing argument, Mr. Carson," Ned said. "We'd like to ask you all some questions."

"How long will this take?" Dr. Hicks said, looking at her watch. "I have rounds this morning and—"

"Don't worry," I said, closing the door and taking a seat. "We called West Briar and told them you and Dr. Tolliver will both be delayed."

"What's this about?" Hicks said nervously. "I don't understand."

"I think you do," I said. "I think it's why you're all here."

"We were discussing taking on West Briar as a client," Carson began.

"West Briar has been a client of this firm

for twenty-five years," Mahoney said. "Since the very first day the institution opened."

"A client in other ways," Tolliver said. "We—Dr. Hicks and I—have been discussing an expansion of our facility or a second one, and we need legal work done at the state level to make that happen in a timely and…"

Mahoney opened the file he was carrying and set two separate piles of documents on the table in front of the doctor. He sat down and stared at Tolliver, who'd gone silent.

They were all trying not to look at the documents, but four out of four stole glances at them as we waited and watched. It didn't take long until Carson said, "I thought you were here to ask questions."

I waited a beat, then said, "I get that there's a wink-and-a-nod, good-ol'-boy way of getting things greased and done down here in Alabama. But we're federal and we don't take kindly to being shot at or to people trying to kill our witnesses."

"Whoa, whoa, whoa!" Carson said. "What in Sam Hill are you talking about?"

Mahoney said, "We were attacked by heavily armed gunmen on the north point of the cove at the plantation three evenings ago. Althea Lincoln was badly wounded and would have died if Dr. Cross had not been able to get her to the hospital."

"Wait!" Dr. Hicks said. "We haven't heard a thing about this!"

"Because we did not want you to hear about it," Mahoney said. "Althea's in a hospital in Florida under FBI protection."

Carson said, "Well, we had nothing to do with you getting shot at and Althea getting wounded. I think this is her past catching up with her. Her family has been involved in drug dealing and other criminality for generations."

"She said you'd say that. She said a lot, actually."

Dr. Tolliver started to get up. "I see no connection whatsoever between the affairs of West Briar and this shooting event, so I am leaving."

Mahoney put on his angry face and said, "Sit down, Doctor, or you will have no chance of seeing life outside prison walls for decades."

CHAPTER
71

THE PSYCHIATRIST ACTED LIKE HE'D been gut-punched. He sat back down, saying, "Prison? I...I believe I want an attorney present."

"I am an attorney," said Nina Larch, who'd been quiet up until now. "I advise you not to say another word, Dr. Tolliver."

"Then I will," I said, gesturing across the table at the two piles in front of Mahoney. "It took five agents from the local office a lot of hours to help us run down what we needed, but there it is. The weight of evidence against you."

Dr. Hicks stared at the documents like they could damn her, but Carson had not lost his cool. "I think this is a stunt."

Mahoney slid the first pile to me.

I spun it around in front of me. "Thanks to Ms. Larch's fine assistant, we have the letters that Kay Willingham sent to Ms. Larch to amend her will the last two times. And we have the documents authorizing Mr. Carson to conduct the timber sale on the plantation. And thanks to Kay's medical record, we also know the time periods when she was a patient at West Briar on powerful antipsychotic drugs that left her incompetent to make sound legal decisions."

Mahoney said, "Isn't it interesting that they overlap? The letters amending the will five years ago and twenty months ago were all signed and dated when she was at West Briar. So were the timber-sale documents."

I said, "The least you could have done is postdate the letters. But you must have thought, *Who's going to try to match up dates on a legal document with time spent in an ultra-secretive, ultra-exclusive psychiatric facility?*"

The junior attorney, Nina Larch, said forcefully, "I am not a part of any fraud. I had no idea whatsoever that Kay Willingham was at West Briar when she wrote those letters. They all bore a Montgomery postmark on the envelopes and a Montgomery notary's seal and signature on every letter."

"We saw them," Mahoney said. "We called the notary, who's retired and living down on the Gulf now. She said Mr. Carson sent her up to West Briar multiple times to get Kay Willingham's signature on documents. She said you were there once or twice, Dr. Tolliver, and you too, Dr. Hicks."

Dr. Tolliver had a tremor in his voice when he said, "Yes, well, I remember documents being signed, but I also recall Kay being exceptionally lucid at those times. She asked sharp questions that showed she understood what she was doing."

"Very sharp," Dr. Hicks said.

"Questions to who?" Mahoney said. "The notary who had no law degree? Or the shrinks with no law degrees?"

The psychiatrists said nothing. Carson stared at the table.

I said, "You, Mr. Carson, took advantage of your cousin's frequently fragile mental state to alter her will so the plantation would become not a park, but land for sale, and then you altered it again to make yourself the sole beneficiary. But although Kay had mental problems, she was physically fit. It could have been years before she died of natural causes."

Carson, already seeing his future land deal slipping through his fingers, looked up at me. "What are you trying to say?"

Mahoney said, "That you hired professionals to kill Kay Willingham the same way you hired professionals to kill Althea Lincoln. Randall Christopher just happened to be with Kay when the shooting started. And we just happened to be with Althea."

"So the counts are mounting, Bobby," I said. "Two counts murder for hire. Two counts attempted murder of a federal officer. One count conspiracy to commit fraud, and multiple counts of outright fraud."

"No, no, no!" Carson shouted. "That's absolutely not true. I…I admit to getting Kay to sign those letters and the permission to log the timber. I…I was going to get nothing in the original will! Nothing, and we shared great-grandfathers! My father and I slaved for the Sutter family. Kay could give away the cash and the stocks, but I deserved that land. Who do you think cared for it all these years?"

"You *were* going to develop it," Mahoney said.

"Damn straight I was going to develop it. State park? Are you kidding? It would have been a gold mine."

"If it weren't for Althea Lincoln and Kay Willingham," I said.

"No!" Carson said. "I am not a violent person. I did not have Kay killed. I did not hire anyone to shoot at Althea, and why would I hire someone to try to kill federal agents? They'd swarm the state!"

CHAPTER
72

JUST AS WE'D PLANNED IF the discussion had Bobby Carson admitting to fraud but denying murder, Mahoney waited a few moments and then said, "So who else would have reason to want Kay Willingham and Althea Lincoln dead?"

Carson stared at the table and shook his head. "I have no idea. Other than brief visits to her mother when she was alive and her stays at West Briar, Kay rarely came to Montgomery and it was even rarer that we saw each other. Kay was a socialite. It has to be someone in Washington."

When he looked up at me, I said, "You have a good idea who it is, Bobby."

"I really don't."

Mahoney said wearily, "You know we are going to dismantle your practice, don't you? Take every file, every computer, search every safe-deposit box affiliated with this firm, and go through all your personal property. We are going to find it."

"Find what?" Dr. Tolliver asked.

I looked at my watch, said, "Oh, you and Dr. Hicks can leave now. There are FBI agents in the lobby waiting for you."

"Are we under arrest?" Dr. Hicks said in a whiny voice.

"You will be leaving in handcuffs," Mahoney said. "Yes."

Hicks started to cry, then got up and slapped Tolliver across the face. "You said no one would know. You said we'd just pick up some extra cash to make our lives easier in the middle of East Jesus, Alabama. Now we're probably going to jail and we're definitely losing our medical licenses. You stupid ass."

"You want to see an equally stupid ass?" Tolliver said. "Look in a mirror, Jeanne."

"Leave," Mahoney said. "Now."

Dr. Hicks turned and left, sobbing. Dr. Tolliver followed her, head up as if he were about to go onstage to deliver a research paper. He slammed the door behind him.

Mahoney turned to Carson. "As I said, we will find it, so you might as well give it to us."

Carson held up his hands. "I don't know what more I can—"

"We know about Althea's half brother Napoleon Howard," I said. "We know Kay was down here digging into what happened to him, how he was railroaded onto death row. And we know Kay believed the proof was in the old files of this law firm, your father's old files. Didn't she?"

Carson shifted in his chair. "Yes. She did. But I told Kay what I'm telling you. I had no clue what she was talking about. When Napoleon Howard stabbed his friend to death, I was in the U.S. Army, working as a JAG in South Korea. During Howard's trial? I was stationed in Berlin. But you know, second cousin and all, I went through all my father's files for her. Evidence to free an innocent man? I would have seen something like that, and I did not."

Mahoney sighed and picked up his phone. "Suit yourself, Bobby."

Nina Larch cleared her throat and I noticed her fingers trembling. "He's not lying to you, Special Agent Mahoney. There is nothing to do with Napoleon Howard in his father's files. I know because I also went through Robert Carson Sr.'s personal and legal files for Kay earlier this year. At Bobby's request, I might add."

"See?" Carson said.

Larch ignored him and focused on Mahoney and me. "But it wasn't until after Kay died and you came here asking questions that it dawned on me to go through the files of Robert Sr.'s late partner, Claude Knight."

Mahoney put his phone down.

"Claude?" Carson said. "He's been dead thirty years. Where were they?"

"In a storage unit over on the east side that the firm has rented since the fifties. Boxes of Knight's old files and old files from the Napoleon Howard trial. Vice President Willingham's old files, as a matter of fact. I've spent the past three days there."

Carson stared at her. "Did Claude——"

I cut him off. "Did you find proof of Napoleon Howard's innocence in the files?"

"I am not a criminal lawyer, Dr. Cross," she said. "But I saw evidence that should have come out at Howard's trial and didn't. I think it might have gotten Kay killed. And I am requesting witness protection."

CHAPTER

73

FOUR DAYS LATER, ON THE second to last Saturday in August, I got out of an Uber car with my luggage and trudged up my porch stairs, feeling as exhausted and disillusioned as I have ever felt. Knowing what I now knew, having seen the hard evidence, I could not help feeling sick for the late Napoleon Howard and sicker still for the late Kay Willingham.

The door was flung open. Bree was standing there, grinning, her arms wide.

"My conquering hero returns," she said and kissed me and hugged me.

"I don't feel like much of a hero today," I said. "I actually feel kind of dirty."

My son Ali said, "What happened? You don't look dirty, Dad."

I looked around Bree and saw him standing there barefoot.

"You walk quietly," I said.

He grinned and wiggled the toes of one foot. "I'm getting my feet strong. Going barefoot a lot is supposed to help with rock climbing. Mr. Mury said that."

"I remember," I said.

"Come inside out of the heat and humidity and close that door," Bree said. "We're burning electricity."

"This isn't heat and humidity, by the way," I said as we went inside.

"What happened in Alabama, Dad?" Ali asked.

"A lot of heat and things I can't talk about right now, bud."

His face fell. Bree reached out and rubbed his shoulders. "Ongoing investigation, Ali. Your dad can't even talk about it with me."

"She's right," I said.

Nana Mama called out, "Come give me a kiss, Alex, and have some lunch."

I couldn't help but remember Jannie's theory that my grandmother had microphones and cameras all over the house that she tracked from the kitchen. I smiled. "We have been summoned."

We went to the kitchen. I gave Nana Mama a kiss and a hug. "How is it you look so young and beautiful?" I said. "Do you have a painting in the attic that shows your real age?"

She laughed. "The Picture of Nana Mama?"

"Exactly," I said and yawned.

"You look like you haven't been sleeping much."

"I slept a bit on the plane this morning," I said, yawning again and going to get a coffee cup. "I shouldn't be this beat. Maybe I'll take a nap later."

Bree chewed on the inside of her cheek as I poured my coffee, and Nana Mama put out cold cuts, homemade bread, and potato chips in a bowl.

"Alex, you have an appointment at two p.m. you can't break," Bree said. "One of your patients. Mrs. Hernandez."

I shut my eyes a moment, then said, "I don't remember scheduling her for today. I can't get out of it? I feel like a zombie."

Ali thought that was funny. But Bree said, "I asked her to come. And so did Sampson. We have questions for her about Elizabeth, and there are things I need to show you after lunch."

"Elizabeth Hernandez?" Ali said. "The girl taken before Maya Parker?"

Bree hesitated and then nodded. "But we can't talk about her, Ali."

"Of course." Ali sighed, took a handful of chips, and munched on them.

I made a sandwich, said to Bree, "You sound like you're going back to work."

Nana Mama frowned. "You didn't tell him over the phone?"

Bree smiled, said, "I wanted to tell him in person. But yes, I am going back to work, but not until next month, and not for Metro PD. While you were gone, a headhunter called and asked if I would be interested in a job working in an elite private-sector investigation company. I'd be based in DC but I'd travel the world if needed. I was flattered and said I was interested. An hour later Elena Martin, the president of Bluestone Group, called from her jet en route to Abu Dhabi."

"Bluestone Group. I've heard of them. They do big-time corporate security work all over the world."

"They do, but that won't be me. I made that very clear, and she was very clear that she wanted me to stick to my strengths, which are investigative. She's great, a real visionary, and she basically made me an offer I couldn't refuse. I can work from home or out of their DC office, and the salary and benefits package is significantly better than what I was getting as COD!"

Part of me was sad because Bree had been a fine chief of detectives and would no longer be a force for good inside Metro PD. But she seemed so thrilled and the job sounded so phenomenal that I smiled, leaned over, and kissed her. "Congratulations. I guess I'll have to get used to the idea of you calling me from jets on your way to Abu Dhabi."

"Why not?" Bree said, beaming. "This will be a whole new world for me!"

"So that starts next month. What are you doing in the meantime?"

"Catching a killer and a rapist."

CHAPTER

74

I ASKED BREE HOW SHE was going to solve the series of killings if she was on leave and about to quit Metro PD. She said she had thirty days of leave due to her and when she offered to spend the time working exclusively on those cases, Commissioner Dennison had agreed.

Jannie came home soon after me. She'd been training on hurdles and said she'd posted one of her best times ever in practice.

A few minutes later, John Sampson arrived with Willow, who was looking kind of listless and sad until Jannie suggested they go up to her room to hang out.

Nana Mama insisted Sampson, Bree, and I take coffee and brownies she'd made from scratch that morning to my basement office. Down there, Sampson showed me the map he'd created and explained how he'd found what he believed was the rapist and killer's favorite hunting ground.

"Impressive," I said. "We're going to have to show this to Keith Karl Rawlins if it pans out. The FBI should be looking at this approach. Have you found a common denominator between the incubator, the apartment building, and the school?"

"Not yet," Bree said. "The incubator has changed ownership three times in the seventeen years it's been in operation, and since the incubator is a place for start-ups, the tenant turnover has been high. We've talked to the past two owners, gotten the names of some of the past tenants, and tracked down a few personnel rosters, but we haven't seen anything that links anyone to the apartment building or the streets around Harrison Charter."

Sampson said, "Then again, we're still waiting for the apartment's landlord to dig up records older than ten years, which was when she bought the property."

"How many units there?"

"Sixty," Bree said. "And like the incubator, lots of turnover."

I chewed on that a few moments. The doorbell rang.

"She's early," Bree said.

"Analisa Hernandez is always early," I said and went to the door to let her in.

For the second time in a row, she came in her bubbly self, hugged me, hugged Bree, and even hugged John, who she'd never even met before.

"What's happened, Analisa?" I said. "I'd swear you were a happy lady."

She smiled, sat down, put her hand over her heart, and said, "You know, I woke up this morning and started to worry in bed about everything all over again. Then I said, *No, Analisa, you must stop spending so much time in your head. You must return to your heart to find your peace.* And I did, you know. I put my hand over my heart like this and I closed my eyes and I said, 'Please, God, show me the way. Just for today.'" She got tears in her eyes. "Not long I'm lying there and I feel Elizabeth. Not think of her. I just felt her love, right here in my heart, like she was living in me."

"Of course she is," I said softly. "She always will be."

"Yes, Dr. Cross," Analisa said, smiling through her tears. "But I never felt it like that until this morning, and I got up believing that everything is going to be okay. Elizabeth is not gone. Her love for me and my love for her will be with me always, and like you said, she will give me meaning in my work with the girls in Guatemala."

Bree handed her a tissue and said, "I love that."

Sampson was wiping at his eyes. "I do too."

"And you know what else?" Analisa said, patting her heart. "When I feel Elizabeth here this morning, I also just suddenly knew for certain that you will find him someday. I think so. The one who ended her physical life."

CHAPTER
75

BREE, SAMPSON, AND I EXCHANGED glances. Bree said, "Well, that's why we asked you here, Analisa. Maybe you can help us make that day come faster."

"Okay?"

Sampson pulled up Google Earth and the map of Southeast Washington, DC, on my computer and highlighted the apartment complex, the business incubator, and the charter school.

Bree said, "Have you or Elizabeth ever been to this apartment building?"

She put on her reading glasses to peer at the screen and the address, then shook her head. "Elizabeth, maybe, but not me."

"You've obviously been in and around Harrison Charter," Sampson said.

"Lived in the neighborhood fifteen years."

"What about this building?" Bree asked, tapping on the third location.

Analisa squinted at the screen. "Can you show me the street view?"

Sampson typed and used his mouse, and then we were on the street, looking straight at the building.

"Ahh, the business incubator. I cleaned it for many years in my old job."

Bree, Sampson, and I nodded to each other. We were getting somewhere.

Bree asked, "Did Elizabeth ever go with you when you cleaned it?"

"Many times. She used to do her homework there while I vacuumed at night."

I said, "When was the last time that happened? I mean, when you and Elizabeth were both there?"

"Oh," she said. "It has been a long time since I stopped cleaning the incubator. When Elizabeth was twelve, maybe? So about six years ago?"

Bree asked Analisa if she remembered anyone staying late at the incubator, anyone who might have talked to Elizabeth or taken an inordinate amount of interest in her.

She thought about that. "You know, many young people would be there one night and not so many another, and yes, some talked to Elizabeth. But I don't remember a man being creepy with her, if that is what you mean. And she never told me something like that or I would have told the detectives when she disappeared."

"Did you ever run into anyone from the incubator at the school?" Sampson asked. "Someone who stood out?"

Analisa pursed her lips and her eyes shifted down and to the left. Then she shook her head. "No. I mean, just Mr. Randall."

"Wait, stop," I said. "Randall Christopher was at the incubator?"

"*Sí*, it's where he started the charter school."

CHAPTER

76

ANALISA CONFIRMED THAT SHE AND Elizabeth would often see Randall Christopher at the incubator working late to put the charter school together. Sampson did an internet search and, sure enough, found a brief story from years ago describing the idealistic young educator out to build an education system of his own design.

"I think the last year he was there, he had two classes of kids at the incubator," Analisa said. "Then he moved somewhere else for a year before the city decided to sell the Harrison property and he stepped in."

"Do you think that's why Mr. Christopher got involved in the search for Elizabeth and Maya?"

"I don't know about Maya," she said. "But yes, he told me he was organizing the search because of those nights when he helped her with her math at the incubator." She glanced at the clock. "I'm sorry. I must be at work at three."

"Where do you work?" Sampson asked, turning away from the computer.

Analisa smiled. "I am a hostess in a restaurant at the Mandarin Oriental. It is wonderful. No more cleaning and they are very kind, give me time off to do my real work in Guatemala. I'll see you next week, Dr. Cross?"

"Our regular time," I said, walking her to the basement door. "I look forward to it."

"I do too," she said, stepping through, then turning. "Be careful. Like I said, I feel like you will find him soon."

"We're on alert," I promised. I smiled and shut the door.

Back in my office, Bree showed me a text forwarded from Jannie. Bree had asked Jannie to ask Christopher's daughters if they knew the apartment building in Marshall Heights.

Tina had replied: We lived there four years before moving to our new house.

Suddenly, because he was the only person we could link definitively to all three locations on Sampson's map, the dead principal became a prime suspect in the series of rapes and murders that had shaken Southeast DC for almost fifteen years.

"Lot of flags flying," Sampson said.

Bree nodded. "He worked at the incubator and

lived at the apartment building at the time of many of the earlier rapes and killings. He ran Harrison Charter when the last few victims were taken, including Maya Parker and Elizabeth Hernandez."

I said, "And he got involved in the searches for both of them. Organizing them, insinuating himself into the investigation."

"Classic serial-killer move," Sampson said.

Bree said, "He could easily have guided the civilian searches away from where he did not want people to go."

"Concerned citizen, school principal, family man, upstanding member of the community," I said. "Pretty good cover for a serial killer."

Sampson said, "If Christopher was the killer, we have to at least consider that someone figured it out and shot him to death. Kay was an innocent bystander."

"We're getting ahead of ourselves. We need to rule Christopher in or out as the serial killer before we can determine who killed him."

"I'll start a list of questions to answer," Sampson said, turning to the keyboard.

"Number one," Bree said. "Where's his lair?"

Sampson said, "Alex, you searched his house. If Christopher's our guy, he kept his trophies or souvenirs somewhere, probably where he took his victims."

"Agreed."

Bree said, "Elaine Paulson said Christopher had multiple short-term affairs over the course of their marriage. What if he didn't? What if he was just actively hunting at those times?"

Sampson said, "Could Elaine have known who he really was?"

"Good point," I said. "We'll need to talk to her to match her recollection of the affair time frames to when the victims were taken and then—"

Bree's cell phone rang. She looked at it. "It's Dennison. I have to take this." She walked out of the office, the phone to her ear, saying, "Yes, Commissioner?"

"We'll want to interview all the teachers at Harrison and his administrative staff," Sampson said.

Bree popped her head in. "Not now. We have to leave pronto. Some billionaire celeb was just shot in the ass outside the International Hotel."

CHAPTER

77

THE PROTEST WAS STILL LOUD and raucous when we reached the International Hotel, a five-star luxury establishment in what used to be the Old Post Office building at Eleventh and Pennsylvania Avenue. The length of the avenue between the White House and Capitol Hill had been closed for the legally permitted march, just one of dozens that take place in the nation's capital every year.

Most of the marchers were moving right along, but there was a knot of them across Pennsylvania Avenue protesting a meeting of top Wall Street financiers at the hotel. Many of them carried signs and placards with catchy slogans like TAX THE RICH, THE CHANGE IS NOW, and THE BANKERS DID IT.

According to DC Metro Lieutenant Meagan Reynolds, who met us in the hotel driveway, the Protest March for Social Justice and Economic

Change involved roughly one hundred thousand people who had peacefully gathered outside the White House and then started walking down Pennsylvania Avenue to Capitol Hill.

"Things went smoothly on the march until most of the protesters had left Lafayette Park and maybe a quarter of them were past the International heading east," Lieutenant Reynolds said. "At that point, Rex Dawson shows up on foot on the north side of Pennsylvania, coming south on Eleventh, back to the hotel. He's dressed incognito except for the Hawaiian shirt."

"Stop," I said. "Incognito except for the Hawaiian shirt?"

Reynolds looked at me like I was clueless. "You don't watch *Snake Pit?*"

"I don't watch investor shows."

"Well, Dawson's on it. He wears flamboyant tropical shirts and is really arrogant. So, anyway, before the ambulance takes him, he tells me he's got sunglasses and a San Diego Chargers hat when he starts to cross Eleventh Street against the left-to-right flow of protesters heading to the Hill. He gets bumped hard, loses the sunglasses and the hat.

"Dawson keeps going, but people start recognizing him. And a lot of people don't like Dawson, especially in this crowd. So they start yelling at him, and he starts yelling back at them. There's a couple of shoves. A lot of anger. He reaches the traffic island, still in a crowd, and gets shot in the right glute by a small-caliber gun at close range.

"Dawson thought someone kicked him. He threw a couple of punches and got away from the crowd. He evidently didn't know he'd been shot until he reached the hotel lobby and felt his pants wet with blood."

"Where is he?" Bree asked.

"GW," Reynolds said. "He says he never saw the shooter."

I looked up at the International Hotel and saw several security cameras aimed at the protest. "Let's get the footage from those cameras, every angle, and fast."

"I'm on it," Sampson said and went into the hotel to find the security chief.

Bree kept asking Reynolds questions. I half listened, watching the flow of marchers and that knot of hard-core protesters still there on the other side of the avenue, exercising their right to voice their opinion.

The three signs I'd noticed before and others in the same anti-rich vein were still bouncing up and down in that crowd of eighty, maybe ninety protesters. I was about to turn away when I saw a flash of a different sign at the back of that knot of protesters.

"Alex?" Bree said. "John says he's got the tapes waiting for us."

The sign pivoted and I could see it clearly now: a distinctive and familiar graffiti that read SHOOT THE RICH.

"He's right there across the street!" I shouted to Bree and Lieutenant Reynolds.

"What?" Bree said and came up beside me.

I lost my visual on the sign and stared over there. "Someone in that crowd at our ten o'clock just flashed the *Shoot the Rich* sign at us."

"Where?" Lieutenant Reynolds said.

"Keep watching," I said.

"I see 'Tax the Rich,'" Bree said.

"No, he's there. He's taunting us, hoping the graffiti turns up on the security—"

"I see the sign!" Lieutenant Reynolds said. "Our one o'clock."

I scanned the crowd and the signs.

Then Bree shouted, "I've got him too. Dark bandanna, dark cap, and sunglasses! Reynolds, get him surrounded!"

CHAPTER

78

I'D SPOTTED HIM AGAIN BY then and was already moving north across Pennsylvania, trying to keep my eye on him and hearing Lieutenant Reynolds in my earbud ordering officers to move into position one block north and one block south of Pennsylvania Avenue on Tenth, Eleventh, and Twelfth. They were checking the identification of anyone leaving the area.

A group of protesters with signs blocked my view for several moments. When I got beyond them, the SHOOT THE RICH sign was gone again, and I didn't see anyone wearing a dark bandanna, sunglasses, and dark cap.

"I've lost him," I said into my lapel mic.

"I've lost him too," Bree said in my earbud.

My eyes scanned back and forth, looking for the sign and not seeing it, only that TAX THE RICH placard I'd seen multiple times. I went straight at the spot where I'd last seen the SHOOT THE RICH sign, using my height to look at every protester in that area. There were a surprising number of grandmotherly types scattered throughout the crowd, which otherwise was a cross-section of diversity.

"Tax the rich!" shouted one young man with shaggy, sandy-blond hair near the back of the protesters. "Tax the rich, not the poor, damn it!"

He was fervent about that message, shaking and pumping a sign with the same slogan and wearing a T-shirt that read FREEDOM AND JUSTICE FOR ALL!

Then he changed his spiel and started bellowing, "Life's a bitch! Tax the rich!"

Others in the crowd picked up his chant while I studied person after person, hoping to spot the bandanna or the sign again.

"Life is a bitch!" the crowd chanted, and marchers walking past joined in. "Tax the rich!"

I triggered my mic. "I'm still not seeing him. I think he's getting out of Dodge. Have officers photograph the IDs of anyone acting suspiciously."

"These people are not going to like that," Bree said, her radio voice crackling.

"They will when we catch the guy who shot Dawson in the ass," I said, moving northeast around the crowd toward Eleventh Street. "He'll be a legend. Most of these people will probably put him up for sainthood."

I looked diagonally northwest through the crowd but could no longer see the guy with the shaggy, sandy hair who'd started the chant that was still echoing through the protesters. And his sign wasn't there anymore. The only TAX THE RICH sign I could make out was held by a woman in her seventies wearing a broad-brimmed beach hat. I walked north on Eleventh scanning the flow of people leaving the march. Police officers were standing at the north end of the block checking IDs.

A man who held a sign that said THE BANKERS DID IT was giving one of the officers a bit of a hard time.

"This is the kind of police-state stuff we're protesting, man," he said as I showed the cops my FBI credentials and glanced his way.

Mid-twenties, rust-orange wool cap despite the heat, he was carrying a bookbag bandolier-style and wearing khaki shorts, sandals, and a yellow tank top with the Corona beer logo across the chest.

"It really is a depressing state of affairs, Officer, and with all due respect," he said, "you should be pissed about the economic tyranny growing around us."

"I hear you, Mr. Edmunds, but it's already been a long day for me," the officer said wearily. "And you've got a line behind you. You want to protest it, go back down there. You want to go home, keep moving."

Edmunds sighed and trudged by her, heading north.

I continued around the perimeter and was almost back to Pennsylvania Avenue on Twelfth when Sampson came over my earbud.

"Dr. Cross? Chief Stone? You need to return to the International. We've got the whole shooting on tape."

CHAPTER
79

SAMPSON, BREE, AND I STOOD behind Carlos Montoya, head of security at the International Hotel. He sat before a large screen featuring the frozen feeds of two cameras that looked down on the intersection of Eleventh and Pennsylvania Avenue.

Sampson took a pencil and tapped it on the screen where a man in a black ballcap, dark sunglasses, and a garish red Hawaiian shirt stood at the curb on the northwest corner of Pennsylvania Avenue.

"That's Rex Dawson," he said. He tapped on another man farther west on the sidewalk of Pennsylvania Avenue wearing a broad-brimmed khaki-green hat that hid his face, a long-sleeved olive-green shirt, and matching olive-green pants.

"Watch him too," Sampson said.

Montoya, the security chief, started the recording. The billionaire stepped off the curb
and moved south across Pennsylvania Avenue,
weaving in and out of the flow.

The guy in olive green did too, angling toward
Dawson.

Sampson narrated. "*Boom,* the guy in the green
hat shoves someone, and that guy knocks into
Dawson. Billionaire's hat and glasses go flying as
he falls down. People start to recognize Dawson.
See them all pointing?"

I saw them and Dawson getting up. People
began to shout at him, and he shouted right back.
But the guy in green was moving south ahead of
Dawson when the billionaire threw up his arms
in disgust at the people heckling him and started
toward the hotel.

"Watch green guy slant toward Dawson again,"
Sampson said.

The two men were separated by no more than
eight feet when they reached the traffic island.
Sampson had the security chief slow the feed.

A gap opened up in the crowd with Dawson
facing the hotel. The guy in green's right arm
rose above his hip. The sleeves on the shirt he
wore were overly long, covering his hand.

Dawson jerked sideways to his left, stumbled,
grabbed at his flank, and screamed in pain. Then
he got his balance and flung a few wild punches
and kicks at the people nearest him while Green

Hat moved away against the throng of protesters and out of the frame.

"I want to see that again," Bree said. "I'm not seeing the gun. There's something off about it."

"I want to see it again too, but humor me a second," I said. "Fast-forward, find the guy in the crowd opposite the hotel holding a sign that says *Shoot the Rich.* Just a few minutes after we arrived."

Montoya gave his computer an order and the feed blurred to 3:42 p.m. Our vehicle came to the driveway three minutes later.

We were visible in the lower part of the frame of the feed from the east side of Eleventh at 3:54 p.m. Two minutes passed and there it was: a placard with the SHOOT THE RICH graffiti on it held by a guy in an LA Dodgers cap, dark sunglasses, a khaki-green shirt, and a black bandanna around his neck.

The sign was visible for about thirty seconds before he ducked down and lowered it.

"Lost him," Montoya said.

"The sign returns in two or three minutes," I said, spotting the guy with the shaggy blond hair holding the TAX THE RICH sign now. "Somewhere down here, below this guy and to his right."

The shaggy-haired guy moved deeper into the crowd.

I pointed. "Stay where he was. Blow it up a little."

We waited. I kept looking for the sign. A few minutes later, Bree said, "There he is, Dodgers cap, right side of the screen."

Sure enough, he'd raised the SHOOT THE RICH sign again. But only for ten seconds, then he lowered it and disappeared into the crowd once more.

"Back out," I said. "You should see me in about twenty seconds."

Montoya gave the computer an order and the image gave us a wider-angle view. I could be seen moving in the opposite direction of the marchers toward the fixed group of protesters with Bree behind me.

Shaggy-haired guy started his tax-the-rich chant. Soon people around him were raising fists, yelling with him. When the chant was at its peak, he drifted out of the frame.

At first, I didn't think much about it and kept looking for the Dodgers fan on the opposite side of the screen. But then I noticed the shaggy blond guy walk up to a seventy-year-old woman in a straw gardening hat and talk to her. She was carrying a sign that said THE BANKERS DID IT.

Montoya froze the screen. "More?"

"Yes," I said. "Just a minute or two."

The security chief started the recording again.

Ten seconds into the footage, the old woman and the blond guy traded signs.

CHAPTER

80

I STARED AT THE SCREEN, not quite understanding what I was seeing, as Shaggy Hair bumped fists with the woman, turned, and went out of sight behind other protesters.

A few moments later, a man wearing a rust-colored wool cap, sandals, khaki green shorts, and a yellow tank top walked out of the throng onto Eleventh heading north. He was carrying a backpack and a sign that read THE BANKERS DID IT.

"That's him," I said, pointing at the screen. "I saw him. He's the shooter."

"How do you know that?" Sampson said.

"He's wearing green khaki shorts because he zipped off the legs. He's carrying a sign he traded an old lady for a few moments ago. And I am betting he's got a shaggy blond wig in that backpack and a green khaki sun hat and a green khaki shirt with overly long sleeves with bullet residue on it and a small pistol of some kind. He was wearing a rust-colored knit cap when I saw him. His last name is Edmunds."

I started toward the door.

"Alex!" Bree said. "How do you know all that?"

"Follow me, both of you, and I'll explain."

By the time we exited the hotel, most of the marchers had passed. The police had opened the avenue to vehicular traffic, and the knot of protesters across Pennsylvania had dwindled to no more than thirty.

I was going to head straight up Eleventh to try to find the patrol officer who'd checked Edmunds, but then I noticed that the older woman with the gardener's hat was still there with the remaining protesters.

"I want to talk to this woman first," I said. "She's still got Edmunds's sign. Call dispatch. Find out the name of the female officer who was checking IDs at the north end, west side of Eleventh. See if she took a picture of his ID."

Bree started the call, and Sampson and I went up to the older woman and introduced ourselves.

Her name was Elodie Le Chain. She was seventy-four, a widow from northern Maine who had come by bus to join the protest. "Someone has to stand up and say something when an old lady like me has to chop firewood to heat her house," she said.

"I'm sorry to hear that, ma'am," I said, putting on latex gloves. "Could we take a look at your sign, please?"

Mrs. Le Chain frowned but nodded and held it out. I took it. The handle was a wooden broomstick. The sign itself was made of two pieces of white poster board stapled to the upper broomstick. It was blank on the back with TAX THE RICH on the front and three of the sort of O-rings you see in binders punched through the tops of the poster boards.

"Why the O-rings?" Sampson said.

I thought that was odd as well. I turned the sign sideways and noticed a seam on the front poster board as if two pieces of it had been sandwiched together. Sampson gave me a pocketknife. I worked the blade into the seam and got it apart; they'd been held together with Velcro along the edges.

I got both pieces separated and flipped the TAX THE RICH sign backward on the O-rings, revealing another sign: SHOOT THE RICH.

"What's that say?" Mrs. Le Chain said. "I don't agree with that. I think they should pay taxes like everyone but I don't want them dead."

"I'm sure you don't, ma'am, but we're going to have to take this as evidence. We suspect the man who gave it to you was involved in a shooting earlier."

"No!" she said. "He was a nice young man. He was from Maine too. Portland."

We got her contact information and left her to see Bree trotting our way on the west side of Eleventh. I pivoted the sign to show her the SHOOT THE RICH graffiti.

She smiled, gave me the thumbs-up, and said, "Officer Wells was still there. She remembered Adam Edmunds because he mouthed off. She didn't take a picture of his ID, but she said she knows it was a George Mason University graduate-student ID card because she asked him what he was studying."

"What'd he say?"

"Conflict analysis and resolution," she said.

"George Mason has a school for that?"

"It does."

CHAPTER

81

WE CAUGHT UP TO ADAM EDMUNDS at the George Mason University School for Conflict Analysis and Resolution at the Virginia Square Campus in Arlington. Edmunds was on his way out of an evening lecture on using meditation and tai chi as a path to inner peace and laughing with five earnest-looking young women on the Birkenstock and Patagonia end of the spectrum.

Seeing that he was also carrying the bulging yellow pack from earlier in the day, Ned Mahoney walked up to him, showed him his credentials, said, "Adam Edmunds. FBI. You are under arrest."

The young women all gasped and looked at Edmunds.

"Arrest?" he said. "For what?"

"Three counts of attempted murder, including one attempt on a sitting member of the U.S. House of Representatives."

Now the women were acting as if an oily

creature had suddenly invaded their safe space. "Attempted murder?" one said.

Edmunds shook his head. "I've never tried to kill anyone in my life."

"Try doesn't matter," I said. "You shot all three of them."

"I don't know what you're talking about," he said. "And I want a lawyer."

I took his backpack, opened it, and pulled out the green khaki hat, the blond wig, the long-sleeved shirt, and, finally, a crude weapon, a .22-caliber zip gun, a single-shot weapon so small, it could be concealed in the palm of your hand.

"Oh," I said. "And we have you on camera in front of the International Hotel."

Mahoney began to read him his rights.

Edmunds finally lost it. "You can't charge me with attempted murder. I shot them in the ass, for God's sake!"

All five of the women's jaws dropped. One said, "He was just talking about that!"

"He was!" cried another. "Telling us about Dawson getting shot at the march."

"And you were all laughing about it!" he shouted at them. "Hypocrites. You know that when it comes right down to it, conflict resolution is a no-win. All in all, peaceful change rarely happens. You're living in a fantasy. At some point, someone has to take a stand and act. People take notice when corrupt politicians and fat-cat lobbyists and billionaire criminals like Dawson get shot in the ass. They take notice and they laugh just like you did or they cheer. And maybe, just maybe, they read up on these rich guys and see them for who they are. And in their own way, they start shooting the rich in the ass—metaphorically. And that shift in perception, everybody doing their best to shoot the bad rich in the ass, that's how you make lasting change—enough pain to get them aware of common pain, not some woo-woo conflict analysis and resolution."

"You're sick and delusional!" one shouted as we put handcuffs on Edmunds.

"No, I'm not, Lynn," he shouted back. "I fought in Afghanistan, remember? I know what real conflict resolution looks like."

Lynn and her fellow students were appalled at that.

"You said you came here because of your war experience," another young woman said. "You said you came here to find a way to peace. If that's not true, why the hell are you here?"

"You really want to know, Maggie?" he said. "I had the GI Bill, and the woman-to-guy ratio in the school was like thirteen to three, and one of those three was a gay guy."

The five women were completely shocked.

"You're an asshole, Adam," Maggie said.

"Total," Lynn said and they all walked away.

CHAPTER

82

BY THE TIME BREE AND I had delivered Adam Edmunds to the federal holding facility in Alexandria, filed our reports, and driven home, it was after midnight. We slept in the next morning and got up for a late breakfast with Nana Mama and the kids.

"You're not working today, are you?" Nana Mama asked.

"Not if I can help it," I said, yawning.

Bree said, "I think you deserve a day off after the hours you put in yesterday."

"Agreed," I said and poured myself another cup of coffee, realizing I owed someone a favor. After we'd eaten omelets and a fresh fruit salad, I got my phone and went out on the front porch. The temperature today, the first day of September, was tolerable but climbing.

I found the number I was looking for and punched it.

Clive Sparkman answered. "I thought you'd forgotten me."

"I didn't have anything solid to tell you before."

"And now you do?"

"You are speaking to a 'source close to the investigation,'" I said. "And you cannot release this until later in the day."

"Of course. Which investigation? Higgins's murder?"

"Rex Dawson," I said.

"You got *his* shooter?"

"We did," I said.

Sparkman started laughing when I told him Edmunds was attending a school designed to promote peace and explained his bizarre rationale for the shootings.

"This is crazy," Sparkman said, and I could hear the blogger tapping on his keyboard. "Good, but crazy."

"I thought it would appeal to your sense of irony," I said. "He'll be arraigned first thing tomorrow morning in federal court in Alexandria. Expect a drama. I have to go now, spend some time with my family."

"Wait," he said. "What about Higgins? And Kay Willingham?"

"Still working on both," I said, and I hung up.

Thunderstorms swept in soon after, which kept us all inside watching a Redskins preseason game against the Browns, and then a baseball game between the Nationals and the Cardinals. I couldn't remember the last time we had all just hung out together, and it was nice.

Later in the afternoon, Nana Mama roasted a leg of lamb in a garlic sauce that filled the entire house with wonderful aromas. Sampson came over with Willow before dinner started.

Once Willow was settled with Jannie and Ali, he took me and Bree aside. "The past few days I've been staring a lot at my map. Like, *a lot* a lot."

Bree and I glanced at each other. He caught it.

"I'm not losing it," Sampson said gruffly. "Anyway, for some reason staring at the map this morning made me realize that Billie's death kept me from trying to figure out what happened to the jewelry taken off Christopher and Willingham."

Before either of us could reply, Nana Mama called us to dinner, which was miraculously good. She'd soaked the lamb in buttermilk for a full day before roasting it. The meat fell off the bone, and the bone was all that was left when we were done.

The kids started the dishes. Nana Mama went in to watch *Sixty Minutes,* one of her Sunday-evening rituals.

Sampson was starting to talk about the Maya Parker case again when my phone rang. It was Rawlins, the FBI contractor and cybercrime expert.

I went out on the porch again and answered.

"It took me a week," Rawlins said. "But I got into

Kelli Ann Higgins's computer. My God, I've never seen so much dirt on so many people in my life."

"Anything on Kay Willingham or Randall Christopher?" I asked.

"Both of them," he said, and he described what he'd found.

"Wow," I said soberly when he'd finished. "It's a lot to wrap your head around."

"Wait until you read some of the other files. I'll e-mail you what you need for now."

"I appreciate the effort," I said.

"Glad to be of service," Rawlins said and hung up.

I sat in the glider trying to make sense of what Rawlins had told me. I decided that some secrets people keep are beyond comprehension. Then, in rapid succession, I saw the possible links between what I'd just learned and what we'd learned earlier—

My phone buzzed. I turned it over, expecting it to be Sparkman calling with a follow-up question or Rawlins letting me know he'd e-mailed me the files from Higgins's computers.

Instead, I saw a text from Ned Mahoney:

VP requested briefing. Tomorrow, 7:25 a.m. Be at Naval Observatory gate at 7:15 a.m. Bring multiple forms of identification.

My mind was still buzzing with what I believed I'd discovered, but then I read the text a second time and thought, *Okay, then. Game on.*

CHAPTER

83

U.S. SECRET SERVICE AGENTS Donald Breit and Lloyd Price were waiting in an idling Chevy Suburban when we cleared security at the Naval Observatory on a dismal, rainy Monday morning in the nation's capital.

"Gentlemen," I said, climbing in after Mahoney. "Good to see you both."

Breit, the bigger of the two, said, "Wish the rain would let up, but they're saying downpour all day today and all day tomorrow. It's going to put the VP in a sour mood. He was scheduled to play at Congressional later in the day."

"We'll try not to keep him too long," Mahoney said.

"You couldn't keep him long if you tried," Price said, putting the SUV in gear and driving to the residence with the windshield wipers slapping.

"Barnes keeps him on a tight leash. I think she's given you fifteen minutes."

I glanced at Mahoney, who said, "More than enough time."

"Got anything?" Price asked.

"A few things, nothing definitive on who killed Kay Willingham yet."

Breit puffed out a breath and shook his head. "Damn shame. He'll be sorry to hear that."

"How's he doing these days?" I asked.

"He's still mourning her, if that's what you mean," Breit said.

Price nodded and said, "I suspect he always will. She *was* the love of his life."

We pulled up in front of the vice president's residence, got out, and followed the two Secret Service agents inside, where we were greeted with the smell of bacon cooking and coffee brewing. We went to the same dining room as we had last time, which was set the same way, with the same server, Graciela, bustling about, smiling, and asking if we wanted coffee.

We accepted the offer. Price glanced at his watch; Breit was looking at his phone. I checked the time, saw it was 7:23.

Claudette Barnes, the vice president's chief of staff, entered the room carrying files and looking harried. She greeted us, shook our hands, and thanked us for coming.

Vice President J. Walter Willingham strode

into the room a few moments later wearing black wingtip shoes, navy-blue suit pants, and a crisply starched white shirt with the collar open. At almost the same time, Graciela poked her head out of the back room and he nodded to her.

"Good of you to come, Dr. Cross," Willingham said, shaking my hand, holding my forearm, and smiling in that mesmerizing way he had.

"Thank you, Mr. Vice President," I said. "We just wanted to keep you abreast of the investigation. As you requested."

"I did indeed," he said.

Willingham went to Ned next, shook his hand, and said, "Do you have him, Special Agent Mahoney? Kay's killer?"

"No, sir. Not yet. But we stumbled onto a few irregularities in Alabama having to do with Kay's estate that we thought you should know about."

"Irregularities in Alabama?" he said with mild surprise as Graciela entered and set his usual breakfast before him.

"Montgomery, sir," I said. "Evidence of fraud and coercion going back years, maybe decades."

Barnes said, "Fraud on whom? And by whom?"

"On your late wife by her second cousin Robert Carson Jr. and others."

The chief of staff's jaw dropped at the same time the vice president set his fork down. Then they both said, "Bobby Carson?"

Willingham looked at Barnes. "I told you Bobby was bad news and you wouldn't listen. Not like his old man at all. I told you that fifteen years ago." Then he shifted his gaze to us. "I worked with Bobby at Carson and Knight in Montgomery for about six months after I left the district attorney's office and was getting ready to run for governor. I was not impressed by him, but Claudette worked with him longer."

"Six years," Willingham's chief of staff said, still shocked by the news.

Mahoney said, "Carson was abetted by the head of West Briar and Kay's psychiatrists there."

The vice president gently pounded his fist on the table, looking at his chief of staff and his Secret Service agents. "I knew that too! There was something shifty about those two. Didn't I always say so?"

Agent Breit nodded, said, "The entire time Kay was down there, sir."

Agent Price and Barnes agreed.

Vice President Willingham told us that after the divorce, Kay's mother's death, her most recent nervous breakdown, and her commitment to West Briar, every time he made inquiries about her health and well-being, he was stone-walled by her doctors.

"I wasn't asking for particulars, just concerned, you know, having been through it with her before," Willingham said. "The old doctors at

West Briar would always share information and ask me questions. Those two would not tell me a thing. I mean, where is the benefit of being me these days?"

He glanced at his chief of staff, then sighed and shook his head. "Tell me what they did to her, Bobby Carson and those mental snake-oil salesmen."

We laid it all out. When we finished, Willingham said, "My God, Bobby Carson found it in himself to use Kay so he could destroy that beautiful land to make a buck."

Barnes said, "I imagine it was a lot of bucks, JW."

"With those quacks doping her out of her mind to do it," the vice president said, peering at me and Mahoney. "Explain how you figured all this out."

His chief of staff looked at her phone. "You have an eight-fifteen meeting, sir, with the White House counsel."

"Who will make me sit and stew, Claudette," he said brusquely. "Please continue, gentlemen. How exactly did you figure this out?"

Mahoney said, "Part of it was luck, sir, and Dr. Cross's sense that there was something not quite right about Bobby Carson and Kay's psychiatrists."

Willingham looked over at me. "Good for you. Great minds think alike."

"Thank you, Mr. Vice President," I replied.

"But the real credit goes to Kay's childhood friend Althea Lincoln."

Willingham suddenly grew wary. So did Barnes, who stopped scribbling notes as she said, "You talked to Althea Lincoln?"

"We did."

"She actually talked to you?" the vice president asked with his eyebrows raised. "Because as far as I know, that woman has not uttered a word in years."

"Except to your late wife, evidently," I said.

"And us," Mahoney said.

CHAPTER

84

DEMPSEY'S ALL-NIGHT DINER SERVED breakfast around the clock and was something of an institution in Anacostia, historically the blackest and poorest neighborhood in Washington, DC.

Calvin Dempsey opened the place shortly after returning from World War II, and it had not been closed since except for three hours on the night of Dempsey's wake in 2004 and three hours on the morning of the late owner's funeral.

Dempsey had a brother who served time for armed robbery, and he'd had a soft spot for ex-cons, often offering them their first jobs out of prison. During his time, the food had been uniformly excellent. Since then, the tradition of hiring men and women on parole had continued, but the quality of the cooking had ebbed and flowed, and so had the diner's fortunes.

"I can't believe it's still open," Sampson said as

he and Bree climbed out of his car opposite the diner, a shabby property with a blue neon sign that said DEMPSEY'S in scrolled letters. "Last time I thought I got ptomaine eating here."

"Positive about this tip?"

"Hundred percent?" he said. "No. It was a street rumor, but it came from a usually reliable source, so I figured we'd start here."

There were two signs on the front door. The first said HOTCAKES 24/7 and the second read SORRY, WE'RE STILL OPEN.

Sampson said, "Some things never change."

"Good," Bree said, opening the door.

"I'll go around back."

"Given the picture, I don't think we'll see a runner," Bree said.

"Just the same."

Bree went inside the diner and scanned the narrow, L-shaped room: A long counter on the left with ten chipped chrome and faded red vinyl stools. A pass-through to the kitchen. Six booths by the windows.

Two men, one in his thirties, the other about fifty, drank coffee at opposite ends of the counter. An older woman ate ice cream with two young boys in the nearest booth. The rest of the booths and stools were empty.

There was music playing; the Weekend, Bree thought. And the entire place smelled like frying bacon and onions. A ropy, intense man with lots of forearm tats wearing a stained apron came through the swinging doors at the far end of the diner and went behind the counter.

"Anywhere you like, ma'am," the waiter said with a smile that seemed fake.

"Thanks," Bree said and walked to the middle of the counter, directly opposite the pass-through to the kitchen.

There were two people working back there, an Asian man in his forties and a big, big African-American woman who seemed in charge.

The man behind the counter wore a name tag that said LARRY. He gave Bree a menu.

She showed him her badge.

"You the manager these days, Larry?" she asked quietly.

Larry's expression hardened. "I'm clean. Everyone here is clean. Drug tests seven days a week. We all showed negative yesterday."

"I'm not here about drug violations," Bree said. "I'm looking for Mary Jo Nevis."

He leaned over the counter, fuming. "She's been through enough, and she's the best cook we've got. Don't do this!"

"I'm just here to ask a few questions," Bree said.

Larry glared at her a beat, then turned and shouted, "The Man's here to see you, Waffles!"

The shout startled Bree and everyone else. A pot crashed in the kitchen.

"Bad boy, Larry," Bree said. She got up on

the counter, jumped down behind it, and ran through the swinging doors.

The Asian cook was cursing in a language she didn't recognize and looking down at a large prep bowl on the floor spilling flour and broken eggs. There was no one else in the kitchen.

Bree dodged past him, smelling bacon burning on the griddle, to a short hall that led to the back door. She yanked it open and found Sampson in the alley with his gun drawn, and the big, big African-American cook about ten feet away with her fingers interlaced behind her head.

"Whatever anyone said about me, it's fake news," she said.

CHAPTER

85

SAMPSON TOOK A STEP TOWARD her. "Do I have to put the cuffs on you, Mary Jo?"

She threw him a look. "Does this sister look like she's running anywhere?"

Bree said, "Are we going to find a weapon on you, Ms. Nevis?"

For that, Bree received the sneer of the year. "Come close, little one. I'll sit on you. Smother you. How's that for a weapon?"

"Answer the question," Sampson said.

"No," Nevis said. "And I am clean. Squeaky."

"Then why'd you run, or try to run?"

"You mistook my nicotine craving for quickness. Just out for a smoke. Check my apron. Front right pocket."

"Left a heck of a mess for your buddy to clean up," Bree said.

She shrugged. "Spilled milk happens. It's just

the meaning you give it. Learned that in Narcotics Anonymous."

"Uh-huh," Sampson said. "Well, here's the meaning I give it, Waffles. By the way, where'd you get that name?"

Nevis laughed, wiggled her obese body, said, "Too many Eggos in adolescence. The name stuck."

"In Chicago," Bree said.

"You read my jacket?" she said.

"Why do you think we're here?" Sampson said.

"I don't know why—I'm waddling the straight and narrow. Ask my parole officer."

Bree had to fight not to smile. "We did, and she's concerned about rumors you're back to your old tricks and trade."

"No way, I did my time in Joliet," Waffles said. "When I got out, I wanted a clean break from all that back on the South Side, so I came here. Heard you could find work, start a new life. I'm telling you, I wouldn't mess that up. I got a six-year-old boy back home. I want to hold him someday soon."

"Compelling story," Sampson said. "But there's an old cop saying: once a fence, always a fence."

"Search me, then, if you dare put your hands on this fine temple of femininity," she said. "I got nothing hot on me or at the house or anywhere else, much less in my panties."

"You have good timing," Bree said. "You should have been a comic."

"Instead, I'm a diabetic," Waffles said. "Can I drop my hands? Ten weeks out of stir, I'm not in shape for this. I'm getting a neck cramp."

"Go ahead," Sampson said.

She did, making a soft moan and rolling her shoulders.

Bree said, "So why are we hearing these rumors of you taking in stolen goods?"

Waffles took a deep breath and blew it out slow. "Some people know I used to do that kind of thing. It's what I was in for."

"Who knew?"

"Like a hundred people. I stood up and shared at a big NA meeting a couple of weeks ago."

"Any of them stand out?"

"No."

"Anybody outside AA?"

"NA, and…no," she said, but she was looking at the ground.

Bree could tell Waffles knew more than she was saying, but she didn't comment.

Finally the ex-con raised her head. "That it?"

"You should tell us now while you have the chance," Bree said. "This is bigger than any fence job you've ever seen."

"I told you—"

"No, we're telling you, Mary Jo," Sampson said. "Someone took jewelry off the victims of a double homicide a few weeks back. A pearl necklace. Earrings. Bracelets. A man's Rolex."

Waffles shook her head defiantly. "Like I said, search me. Search my room at the halfway house. Search anywhere I go."

"You could have already fenced them," Sampson said.

"But I didn't."

Bree racked her brain for angles, and it did not take long to find one. "You know, I believe you," she said. "You don't have the jewelry and never have."

Waffles sighed. "There you go. Can I go back to my job now before I don't have one to go back to?"

"After you tell us who *tried* to sell you stolen jewelry in the past few weeks."

"Didn't happen," Waffles said. "Fake news. Can I go?"

"You know what obstruction of justice is, Ms. Nevis?" Bree asked.

"I'm hyper-chubby, not stupid."

"You understand that withholding material evidence to a capital crime is itself a form of obstruction. Knowing something and staying silent *is* a form of obstruction."

"Unless I invoke the Fifth. What's your point?"

Bree took a step forward and gazed up into the woman's eyes. "If we find out you're lying to us, your silence can break the terms of your parole, and the smart funny lady in front of me will be back doing standup for hard-timers in Joliet, still guilt-ridden and dreaming about her son, who just gets older and farther away from his gifted, funny mom every day that passes."

Waffles held Bree's gaze, but her expression shifted toward resentment.

"You don't play fair," she said.

"The murdered woman?" Bree said. "She was the ex-wife of the vice president of the United States. We don't have to play even remotely fair with you."

CHAPTER

86

IN THE DINING ROOM OF his official residence, Vice President Willingham shifted in his seat, took a sip of juice, and said, "When Althea Lincoln spoke to you, she told you about Bobby Carson being a swindler?"

"Among other things," I replied. "As Althea says, when you keep your mouth shut for years, you tend to hear a lot."

"Let me guess," Willingham said. "Her brother? Napoleon Howard?"

"Half brother, and a little bit of that," Mahoney said. "But Althea was more focused on West Briar and how the staff would not listen to her when she brought Kay in this last time. She kept telling them that Kay had been through two traumatic incidents in the weeks before she brought her to the facility."

"What traumatic incidents?" Barnes asked.

"Her mother dying," the vice president said.

"And the death of Napoleon Howard," Mahoney said. "Ms. Lincoln said it was the straw that broke the camel's back and caused the nervous breakdown."

I could see the news had gotten to Willingham.

"Your ex-wife believed Mr. Howard was innocent," Mahoney said.

"Kay sure did not believe that when he was convicted," he said, setting his coffee cup down hard. "It's how we met, you know. She walked up at a party, told me she'd been a childhood friend of Jefferson Ward, and thanked me after I put Howard away."

Mahoney said, "She came around to Howard's position over the years."

"Napoleon Howard wasn't innocent," Willingham insisted. "He killed Jeff Ward in a drug-fueled rage. Cut off the man's head, for God's sake. His prints and Ward's blood were on the knife. He lost every appeal. End of story."

Mahoney said, "There might be a different angle on all of that."

Barnes sat forward. "What sort of angle?"

"Kay evidently believed her mind was being manipulated long before Dr. Tolliver and Dr. Hicks were ever involved in that facility."

Barnes said, "This sounds like Althea Lincoln nonsense and a waste of the vice president's time. Sir, you really do have to be at the White House at—"

Willingham crossed his arms. "I want to hear this, if only to see how delusional Kay managed to make herself this time. Dr. Cross, she used to tie herself in knots with family conspiracy theories. It's why her parents sent her to Switzerland for school when she was seventeen. She blamed Roy and Beth Sutter for everything wrong with the world and she needed some perspective on that."

"When Kay was seventeen," I said. "That would have been after her first stay at West Briar?"

He shrugged. "Sounds right."

"Do you know why her parents committed her to West Briar that first time?"

"Bipolar disorder," he said. "It's a chemical imbalance, treatable with drugs."

I said, "That was the diagnosis. But Althea says there was a traumatic incident that triggered the depression and Kay's first commitment."

CHAPTER

87

"**WHAT DID ALTHEA SAY HAPPENED** to Kay?" the vice president asked, the fingertips of his hands touching to form a steeple.

"She fell in love for the first time," I replied.

"With Jefferson Ward," Mahoney said.

"What?" Willingham said scornfully. "No, not a chance. She would have told me that."

"And yet she didn't," I said. "But we've confirmed the romance with several sources, all teenage friends of Kay and Althea."

"Whoever they are, they're full of it. I know most of Kay's teenage friends and never once did they mention Kay being in love with Ward. That's preposterous."

Mahoney said, "How many of those friends were black, sir, African-American?"

"Well…I don't know."

I said, "Kay's African-American friends, the

ones we spoke with, were adamant that Kay had not only been in love with Ward but was in a sexual relationship with him. Kay's parents found out and forbade her to see him. That's what caused the depression. Not a chemical swing."

"According to Althea Lincoln," Barnes said, dismissively.

"And six other women, Ms. Barnes," Mahoney said. "We have sworn affidavits."

The vice president stared off as if seeing his late ex-wife in a different light. "Roy and Beth put her in West Briar for sleeping with Ward?"

"That's our belief," I said. "The problem was, Kay went right back to Ward after her release from West Briar, which was really what got her sent to school in Switzerland. Two years later, she came home to Montgomery at Christmas, polished, multilingual, and extremely well educated, on her way to being fully prepared for her future life. Jeff Ward had fallen on harder times. He'd lost his job. He sold drugs. Still, during that visit, Kay told Ward that when she'd finished her studies abroad and gotten her inheritance, she would return. They'd go away, make a life for themselves."

Willingham stayed silent, watching us, while Barnes scribbled furiously. Then he shook his head. "We had investigators all over that case. We would have known this."

"But you didn't," Mahoney said. "With all due respect, sir, we believe the Montgomery investigators were understandably lax about pursuing other explanations for Ward's death. They had the weapon, the motive, and eyewitnesses who put Howard at the scene. Why would the detectives have looked at other theories?"

"Bill Miller, Howard's public defender, was very good. He would have brought the relationship up at trial if it had been pertinent to Howard's case."

I said, "We asked Mr. Miller about that. He said he vaguely remembered that Kay had been in love with Ward when they were young but did not know about her visit home at nineteen and believed she'd been in Switzerland almost six years and was living with a Swiss man when Ward was murdered."

"Henri," Willingham said with a head bob to Barnes. "I met Henri once. A twit. But Dr. Cross, Special Agent Mahoney, I still haven't heard anything that presents a new angle here. One night when Howard and his friend were high on booze, meth, and coke, tempers flared and Howard went berserk."

"Or someone else did, Mr. Vice President," Mahoney said.

He crossed his arms again, said, "You going to tell me Bobby Carson did it?"

Mahoney said, "No, sir. Bobby's good for fraud and racketeering but not murder."

I said, "We believe a hired assassin was watching Ward and Howard the night of the murder. The assassin saw them higher than kites and arguing. When they passed out, he took advantage of the situation, went in wearing gloves, cut Ward's head off, and framed Howard for it with the knife."

"C'mon," Barnes moaned. "An assassin? Who's going to believe that scenario?"

Arms crossed, frowning, the vice president sounded equally skeptical when he said, "Who do you think this assassin was?"

"I don't think we'll ever know exactly who, sir," Mahoney said.

"That's convenient," Special Agent Breit said.

"Right?" Special Agent Price said and sat back, unimpressed.

Barnes's phone buzzed. She looked at it, closed her eyes, said, "Great. That's the White House counsel wondering where we are."

"Tell him we are attending to a personal issue that's just come up."

"Sir, I—"

"Do it, please," Willingham said. He looked at us. "If you don't know who the assassin was, how do you know he was hired? That's what you said, wasn't it?"

"Yes," Mahoney said. "We know he was hired because we know who hired him."

The vice president, his chief of staff, and his security detail all leaned forward.

"Who?" Willingham said.

"Roy Sutter," I said. "Kay's father."

CHAPTER
88

AT THE SAME TIME OVER in Southeast DC, not far from Dempsey's All-Night Diner, Bree and Sampson pounded on the apartment door of Angela Monroe, mother of Devon Monroe, a seventeen-year-old junior at the late Randall Christopher's Harrison Charter School.

Devon Monroe had no prior history of criminal activity, a minor miracle for the neighborhood, but Mary Jo Nevis, aka Waffles, had told Bree and Sampson that Monroe and a friend of his named Lever Ashford came to her two days after the murders.

Several weeks before, the boys, who washed dishes part-time at Dempsey's, had asked her about being a fence. Waffles told them being a fence had landed her in a penitentiary and that's all they needed to know.

She'd meant it as a warning, so when they

showed up at the diner looking for her to fence some jewelry that had "come their way," she refused. Which meant either they'd sold the stolen goods elsewhere or they still had them.

Sampson knocked again on Monroe's door.

Devon's mother, Angela Monroe, who worked nights as an EMT, answered the door in a robe looking exhausted and confused. "Devon?" she said when Sampson showed her the search and arrest warrants. "No, my boy has never been in trouble a day in his life."

"I'm sorry to say that day has come," Sampson said. "Where is he?"

"No, no, Devon's a good boy, a good student," she said, her anxiety rising. "He's going to go to college someday. He—"

"Stole jewelry off two dead people," Bree said. "One of them his high-school principal."

"Mr. Christopher?" she said, appalled. "No, that's—"

"Ma'am, please," Sampson said. "Can we make this easy? For his sake?"

Mrs. Monroe nodded. With tears welling in her eyes, she pointed to a hallway. "Third door on the right."

Sampson didn't bother to knock, just went in and turned on the lights. Bree followed him and almost gagged at the smell of a seventeen-year-old boy's bedroom, a mix of body odor, sneaker toe punk, and dirty-clothes stink.

And the tiny space looked like a bomb had hit it.

Across the wreckage, on the lower of the bunk beds, something moved. Clothes fell to the floor, and then schoolbooks, then Devon Monroe's head appeared, eyes shut, grimacing.

"Not again, Ma." He moaned. "Shut the light off. I said I'd pick up in the morning."

"Metro Police!" Bree said. "Get up. Now!"

The kid's eyes flew open and his face registered shock at seeing Bree and Sampson standing there in their bulletproof vests. "What? Wait! What is this?"

"You're under arrest, Devon," Sampson said, going to him and throwing aside the small mountain of clothes and blankets he'd been burrowed under. He was naked.

"Dude!" he yelled, covering himself. "Not cool!"

Bree looked around, saw a pair of jeans, threw them at him, and listened as Sampson read him his rights.

"Do you understand, Devon?" Bree asked.

He nodded morosely.

"I sacrificed everything for you!" his mother yelled from the doorway. "Your father left, and I lived for you, boy!"

"Ma!" he said. "Please!"

"Please, nothing," she said, weeping. "You've thrown it all away. Everything I worked for."

"Maybe not," Sampson said, looking at the kid.

"We have a search warrant, but honestly, Devon, we'd rather not dig around in here. Show us what we want, *now*, and just maybe the judge will cut you some slack."

His gaze shifted from Sampson to Bree to his mother, who shouted, "Show them! Tell them, Devon! Whatever they want, you do it!"

The teen's shoulders drooped in surrender, and he sullenly pointed to a pile of debris in the corner. "I tried telling Lever it was too good to be true, but he just wouldn't listen."

Sampson put on latex gloves, went to the corner, and started digging.

Bree said, "Was that before or after you shot Mr. Christopher and Mrs. Willingham?"

"What?" his mother shouted. "No! Do not answer that, Devon."

"Ma," he said angrily. "We didn't shoot anyone. We—"

"I don't care," she said, sounding on the verge of hysteria. "I know where this is going now. Not another word until we've talked to a lawyer, you hear me, young man?"

CHAPTER

89

VICE PRESIDENT WILLINGHAM'S BROW FUR-
ROWED after we'd told him that Kay's father had
ordered the murder of Jefferson Ward and the
framing of Napoleon Howard.

"Roy Sutter?" he said, shaking his head. "I'm
sorry, my late ex-father-in-law might have been
a racist but I can't believe he'd—"

"Why not?" Mahoney said. "He put his
daughter in a psych ward and had her
doped to the gills, and then he sent her to
Switzerland for years to keep her and Ward
apart."

"Why have Ward killed, then? As you said, Kay
had been in Switzerland for nearly six years by
that time. She had a life over there."

I said, "Kay was coming home, returning
to Montgomery because her grandmother was
terminally ill with cancer. And she was going

to reunite with Ward. She told her father as much in a letter two months before Ward was killed."

"Says who?" Barnes said. "Althea Lincoln?"

"No," I said, flipping my file open. "Kay's letter states it clearly."

"You have the letter?" Willingham said, shocked.

"Mr. Vice President," his chief of staff said. "I don't like where this is—"

"We have a copy of it, sir," I said, pushing the document to Willingham.

He said, "And where did you find this letter Kay allegedly wrote?"

Mahoney said, "In a storage unit in Montgomery. With your old files from the Ward trial, sir. You must have left them behind when you ran for Congress."

Willingham stared at Ned and me, blinking, then he put on reading glasses and scanned the letter and the envelope Mahoney slid across to him.

Barnes shifted in her chair, said, "Mr. Vice President—"

"Give me a damn minute, Claudette," Willingham said, his eyes on the letter as he read and reread it. After a moment, he lifted his head. "I can tell you, gentlemen, I have never seen this before in my life. And you say it was found in *my* trial files? That is impossible. If authenticated, this letter might have been exculpatory at trial."

"Exactly, sir," I said.

"Stop!" Barnes said. "This conversation is over, Mr. Vice President!"

Willingham glanced in bewilderment at the letter again and then at her. "Why?"

"Because I am also serving as your counsel here, sir," Barnes replied, agitated. "Whatever that letter says, they found it in *your* files and they are, in effect, accusing you of withholding evidence in a capital crimes case, a violation of Napoleon Howard's constitutional rights as well as a gross obstruction of justice."

The vice president blinked again and shook his head. "But Claudette, I have a near-photographic memory, and I have honestly never seen this letter before. And I remember going through those trial boxes before I had them moved to storage. There was an index of everything. I would have seen this in the index or in the evidence log, and I didn't."

Mahoney cleared his throat. "I never said the letter was *in* your files, sir. We said the letter was *with* your boxes in the Carson and Knight storage unit. But the files that contained the letter and other documents were markedly different than yours. They were light blue and had a different labeling and coding system."

"Whose files were they, then?" he demanded. "Who did they belong to?"

Mahoney and I turned our full attention on Barnes, who was staring at us like we'd morphed into a firing squad.

"They belonged to Claude Knight, sir," I said. "Your chief of staff's late father."

CHAPTER

90

CLAUDETTE BARNES'S LIPS BARELY TREMBLED as she said softly, venomously, "How dare you impugn the reputation of my father. He was one of the finest—"

"—liars, cheats, and legal con artists Montgomery has ever known," Ned Mahoney said. "At least, that's his reputation among people old enough to remember him in his early days. 'A bag man' was how some described him."

"Corrupt," I added. "A man without a conscience. A man willing to sell his soul."

Barnes's face flushed and she shouted, "Do not talk about my daddy like that! He was a good man and I'm not listening to any more of this."

She got to her feet. Willingham put his hand on hers and said, "Sit down, Claudette. You've said yourself he was a lousy lawyer."

"He was *not* a criminal," she said, sitting down,

not looking our way. "I went through his files before he died and he *was not* a criminal. I would have seen evidence of that and I did not."

"Why did you go through his files?" I asked.

"It's what you do when your father has died," she said.

"Except you went through the files *before* he died," I said. "We've seen the sign-out sheets. Why before?"

Barnes shook her head. "I don't remember it that way."

"Your sister remembers it that way," Mahoney said. "She says a week after your father's first stroke, she overheard him ordering you to go through his old files and destroy anything that linked him to any criminality."

"My sister's lying," Barnes said. "But it's moot. I didn't find anything."

"Because someone else got to the files first, someone who had suspicions about their contents—a paralegal at Carson and Knight named Belinda Jackson."

"I remember her," Willingham said.

I said, "In the hours after Claude Knight had his first stroke, and three days before you went to the storage unit, Ms. Barnes, Belinda Jackson went through your father's files on Kay Willingham, Roy Sutter, Jefferson Ward, and Napoleon Howard. She put what she discovered in with your files, Mr. Vice President, figuring that they would be seen at some point soon in Howard's appeals process."

Mahoney said, "But those files were put in storage. Belinda tried to tell several investigators that there was information pertinent to the case somewhere in the trial boxes. But no one looked. And then Howard died in prison."

I said, "When Belinda heard, she tried to call Kay to tell her about notes she'd seen, written in Knight's own hand, that referred to meetings with Roy Sutter after the letter arrived from Switzerland along with specific times and dates where Kay's father talked about having Ward 'eliminated.' But Kay couldn't take Belinda's calls because she was in West Briar and not allowed any outside contact at the suggestion of Ms. Barnes."

"What?" Willingham cried.

"That is not true," Barnes said.

"But it is, and we'll get back to that in a few minutes," Mahoney said, tapping his file. "Right now, it's important to know that Kay was released from West Briar and finally called Belinda Jackson, who had just broken her hip at age ninety-two."

I said, "She was on painkillers and out of it, but she managed to tell Kay about the notes and their location. It was late in the last campaign cycle. It could explain Kay's meltdown as the election approached."

Barnes said, "I want to see these documents. I have no idea where you could have heard thirdhand about Belinda Jackson's crazy fantasy, but—"

"From Belinda Jackson herself," Mahoney said. "She lives in a rest home in Tallahassee. Hip's good. Not on meds. Sharp. Another interesting thing? Someone else talked to Mrs. Jackson before we did."

"Who was that?" Vice President Willingham asked.

"Kelli Ann Higgins," I said. "A dealer in political dirt."

"I know who she is," Willingham said.

"*Was*, sir. She was beaten to death in her apartment not long ago."

He looked shocked, then glanced at Barnes. "How did I not know that?"

"You were in Cambodia, sir," Barnes said, shifting uncomfortably in her chair.

I said, "But you weren't, Ms. Barnes?"

"No. I, uh, was here, working."

Mahoney looked at the two Secret Service agents. "Were you part of the overseas detail?"

Special Agent Breit hesitated, then shook his head. "Not that trip."

His partner, Price, the stocky one, said, "I remained behind as well."

Mahoney said, "That helps."

"With what?" Barnes asked.

He opened a file and pulled out a still shot of Special Agent Price walking down a sidewalk.

"That's from a security surveillance camera down the street from Kelli Ann Higgins's town house," Mahoney said. "The day she died."

CHAPTER

91

PRICE LOOKED CORNERED, BUT THEN he said, "Like eight hours before she died. I went and knocked on her door. Got no answer."

I said, "Why were you knocking on Higgins's door?"

Price glanced at Barnes, who said, "Because I asked him to. Because Kelli Ann was dropping hints that she had something potentially damaging to the vice president. If that was true, we wanted to know what this information was so we could prepare."

Willingham stared at her. "You never told me that."

She smiled at him a little coldly. "Sometimes my job is to not tell you, sir."

"What else haven't you told me?" he demanded, looking at Barnes and then his Secret Service agents.

Breit and Price appeared ready to say something, but before they did, Mahoney asked Barnes, "Have you told the vice president about your arrangement with Bobby Carson and the good doctors of West Briar?"

Willingham's chief of staff swallowed hard. "I have no arrange—"

"They're all under arrest," I said. "You didn't think they were going to talk?"

Barnes said nothing but I could see the fight-or-flight reflex kicking in.

Mahoney looked at Willingham. "It was her idea to use Kay's visits to West Briar to get Bobby Carson named as the heir of the old Sutter plantation."

"That's a lie!" Barnes cried.

"No, it's not," I said. "They've all turned against you, Ms. Barnes, said you were the one who thought the land should be logged and then subdivided for trophy homes. They also say you hired the professionals to take out Althea Lincoln because she was the one closest to Kay, the one who heard everything. She just didn't count on Special Agent Mahoney and me being there when they tried to kill her."

"Absolutely not!" Barnes said. "This is preposterous and I want a lawyer."

"You're going to need one," Willingham said, looking at her coldly.

"You don't believe them, do you?" she said.

"If he doesn't now, he will in a moment," Mahoney said, sliding another file across the table to the vice president. "That's the formation papers of a Delaware shell company that owns two other shells within shells that all lead to the original partners of Sutter Development Ltd. They're listed on the last page. You'll see Robert Carson Jr. and Claudette Barnes as the senior partners."

Willingham rifled through the pages to look at the last one. Then he glared at his chief of staff. "I believe them."

"Walter," she said. "Mr. Vice President—"

"Did you kill Kay and Randall Christopher?" he demanded and then he smashed his fist on the table so hard, several of the coffee cups tipped over.

"What? No!"

"You weren't there?" he shouted. "You can prove it?"

"Prove it?" she shot back. "Of course."

"What about these papers? Do you deny knowing about them?"

Barnes stared at the documents, now stained with coffee. "I know about them. I was part of it, and it was Bobby's idea. But I had nothing to do with Kay's death and nothing to do with whatever happened to Althea. Nothing!"

"I don't believe you," Willingham said. He turned to his Secret Service agents. "Since you two seem more loyal to Claudette than to me, I'll ask you once. Did she kill them? Or were one of you two there in that schoolyard on her behalf? Or both?"

Breit held up his hands. "We didn't kill anyone, sir. We followed them that night—Kay and Christopher—at Claudette's request but ended the surveillance when we saw them drive into that schoolyard around three thirty that morning."

"It's true, sir," Price said.

"Why in God's name were you two following them?" Willingham demanded.

The Secret Service agents looked like they wanted to crawl away from the question and said nothing.

The vice president turned his glare back on his chief of staff, who said coldly, "Because you would not have done it yourself, Walter. Because you always had a blind spot when it came to Kay. But I didn't. I saw Kay for who she was from the get-go: a threat to you, your eventual presidency, and the future of this country."

Willingham tried to interrupt, but she waved him off angrily. "Wake up, Walter! Your socialite ex-wife was a loose cannon on her best days. And then Kelli Ann came calling with supposed whispers from Kay about your past prosecutorial misconduct. *That's why* they were following her."

Willingham stared at the table, drumming his fingers.

I took the opportunity to say to Price and Breit, "Two men in hoodies were seen running from the murder scene."

"Not us," Breit said sharply. "No way. There have to be videos of our Suburban in the streets around that school. We drove right past the school a good thirty minutes before they were killed, and we never went back."

CHAPTER

92

THE FOLLOWING MORNING, BREE SAT on a bench in the hallway of juvenile court reading a newspaper article, Clive Sparkman's big scoop on the arrest of Vice President Willingham's chief of staff for conspiracy to commit murder and fraud in Alabama.

Sparkman's article also described the letter from Kay to her father and other evidence that might have proved Napoleon Howard did not murder Jefferson Ward.

Willingham had told Sparkman, "My heart breaks for the families of Napoleon Howard and Jefferson Ward. Had I known about this evidence, had the grand jury known about this evidence, Howard might not have been convicted so easily and might not have died in prison. My heart also breaks for my late ex-wife, Kay, and for myself because she died believing I had willfully ignored evidence that would have benefited Howard, which is fundamentally not true. As for my chief of staff, Claudette Barnes, I will let the justice system in Alabama do its work before commenting further."

"Bree?"

She looked up from the article, which I'd read earlier, to see the cup of coffee I was holding out.

"Careful," I said. "I don't think I got that lid on tight enough and it's hot."

Bree set the paper down and took the cup. "Thank you."

"Anytime." I took a seat beside her on the bench.

Bree tapped the paper with her knuckles and whispered, "Are you the anonymous source saying Barnes is also under suspicion for Kelli Ann Higgins's murder and her own husband's death?"

"Not me, but it makes sense," I said. "If she hired hit men to take out Althea Lincoln, maybe she'd hire someone to beat Higgins to death. And maybe she was the one who hit her husband while he was out riding his bike."

Sampson walked up. "Ned says they've agreed to talk."

We got up and followed him into a conference room where Devon Monroe and Lever Ashford sat flanked by their mothers and public defenders. Bree sat beside Ann Dean, the prosecuting attorney. Sampson and I stood at the back with Mahoney.

Devon Monroe looked haggard and resigned to his fate after a night in custody. Lever Ashford, the taller of the two, had his head up and was taking it all in, acting almost cocky.

The boys told us that they snuck out after their mothers were asleep and went to a friend's house on Fourth Street. Her mother had been away for the weekend and the girl decided to host a party. The boys did not leave until four fifteen a.m. and decided to take a shortcut through the school grounds on their way home.

"Who was the girl?" Bree asked.

"Dee Nathaniel," Monroe said. "We were both kind of wasted, and we cut through the campus diagonally across the football field and went under the stands. That's where we were when we heard, like, faint thuds. Four of them."

"Like, they could have been anything," Ashford said. "Not real loud, but enough that you could hear them."

The boys said they continued walking out.

Monroe said, "I look way down the field and I see the front end of the car sticking out behind the dumpsters, kind of a little in the light, but not under it. So we walked toward it 'cause we had to go that way."

Ashford said, "Straightest way to the alley and home. We were maybe forty yards from the dumpster, and we both saw this person moving in the shadows way off to our right."

"Male? Female?" Bree said.

"Couldn't tell," Ashford said.

Monroe said, "But not a big, big person, you know."

Remembering that Elaine Paulson had also claimed to have seen someone moving in the shadows near the football stands headed northeast, I said, "If the school was to your east and this person was to your west, what direction was this person moving in?"

Ashford thought about that, curved his right hand hard right, said, "Like, circling back away from us. North, I guess."

"Northwest toward Dee's home? Or straight north? Or northeast?"

Monroe said, "Headed back toward the football stands. I guess that's northeast?"

Exactly where Elaine had said the person was moving. But did it matter when the gun that killed her husband and his girlfriend belonged to her?

"Back up," Sampson said. "Did you see the bodies before you saw this person?"

Both boys shook their heads. Monroe said, "That wasn't until we heard the car engine still idling and we came around the dumpsters to see them."

"Close enough to see two dead people and

decide to take their jewelry?" Sampson growled. "One of them your high-school principal?"

Ashford squirmed in his seat but didn't look or sound remorseful when he said, "I don't know. Mr. Christopher...he—they were dead. They couldn't use their glitter no more."

His mother swatted his head, said, "Should have kept you in Sunday school."

Sampson said, "It seems awful convenient, you two seeing someone flee the scene just before you decide to go graverobbing."

"No way," Ashford said. "That's for real, man. Tell 'em, Dev."

"We saw someone going northeast, for sure," Monroe said. "And, like, after we took the stuff, we were leaving, going through the fence to the alley, and we most definitely saw someone coming from behind the north end of the school. That's when we ran."

Ashford nodded. "Because we knew her."

Bree asked, "Who?"

"Tina and Rachel's mom," Monroe said. "Mr. Christopher's wife."

Ashford said, "It didn't make sense to us. I mean, I know she's in jail for it with the gun and all. But why would she come back like that after she just shot two people?"

CHAPTER

93

OUTSIDE THE COURTHOUSE a half an hour later, Ned Mahoney chewed on the inside of his lip when I said, "They have a point."

"And I have a murder weapon that you took from the hands of the killer!" Mahoney shot back. "Explain that."

"I can't," I said, feeling my cell phone buzz in my pocket. "Can you explain how two reluctant witnesses describe the events of that night the same exact way, with the same third person in the shadows circling around to the northeast?"

"Elaine Paulson was lying," he replied. "She was describing herself. She wasn't by the side of the school when the shots went off. She was right in front of the Bentley and then she snuck around west and then northeast to get around the boys."

Bree shook her head. "Why come back?"

"To make sure they're dead."

Sampson shook his head this time. "No. I can't see that, not if she shot them at close range like an assassin would. If she's the killer, she gets out fast and does not return."

Mahoney said, "But other parts of her story don't match. She told you she came onto the campus from the northeast. I looked at the bodega security footage last night. I saw the Bentley turn onto the school grounds at three forty-six a.m. and the Suburban with the two Secret Service agents go by a few moments later. But I did not see Elaine Paulson run by at all."

Sampson said, "I didn't see her either."

"We've got the right person in custody facing trial," Mahoney said.

My cell phone buzzed again. I pulled it out, saw a number I did not recognize and this text: Dr. Cross. Can you call me, please? It's urgent. Gina Nathaniel.

Bree said, "Home?"

"Let me make a call first," I said, dialing.

Gina picked up. "Dr. Cross?"

"I was just about to call you," I said.

"Then you found her?" she cried.

My stomach sank a little. "No."

"Dee went to bed last night around ten," Gina said, frantic again, on the verge of crying. "When I got up this morning, she was gone. Not a trace. And she's not answering her phone. I called the police, but they say they can't do anything until she's been missing twenty-four hours. Tell me this isn't like Maya Parker, Elizabeth Hernandez, and the others! Please, Dr. Cross, she's the only child I have!"

"Mrs. Nathaniel, I am on my way to you right now. Do not touch her room. And I promise you, we'll find her."

CHAPTER

94

THE STORY OF DEE NATHANIEL going missing exploded and went viral because she was yet another young woman to vanish in Southeast Washington, DC, in the past fifteen years and she was also a longtime friend of the most recent victim, Maya Parker. The media played up the fact that in the past, the killer had dumped his dead victims within forty-eight to fifty-six hours of grabbing them. If Dee had gone missing after midnight, she had between a day and a day and a half to live.

By four p.m., Verizon had given us Dee's most recent data. Just as her mother had said, the GPS in the phone had Dee at home at seven. She'd texted friends and surfed the internet until 10:45, when her phone was shut off in the Nathaniels' home.

She got on her laptop in her room five minutes

later but used a private browser that gave us no history of what she did between 10:50 and 11:20, when the laptop was put to sleep.

Sampson and other officers had gone in search of security footage and discovered that every camera in a two-block radius around the Nathaniels' home had been smeared with Vaseline, distorting the footage.

"That's the same play the killer made with Kay and Christopher," Sampson said in the middle of the afternoon. "Maybe we've got it wrong, Alex. Maybe Christopher and Kay were shot by the serial killer."

That threw us. Were they killed by the same person responsible for the deaths of Elizabeth Hernandez, Maya Parker, and now, possibly, Dee Nathaniel?

Sampson had to leave to pick up Willow around five and deliver her to Jannie, who was arriving at his house around six. We went outside the mobile command post to where Bree was talking to a crowd of people over a megaphone.

"If you are interested in helping us search, go to Detectives Newton and Martin here to give them your name and phone numbers," she said. "They will assign you a specific area to go and knock on doors. And thank you. Metro PD and Mrs. Nathaniel deeply appreciate your help."

Sampson left and I waited for Bree. She came

over to me, took a deep breath, and blew it out. "I don't know how Gina Nathaniel is holding up the way she is. I'd be a basket case if I knew someone was going to kill my daughter sometime in the next two days."

"So would I," I said. "But she has hope and so do we. And I'm leaving."

"Oh?" Bree said.

"I don't think I lend much to a door-to-door search," I said. "And I think Sampson might be right. The same person who's got Dee might have killed Kay Willingham and Randall Christopher."

"Where are you going?"

"To see the only person in this case who I absolutely know did not put Vaseline on security cameras and grab Dee Nathaniel last night."

"Who's that?"

"Elaine Paulson," I said and walked away, heading for my car, which was parked down the street.

The sun was getting low, but the heat had not dwindled a bit. Even so, there were at least a hundred people lined up to register to be part of the search.

As I skirted the crowd, I heard a female voice call, "Dr. Cross?"

I turned to see Tina and Rachel Christopher at the end of one line. Rachel was stone-faced, as usual. Tina reached out to shake my hand.

"You're going to help look for Dee?" I asked.

"Yes," Rachel said. "We went to middle school together."

"Your grandmother know you're here?"

"Yes," Tina said. She looked pleadingly at me. "Dr. Cross, please prove our mom's innocent. They won't let us see her and…it's just too…"

When she couldn't go on, Rachel put her hand on her twin's shoulder and stared at me. "Brutal. Harsh. Cruel."

"I can't begin to understand what you're going through," I said. "And I will do everything I can. In fact, I'm on my way to see your mother about some things that may work in her favor."

"Really?" she said, her stony demeanor softening. "Right now?"

"Right now," I said.

Tina said, "Please tell her we love her. We don't know if our letters are getting through."

"I'll tell her," I said. "And I'll tell her how much we appreciate you searching for Dee. Please go together. Stay safe. If something feels off, back away and notify us."

"Off?" Rachel said.

"You'll know it when you feel it," I said and wished them luck.

CHAPTER

95

FORTY-FIVE MINUTES LATER, I was in an interrogation room at the Alexandria detention facility as a sheriff's deputy brought in Elaine Paulson. Even dressed in her orange jail jumpsuit, Christopher's widow looked much better than the last time I'd seen her, in the psych ward.

"You're the last person I expected here," she said, taking a seat opposite me.

"Why's that?"

She shrugged. "You save my life. You send me to prison for life. Another notch in the belt for the great Dr. Cross. Out of sight, out of mind."

"It doesn't work like that. Not with me. If there is any gap in a conviction story that I cannot explain, I consider the case open."

Elaine looked at me with a glimmer of hope. "Is there a gap?"

"Maybe. Which is why I'm here. And your daughters say they love you, by the way."

"You saw them?" she said, smiling. But then her lips twisted bitterly. "I haven't been allowed."

"I saw them an hour ago," I said. "Your mother's taking good care of them. And they're helping to look for another girl who's missing."

"Dee Nathaniel," she said. "I know her. It's all over the news. Is that part of the gap that brought you here?"

"Maybe," I said and then told her about the two boys who'd seen someone moving toward the football bleachers before they'd stolen the jewelry from Kay's and Randall's bodies.

"I told you I saw them," she said. "And they saw me?"

"They did and identified you by name," I said. "They were students at Harrison."

You could tell that did not go down well but she swallowed it and said, "But that's good for me, right?"

"It means three people, including you, have said there was another person on the campus shortly after the shooting," I said.

That got her hopes up. She straightened and said, "That has to be good for me."

"Unless you're lying and you yourself circled toward the stands after shooting Randall and Kay and then you went back to make sure you'd gotten the job done."

She stared at me and then laughed. "Why would anyone do that? Go back?"

After a moment, I shrugged, said, "Let's say you didn't. How do you explain the gun?"

"There's nothing to explain," she said. "I did not have that gun with me that night. I…I realized after taking it with me the first time what a dumb move having a pistol with me would be. I mean, I might be a little touched upstairs, but I'm not stupid."

"When did you get the gun before you went out to the Eastern Shore?"

"You mean what time?"

"I do."

Elaine thought a few moments. "Ten minutes to six? It was after I'd taken a shower and thrown some clothes in a bag along with some cash. By then I was already thinking that my life was over."

I took out a notebook and wrote that down. "When did you leave the school? I'm trying to understand the timeline here."

She nodded, thought again. "I ran out of there at maybe four twenty. More like four eighteen."

"And you ran by the bodega and onto the campus earlier when?"

Elaine squinted. "Eight or nine minutes past four?"

"We've looked at the bodega's security footage but we've never seen you run by."

She looked puzzled. "I do change routes but I'm pretty sure I went that way. But maybe not?"

I let it slide for the moment. "And what time did you get home that morning? When you ran into your neighbor Barbara Taylor?"

"Quarter to five?"

That actually fit with what Taylor had told me. "So there is a gap," I said. "Roughly a half an hour between you leaving the campus and coming home."

She didn't get it at first but then said, "Thirty minutes for the real killer to come to the house and put the gun back."

"Right. Who has access to your house and might have wanted to kill your husband?"

She didn't hesitate. "No one."

"No one has access or no one who has access would want to kill him?"

"The second one."

"You're saying people besides you and your husband had access," I said.

She nodded. "They knew where the spare key was."

"Who?"

"My mother. My sister, but she lives in Texas now and loved Randall. The cleaners. And our contractor. We had the kitchen done in the spring. There were people in there all the time. I'd come home and there would be a new guy installing the floor and another one the countertop."

I slid my notebook across the table at her. "I need names and numbers if you've got them."

CHAPTER
96

MY ALARM WENT OFF AT six fifteen the following morning. On any other day, after sleeping less than five hours, I would have hit snooze. But I bolted upright immediately. More than thirty hours had passed since Dee Nathaniel was taken. If the serial killer's signature style held, she had only around eighteen hours before he killed and dumped her.

I got up quietly because Bree had been up even later than me and dressed for a jog to try and clear out the cobwebs. Outside, the heat was just starting to build again.

As I ran, I went over the idea I'd had the night before, that the Southeast serial rapist and killer who probably had Dee might also have murdered Kay and Christopher. One person—that figure who'd lurked in the shadows near the football stand that night—might have done it all.

But why shoot them? Killing a couple was not his usual modus operandi. He snatched single young women, raped them, and killed them. He didn't gun down random people in school parking lots. So why now?

As I slowed to a walk and climbed onto the porch, the only answer I could come up with was that either Kay or Christopher had gotten suspicious about him. Maybe the killer realized it and cold-bloodedly executed them?

In the foyer, I grabbed a towel, wiped off my face and head, and put it around my neck before going into the kitchen. Nana Mama had already brewed a pot of coffee and was making omelets for Ali and Bree. Jannie was still upstairs sleeping, which was not unusual for a seventeen-year-old.

"Where to first?" I asked Bree as I poured a mug of coffee.

"Back to the Nathaniels' house," she said. "You?"

Before I could answer, my cell phone buzzed and rang on the counter. Another unfamiliar DC number. "Alex Cross," I said.

I got no reply, only a choking noise.

"Hello?" I said. "Who is this, please?"

"It's Elinore Paulson," she finally said in a voice shot through with anxiety and loss. "Elaine Paulson's mother. My granddaughters are missing, Dr. Cross. They never came home last night and they're not answering their phones."

CHAPTER

97

AFTER I GOT OFF THE phone with Elinore Paulson, I informed Bree of what had happened and called Ned Mahoney. I thought that with three young women missing, two of them the daughters of a victim in a federal murder investigation, the FBI should take over the entire probe.

Ned agreed and said he'd pick me up in half an hour. Bree was on the phone with Commissioner Dennison, keeping him abreast of the situation and asking for help in getting all data from the twins' cell phones.

I called the detectives who'd helped organize the civilian searches the night before and got Maria Newton, who was shocked when I told her.

"So he was right there in the streets with us?"

"It appears that way. When was the last time you heard from Tina and Rachel?"

"Hold on," Detective Newton said. "Christopher, Tina and Rachel. Here's the list of addresses they contacted and times. Last one, eleven ten p.m., they talked to a Marian Rodgers on Sixth Street in Southeast. Then they texted me at eleven twelve p.m. to say they'd found nothing and were going home for the night. They wanted to come back and help this morning."

I was taking notes furiously on a pad on the counter. "Can you send that text to me with Marian Rodgers's address?"

"Absolutely," she said, then cleared her throat. "Dr. Cross, given what's happened, I...I don't know if I feel comfortable asking civilians to do more canvassing."

"I'm with you," I said. "We don't want *four* missing girls on our hands. Besides, the FBI's taking over now. They'll want special agents going door to door. But, seriously, Detective, thanks for your efforts."

"Well, you're welcome," she said sadly. "I just wish it had worked."

I hung up to find Bree still on her phone. She gave me the thumbs-up, a good sign. With the GPS data, we'd soon know where all three were when they vanished. Upstairs, as I took a quick shower, I thought, *One and then two more right away. That's another break in his pattern. All the other girls were taken one at a time at long intervals. Why change now? And why take the chance of being caught grabbing two girls in the middle of a canvass, when there were all sorts of eyeballs on the streets? It's such a brazen act.*

Maybe he was showing us how clever and invincible he is. Or maybe he felt threatened with discovery and wanted to make a statement: He killed the girls' father and their father's lover, and now he has the dead man's girls.

I couldn't help but think of Jannie and what this was going to do to her. She knew Dee Nathaniel, Maya Parker, and Elizabeth Hernandez as acquaintances. But she was friends with Tina and Rachel Christopher. She was…

It hit me so hard then, I almost doubled over.

Jannie's a possible target. She has to be.

I panicked at the thought that my daughter might also have been grabbed during the night. I turned off the water, jumped out of the shower, grabbed a towel, wrapped it around my waist, and charged out of the bathroom.

I threw our bedroom door open, ran across the little landing, and raced down the short hall to Jannie's room. I opened the door without knocking and felt queasy almost immediately.

Jannie's bed looked like it hadn't been slept in.

"Jannie?" I shouted. "Jannie!"

The bathroom door across the hall opened a crack, and Jannie looked out, saw me in the open doorway to her bedroom, and frowned.

"No need to shout, Dad," she said. "I'm right

here and I'm on time. Weight training's not for an hour. What's with the towel?"

I looked at her, my heart beating with relief and joy. "Sorry, I'm just being a dad making sure his daughter's safe."

"Why?" she said, opening the door all the way. "What's happened? Did they find Dee?"

I didn't want to, but I told her about her friends.

CHAPTER
98

BREE AND I HAD DRESSED and were wolfing breakfast down when Jannie came into the kitchen, still upset.

"Does Tina and Rachel's mother know?" she said.

"Not yet."

"How do you live through something like this?"

I swallowed a chunk of egg and said, "Faith. You, me, Bree, Ned, John—we all have to have faith that we will find them. That's how we get through and take smart action to locate them as fast as possible."

"You'll find them, Dad. I have faith in you."

"Thank you," I said. "But for now, other than training, I want you to stay close to home. And don't go anywhere without telling me or Bree or John. Okay?"

"Now I am scared," she said.

Bree said, "Being scared is good sometimes. Again, keep a low profile. If you have to go out, we'd prefer you to travel in threes and with a male if you're with friends."

Jannie crossed her arms but nodded.

Nana Mama said, "Hungry?"

"Not really," she said.

"If you're going to train, you need to eat," my grandmother said.

"Okay," Jannie said with little enthusiasm. "I guess I'll take an omelet too, Nana."

Bree's phone rang. She answered, listened, and said, "Thank you, Commissioner. We'll download it as soon as it gets here." She hung up and opened her laptop on the counter. "Dennison got us the twins' data."

"That was fast," I said.

"He's handy at times," Bree said, logging into her Metro e-mail account. "Here are the files. One for Tina, one for Rachel."

She opened the files, which gave us not only the twins' GPS locations over the last twenty-four hours but their texts, social media, and internet searches. Mahoney arrived while Bree was working with the GPS coordinates on Google Maps.

"Here they are at Mrs. Rodgers's house at Sixth and L at eleven ten last night," she said.

"Jibes with what Newton told us," I said.

She nodded and gave her computer a few more

commands. The map now showed the route they took heading home to Eleventh and E. But they made it only four blocks, to Ellen Wilson Place and Seventh, before they left the direct route, got on the Southeast Freeway, and started covering ground.

"They're in a vehicle and going by CCTV cameras on that on-ramp," Bree said, typing again.

Ned said, "I'll get agents there ASAP."

We had GPS coordinates every few minutes for the twins' phones for almost two hours after they got in that vehicle, which traveled down I-295 and then took I-95 south to Virginia Route 54 and a street in Ashland, Virginia, where their phones had stopped moving. On Google Earth it looked like the phones were in a mixed neighborhood of light industrial and residential apartment buildings. Forty minutes later, Rachel's phone died. Eighteen minutes after that, Tina's phone stopped transmitting its position.

"Okay, we're heading to Ashland," Mahoney said.

We heard the front door open and shut, and Sampson rushed in, breathing hard. "I got her. Dee Nathaniel."

"What?" Bree said.

"Where?" Mahoney said.

"Three blocks from her house at eleven forty-five p.m.," he said and put still shots in front of us showing Dee climbing into the passenger side of a black panel van with tinted windows and a Virginia license plate.

"I'm already running it," Bree said, calling up the Virginia DMV on her computer and entering the plate. Up popped a 2011 Toyota Camry belonging to a forty-five-year-old woman in Fredericksburg, Virginia.

"Stolen," Mahoney said. "On the way to or from Ashland. Do me a favor, Bree?"

"Anything."

"Look at Virginia's registered sex offenders list and see if any of them live within a six-block radius of where the phones stopped signaling."

"Great idea," I said.

Sure enough, two minutes later, Bree located a level 2 sex offender living in an apartment complex three blocks away.

"Eric Boone, fifty-four," she said, throwing up her fist in victory. "Convicted of statutory rape in Kentucky in 1998. Goes to Kentucky state penitentiary and…released in 2004! Moves to Ashland in 2005."

"The year the first girl disappears here," I said.

"We've got him," Ned said. "And if we have him, we have the girls."

CHAPTER

99

BREE TOOK SCREENSHOTS OF THE maps and satellite views while Mahoney got on the phone to arrange for an FBI helicopter to fly to Ashland. Alex went upstairs to retrieve his service weapon and sunglasses.

Bree was about to log off her computer when she saw another e-mail from Verizon. Subject line: *New data.*

She clicked on it as Alex returned to the room and Mahoney hung up.

Ned said, "Chopper will pick us up on the roof of Bureau headquarters in twenty. I assume you all want to be there when we cuff him?"

"I do," Sampson said.

"Yes," Alex said.

"Bree?" Mahoney said.

Bree barely heard him. She was staring at the screen of her laptop, frowning and biting on a nail. "According to this e-mail I just got from Verizon, Dee Nathaniel's phone turned on briefly about three hours ago and transmitted a 911 signal before dying."

The three men came up behind her.

"GPS coordinates?" Alex asked.

"I'm trying to see," she said, clicking on various links. "Says the signal went through to Morgan County, West Virginia, sheriff's dispatch. There's the coordinates!"

She copied the GPS data and plugged it into Google Maps. The app immediately lifted off Ashland and went northwest to what looked like an old industrial factory on the east bank of the Potomac River, several miles north of Berkeley Springs, West Virginia.

Alex said, "Can you get two helicopters? That's a four-hour drive."

Mahoney said, "We've got a man convicted of raping an underage girl six blocks from the twins' last known location. Call the sheriff's office first. See if they responded."

Bree did and talked to a Deputy Janet Cafaro, who said that after getting the 911 call, she ran out to the location, an old silica-processing plant south of the current modern facility, but found the place buttoned up tight.

"It's been condemned for two years now," the deputy said. "They're going to raze the place this fall to make way for an expansion."

"How big is it?"

"Oh, covers forty acres, easy."

"Buildings?"

"Four. But like I said, I checked the locks on the main gate and on every one of those buildings and I talked to security at the new plant. They haven't seen any suspicious activity down there, and they go through the area twice a day."

After she thanked the deputy, Bree hung up.

Mahoney said, "I'm leaving for Ashland."

"I'm with you," Sampson said.

"I think we should split up," Bree said. "Alex and I will use a Metro helicopter to fly to Berkeley Springs while you go to Ashland."

"You're sure?"

"Do you want to tell Dee's mother we ignored it?"

"Point taken," Mahoney said. "Let's stay in close touch."

CHAPTER

100

TWO HOURS LATER, BREE AND I landed in a field outside Berkeley Springs, West Virginia, a rural, heavily wooded, unincorporated area no more than a mile and a half from the Potomac and two miles from the silica-processing plant. Mahoney and Sampson had already arrived in Ashland, and with FBI agents from the Richmond office, they were on their way to the last known location of the Christopher twins' phones.

Morgan County Sheriff's Deputy Janet Cafaro was waiting for us outside her Chevy Suburban patrol vehicle. Beside it was a Chevy Tahoe rental Bree had arranged to have delivered from Hancock, about twenty miles north.

Deputy Cafaro was a big woman who'd played basketball at Pitt University. It was beastly hot, and she was in her body armor, sweating, so she was unhappy with us at first.

"I checked that old plant," she said briskly after shaking our hands. "I think this was a waste of a trip for you."

"Probably," Bree said. "But we have two mothers with missing girls back in DC and I'd like to be able to tell them we did everything we could to find their daughters before he tires of them and decides to kill and dump them."

That softened the deputy. "Not much time left for the first one, Dee?"

I shook my head. "Twelve to twenty-four hours if he sticks to his MO."

"Okay," Deputy Cafaro said, holding her palms up. "I get it now and I'm sorry for the attitude. Let's go."

"No worries on the attitude," Bree said. "No one likes being second-guessed."

The helicopter lifted off to refuel in Roanoke; the pilot would be back in an hour and wait for us. Bree and I got in the rental, listened to the country station the radio was tuned to, and followed Deputy Cafaro in her cruiser north on the road to Hancock. After a few miles, a high chain-link fence appeared on our left. Beyond it, to the west, the trees gave way to open ground and then a hill that had been cleaved by a pale white open-pit mine running north for almost a mile. At the other end of the pit, machines were boring and extracting tons of raw silica.

The old processing plant on the east side of the street was surrounded by a tall chain-link fence with razor wire on top. The gate was barred, chained, and locked with three padlocks. A condemnation and demolition notice hung on the gate beside a No Trespassing sign.

Before we arrived, Deputy Cafaro had gone to get keys from the plant security manager, who wanted to be there but had to leave to see his mother in a hospital in Pittsburgh. Cafaro fiddled with the keys and finally got the gate unlocked and opened it.

We drove in and parked, then walked across cracked and busted pavement toward railroad tracks that ran by a large complex of old, abandoned factory buildings. A pair of them were two-story, steel-sided, steel-roofed, and rusting badly.

The other two buildings were much larger. They sat parallel to each other and were built of crumbling brick, three stories high at the near end and a good hundred yards long before the roof jumped another four stories to two tower-like structures.

Deputy Cafaro said the silica plant had been around for close to a century and produced fine sands and clays from its mine on the hill across the street. The modern facility had been built a few years ago and had double production.

"They're thinking they can double it again

once they've built the second plant on this site," she said. She gestured at the buildings. "In the meantime, take your pick. I've got keys for all of them."

"The small ones first," Bree said.

CHAPTER

101

HEADING TOWARD THE CLOSER OF the two small, rusting buildings, we crossed the railroad track.

"This still used?" I asked.

Deputy Cafaro nodded. "Four, five times a day, north and south. There's a spur off the main line that goes to the current plant and rejoins it on the other side. The processed sand is loaded into hopper cars and off it goes."

I looked down the tracks south toward Berkeley Springs and a road the rails crossed. There were houses beyond. In the other direction, I could see past the old towers to the newer plant. We crossed more busted pavement and places where it was gone completely and down to sand and weeds.

I let my eyes move back and forth across the ground, trying to spot any indication of recent vehicle traffic. But there was no evidence of it that I could see.

The first building was roughly six thousand square feet and had processed specialty clays back in the day. Cafaro opened it, revealing the interior of the shell and little else. It had been stripped of all its machinery nearly a decade before.

"They all like this?" I asked. "Empty?"

"Pretty much," she said. "Like I said over the phone."

"What's not empty?" Bree asked.

The deputy gestured north toward the larger buildings. "There's still big pieces of the old conveyors and lifts in the towers to reclaim. But everything else is long gone."

I was about to suggest we go in the big buildings when my cell phone and Bree's went off together.

"Mahoney," I said.

"And Sampson," Bree said.

We got onto a four-way call with terrible, crackling reception.

"We've got nothing," Ned said. "Phones are not there and Boone has an airtight alibi. He's a telemarketer in town and worked the late shift. His supervisor confirmed it."

"We're still looking," I said. "We'll let you know."

"We're heading for the helicopter," Sampson said.

We hung up and told Deputy Cafaro that we needed to search the entire complex. You could tell she wasn't thrilled, but she got out a key and unlocked a chain wrapped around double doors at the near end of the farthest long building. We pushed them open, flushing pigeons and revealing a long, lofty space with rusting conveyor systems and cables hanging from the girders that supported the roof.

"You go down to that tower when you were in here?" I asked.

She shook her head. "Look at the floor. That's a quarter of an inch of dust and pigeon poo; don't you think we'd see tracks?"

"Any other way into the tower?" Bree asked.

"Where the railcars used to come in," she said. "But we'll have to go around. They're chained shut too."

She locked the double doors and led us around the side, and we started down an overgrown walkway between the two buildings, which Cafaro said had been used to screen and wash the sand. The towers had compartment-like rooms that held the sand and there'd been a complex of lifts and chutes that drained it into the hopper cars.

"How do you know all this?" Bree asked.

"My father worked here. Grandfather too."

There were narrow horizontal slits in the sides of the towers where pigeons were fluttering in and out. She said they were ventilation windows that had let the plant workers control the humidity and allow in light on those rare occasions when the storage rooms were empty.

Then her radio squawked.

"Janet Cafaro?" the dispatcher said. "You by the radio?"

"Right here, Imogene," the deputy said.

"We got a motorcycle wreck south of town, mile marker two. Fire and ambulance responding. I need traffic control."

"On my way," she said, and she looked at us. "We good?"

I hesitated, then said, "Give us the keys to the two towers. We'll finish and bring the keys to you."

Cafaro didn't like that but shrugged and handed us the keys on the ring. "Just don't sue the company if something collapses on you," she said. "I'll be back as soon as I can."

CHAPTER

102

RUSTY TRAIN TRACKS LED THROUGH double doors on the east and west sides of both towers. The lock to the rear tower's west door was rusted and it took us three or four tries to get it open. The double doors screeched when we pushed and dragged them back to reveal a yawning space, one hundred feet long and forty feet wide, with multiple chutes coming out of the high ceiling above the tracks.

"I suppose they loaded the hopper cars here?" Bree asked.

"Good guess," I said. "I'm not exactly an expert on aging silica plants."

She turned on a flashlight and shone it on the trash-strewn ground and toward the back of the space, where there was a steep, narrow steel staircase next to a big industrial lift with stout steel cables descending out of a gaping open shaft in the ceiling. Somewhere above us, we could hear birds rustling around.

"Doesn't look like there has been anyone in here in years," Bree said.

"Let's call it, go find some shade, and wait for Cafaro to come back."

She nodded. We closed the double doors, locked them, and walked around the back of the tower closest to the road.

A train was coming from the south. It rumbled into the old silica yard and went right by us, so loud I had to cover my ears. The engineer waved and we saw the hopper cars Deputy Cafaro had described. The train went onto the spur that led to the newer plant and stopped with fifteen hopper cars still on the old plant's grounds, cutting us off from the gate and the main road.

"Think we can climb over the couplings?" I said.

"What if the train moves?"

"We'll wait," I said, looking down at the old spur rails where they left the main tracks and went toward the first tower.

I saw something and squatted down to be sure.

"What?" Bree said, stepping up beside me.

I stood and lowered my voice to a murmur. "Look down at the spur rails. They are nowhere as rusty as the rails going into the far tower. See where the rust has been rubbed off? Almost buffed to a brown versus the orange-red over there?"

Bree looked down for several seconds and then nodded. I scanned the area around the rails, seeing broken weeds and a small chunk of black. I bent down, picked it up, squeezed it.

"Tire tread," I whispered, feeling my heart beat a little faster. "I think someone's been driving a car on these tracks."

We both turned and looked at where the rails disappeared beneath the double doors into the near tower.

CHAPTER
103

THE TRAIN GROANED INTO MOTION as we went to the double doors. I put the key in the lock. It turned easily and popped open with a soft snap, not like the lock on the other tower at all.

Bree understood, bobbed her head at me, and drew her service weapon. I did the same. We each got a free hand on one of the doors and hid behind them, shielding our bodies as we tugged them open. They slid back easily and quietly, as if the tracks the old doors ran on had recently been oiled.

Behind us the train stopped again. We both got out flashlights, held them beneath our pistols, and, on the count of three, eased inside. The base of this tower was set up exactly the same way as the other, with chutes coming down from the ceiling, a narrow metal staircase in the far corner, and an industrial lift beside it. Except the lift itself was not there, nor were there any cables hanging from the large hole in the ceiling.

Bree pointed at the concrete floor to either side of the rails and whispered in my ear, "It's been swept and then trash thrown on it."

I saw the brush marks beneath a piece of yellowed newspaper and nodded. We crept across the floor to the staircase and slowly climbed the steep, narrow stairs, trying to stay to the outsides of the risers to keep squeaking to a minimum as we eased up to where the staircase went through the ceiling.

We stopped below the first ceiling, listening and hearing nothing except the train starting to squeal again. Finally, I took a step up, peeked over into the space. Empty.

Like the ground floor, the floor of the upper room was heavy plank wood that looked swept. The third floor was empty and filthy, no signs of sweeping.

The fourth floor was infested with pigeons. So were floors five through seven. Nothing but pigeons.

Deeply discouraged, we went back down the staircase and looked at the broom marks in the dirt on the second floor and the first.

"Dee was here hours ago," Bree said. "She dialed 911 in here. I can feel it."

"I'm feeling it too," I said, hearing the train start up yet again.

By the time we got outside and were chaining and locking the double doors, the train had left the old silica processing yard. The caboose was now well up the track toward the new plant. We sweated as we trudged toward the Tahoe.

Bree sighed, said, "I guess we're back to square one."

"On borrowed time," I said and checked my watch, feeling anxiety and frustration build inside me.

Wanting to punch something, I jerked open the driver's side of the Tahoe and climbed into the SUV. Bree got in, slammed her door, and threw her head back against the rest in frustration.

"He's good," she said.

"I am good, aren't I?" said a male voice behind us in the back seat. "The best."

My hand started toward my pistol before I felt the muzzle of a gun against the back of my head.

"Don't even think about it, Dr. Cross. Or you, Chief Stone," he said, and I finally glanced in the rearview and saw the homely face of Ronald Peters smirking back at me.

CHAPTER

104

BREE TWISTED HER HEAD AROUND and saw the bodega owner grinning at her, his eyes shiny with excitement as he pressed the muzzle of a nickel-plated Colt revolver to the back of Alex's head.

"Chief Stone, remove your weapon and drop it out the window. Backup too."

"As a matter of policy, high-ranking officers in Metro PD cannot carry a backup."

"Prove it," Peters said. "But dump your pistol first."

Bree rolled down the window, removed her Glock from her belt holster, and dropped it to the pavement. Then she tugged up her slacks and showed Peters her ankles. She shrugged her jacket off her shoulders to show no holster, then rocked forward and raised the back of her jacket to show nothing at the small of her back.

"Good," Peters said. "Now you, Dr. Cross. Slowly."

As Alex reached into his shoulder holster, Bree let go of her jacket and sat back, her hands in her lap, palms up. She forced herself to breathe as Alex removed his Glock with his thumb and index finger, rolled down the window, and tossed it out.

Then Alex bent over and removed his backup nine-millimeter from its ankle holster and tossed it as well.

"Cell phones," Peters said.

They both reached for their phones and dropped them to the broken pavement.

"Windows up," Peters said, still pressing the gun against Alex's head.

"Where are the girls?" Alex said.

"In airless places," Peters said, sitting back. "Where they won't be found until I want them found. Now start the car. Put it in drive. Go out the gates. Turn right."

Alex started the car. Country music came on. He put the Tahoe in reverse, saying, "You killed them, Kay Willingham and Randall Christopher, didn't you?"

"Randall wouldn't let it go and he got too close for comfort," Peters said. "The vice president's ex was collateral damage."

"Did you doctor the security footage you gave Detective Sampson?" Alex asked, braking to a stop and turning the wheels toward the gate.

"Having an associate's degree in film helps."

"What about the gun?"

He smirked again as Alex put the car back in drive. "I own the little company that cleans Elaine Paulson's house. She mentioned she and her husband were separating when I happened to stop by to inspect my workers' job. The rest was sheer creativity."

The fingers of Bree's right hand crawled up her jacket's left sleeve and found the Bond derringer in its clever holster snugly beneath her upper forearm. She released the simple stretch band that wrapped around the hammer and kept the gun in place.

Alex drove toward the gate, slowing to avoid potholes, and said, "Don't you want to know what got us here?"

Peters chuckled and pressed the pistol barrel harder against Alex's head. "I figured Dee got out a 911. Not that it really matters to either of you now. You won't be around to do anything about them. Speed it up!"

That sealed it in Bree's mind. She shifted her upper body toward Peters, hoping the sound and the country music would be enough to cover the rustle of jacket fabric as she drew the derringer and the soft click when she cocked the hammer.

Peters sat directly behind Alex. He looked at her as she shifted and then moved his gun her way. "How can I help, Chief Stone?" he said.

Bree pressed the double barrels of the derringer against the seat fabric and said, "You could tell us if they're alive, for starters."

"I could, but I won't," he said before shifting his aim back at Alex. "Out the gate. Take a right. It's time to finish this."

"It is," Bree said and squeezed the trigger of the derringer.

The little gun barked and bucked in her hand as two .45-caliber bullets blew through the seat. Both hit the rapist/kidnapper/killer square in the chest from less than three feet away.

Peters died instantaneously and the Colt dropped to the floor.

CHAPTER

105

FIVE MINUTES LATER, SIRENS WAILING and lights flashing, Deputy Janet Cafaro's patrol car squealed up to the entrance of the old silica plant. She jumped out, eyes wide and staring at the Tahoe, which we'd parked and left running with the dead man inside.

My ears were still ringing from the double-barreled pistol going off in the car. I said, "He was going to take us somewhere and kill us. Bree saved our lives with that derringer. His gun's there. Back seat on the floor."

"That's him?" she said. "The psycho you were after, for real?"

"For real," Bree said. She was standing with her arms crossed in the shade about ten feet from the Tahoe. The derringer was on the hood. Our service weapons were back where we'd dropped them on the ground.

I said, "We need to search his body."

Deputy Cafaro shook her head. "Not before a state homicide investigator is on the scene."

Bree started toward her, feeling shaky from having to kill Peters but determined that no more girls would die because of him. "His victims are somewhere close by. He told us he had them in 'airless places.' He came on foot. He's got dried mud caked on his lower pants and boots. Take photographs in situ with your phone and then let us search him. Please. If those girls are in airless places, do it for their sake."

Cafaro hesitated. "I have to make a call, but then we'll do it your way."

She returned to the patrol car, called dispatch, and requested another patrol car, a county coroner, and a state homicide investigator sent to the scene. Then she pulled out her phone and got to work.

We helped her, taking photographs with our own phone cameras from multiple angles. Cafaro crouched down to study Peters's lower legs and hiking shoes. She took a gloved finger and smeared the dried mud. It darkened slightly.

"Still some moisture in it," she said. "So it hasn't been there long. Looks like river bottom. Lot of wet clay down there now."

Bree pointed across the road. "How far is the river?"

"As the crow flies, a mile, mile and a half?

Other side of the silica hill. A lot of ground down there, all the way south to the wildlife sanctuary and north to the river bend by Hancock."

I said, "He knew about Dee's 911 call five hours ago and the mud's fairly fresh. I don't think they're far."

Bree nodded. "It makes me believe he was over there, across the street in those pines, watching us when we came in."

"I'll look there, you search his body," Deputy Cafaro said.

"We'll photograph everything we find," Bree promised.

The deputy walked away from the Tahoe, head down, peering at the ground.

I put on latex gloves and reached into the pockets of the light windbreaker Peters wore over his T-shirt but found nothing. There was nothing in his left pants pocket either.

But I got charged up when I found keys and an electronic fob in his right pants pocket.

"Chevy," I said, looking at the fob. "Probably a black panel van."

"We're close."

"Five-mile radius. Maybe less."

Deputy Cafaro came trotting back to us. "Found some dried mud on the curb over there. I called for a state trooper with a tracking dog, but it will take him at least an hour to get here."

I said, "In the meantime, show us every road or

path within five miles of here, north and south, that goes down into that river bottom."

Cafaro went to her patrol car, came out with an iPad running Google Earth. She showed us the tracts of forests along the upper Potomac from south of the wildlife refuge and north to Hancock.

Two county roads gave access to the refuge. Another four dirt roads and improved tracks wound through the widest part of the forest behind the pit mine and north of one of its holding ponds. There was also a two-track maintenance trail running directly along the river next to the CSX rail lines.

Bree's phone rang. She looked at Cafaro, who nodded. She picked it up, answered, and listened while the deputy and I looked at an aerial view of the forest on her iPad.

I said, "I say we go up the nearest roads first."

Cafaro tapped her finger on the iPad north of the plant's holding ponds. "These two roads."

"We've got a helicopter," Bree said. "Our pilot's five miles out. He'll take a look from up high and we'll go low."

The second patrol car arrived. Cafaro had the deputy seal the crime scene pending the arrival of the state homicide investigator and told us to get in her patrol car. She said, "What exactly are we looking for?"

"A black Chevy van with tinted windows," I said.

CHAPTER
106

AIRLESS PLACES, I THOUGHT, FEELING sickened that our window to save the girls might have shrunk to minutes as Deputy Cafaro flipped on the sirens and lights and went burning north to the dirt roads that ran parallel to the plant's holding pond.

We stopped at the entrance to the plant, described Peters to the guard, and asked if he'd seen a man resembling him or a black van out near the pond. He said he had not, but then again, he'd just come on shift.

We drove the length of both roads, saw nothing, then headed south of Berkeley Springs and picked up the Grasshopper Hollow Road heading into the deep forest behind the silica mine.

Our helicopter roared overhead. "Nothing yet," the pilot radioed down. "Lot of leaves though. Hard to see under the canopy."

Where the pavement ended, I had Cafaro slow and turn down her radio so I could hang out the window with the electronic fob I'd found in Peters's pocket. I pressed the panic button every hundred yards or so, hoping to hear the van's alarm go off.

We heard nothing the first mile or the second, where we reached a Y in the road. The deputy said the right fork went in tight to the back of the mine, while the other wound out onto a ridge above the river.

"Which one gets more activity?"

"The right during the day. The left at night, mostly kids back in there partying. You also get more of an elevation gain going left."

"Left," Bree said.

"Left," I said.

Cafaro went that way. The woods became very dense. By then the temperatures had soared into the low nineties and were bordering on stifling. In my mind, I kept hearing Peters: *Airless places.*

It was more than likely that the bodega owner had hidden the van or camouflaged it, so we peered at every pullout along the route and I just kept hitting the panic button. Whenever we hit a high spot, I had Cafaro stop and turn the Suburban off before I hit the button. But all we heard were cicadas whining in the heat.

Near the end of the road, it curled back left and south, almost forming a question mark before coming to a dead end. Four miles and we hadn't heard so much as a peep in response to the panic button.

I studied the Google map on Cafaro's iPad again, trying not to feel defeated when the deputy turned around. She headed back the other way at a much faster clip. We'd check the roads into the wildlife refuge next.

Where the road was starting to curl back to the right, I blew up the satellite image of our position and saw a razorback spine of rock in the woods to our left and, well above but running parallel to a CSX railway maintenance trail, the rail tracks, the bottom, and the river itself.

"Stop," I said.

Cafaro slowed, put the vehicle in park. "We hit the panic button here."

I showed her the satellite image. "Through those trees about sixty yards and parallel to the road, there's a ridge. See how it could block the fob's signal?"

She nodded but didn't move. "You go on and try if you want to. Lot of ticks in there. And I am done with Lyme in my life."

I thought of Billie Sampson, looked at Bree, then opened the door. Bree got out after me.

We pushed and forced our way into the woods through brambles and thorns and cobwebs and, no doubt, ticks until we reached that spine of rock. It was sheer-faced and about seven feet high.

After making three unsuccessful attempts to get up on the razorback, I remembered something our climbing instructor taught me, Jannie, and Ali. I found a significant crack in the rock, which gave us a way up.

The top of the spine was wide, easy to stand on. We still couldn't see the river, but we could hear it below us.

I aimed the fob south, punched the panic button, and got nothing. I turned it north and tried again. No sound other than the whine of insects and biting flies attacking us.

Bree slapped at one. Feeling defeated again, I was about to head back to Deputy Cafaro's Suburban when the wind shifted from out of the east to out of the west and straight up the steep bank below us.

With the breeze came the smell of the river and then something fouler, a rank and rotting scent, the odor of decaying flesh.

"Please don't be those girls," Bree said, covering her nose.

Not wanting to, I aimed the fob straight down the steep bank through the trees toward the tracks and the river. I thumbed it hard, three times.

Somewhere far below us, the sounds of the river and cicadas were drowned out by a car alarm beginning to wail and rage.

CHAPTER

107

BEHIND US AND OVER THE howling of the car alarm, I heard Deputy Cafaro bellow, "I hear it! I'm heading for the maintenance trail!"

"Airless places," I said to Bree and jumped down off the spine and onto the steep side hill, absorbing the shock of the fall but then slipping in the slick mud, hitting hard, and sliding.

I went fifteen feet down the side of the bank through thorns and ferns and over a few downed saplings before I could grab a tree and hold on. I looked back. Bree was creeping down off the spine.

She yelled, "Go on! I don't want to break a leg."

After getting upright again, I kept the wind and the smell of death right in my face as I descended, grabbing every tree trunk I could to slow me on the way down. When I reached the bottom, my hands and face were bleeding from being whipped and gouged by branches and vines.

There was a good thirty feet of thicket and thorn left there before the trees gave way to the CSX trail, the railroad tracks, and the Potomac River. The wind and the stench was to my eleven o'clock now. So was the car alarm.

I pushed into the brambles, feeling my pants and shirt catch and tear but not caring. I was getting to that van one way or another.

Soon I was so close, the wailing hurt my ears, and the stench was so bad I thought I'd vomit. But I separated a hanging tangle of vines and found a wall of recently cut, leafy branches and saplings.

I began pulling at them, trying to throw them aside, trying to get to the—

There it was, the side of the black van. I pressed the panic button and heard it die. "It's here, Bree!"

"Coming," she called, still up the side of the slope.

I began hurling aside everything in my way until I reached the van's back left bumper. Green blowflies were swarming there and thick.

"Alex!" Bree shouted, closer.

"Here!" I called.

I knew I should stop, wait for her, Deputy Cafaro, and a state homicide investigator. But I didn't.

I began to tear apart the wall of vegetation that Peters had piled against the rear of the van and up over the roof. Bree stumbled in beside me and began to help.

The flies were infernal and everywhere. I thought of the girls' mothers, wondered how in God's name I was going to tell them what we'd smelled and found in the West Virginia woods.

We could hear Deputy Cafaro's sirens coming from the south as Bree moved the last of the branches and saplings while I battled the tornado of flies swirling behind the van and hit the unlock button on the fob. I heard the mechanism work before I put on latex gloves again and opened the rear double doors.

The first things we saw in the back of the van were three rectangular wooden boxes built of three-quarter-inch plywood and wood screws.

Airless places.

Coffins.

"No," Bree moaned.

CHAPTER
108

I FELT CRUSHED AT THE sight of the coffins. In the heat, dehydrated, with all the blowflies swarming and the smell of death all around me, I got claustrophobic, nauseated, and then dizzy.

I had to go down on one knee to stop from falling.

The flies were worse down low, an aerial hive that spun by the rear bumper. Several flew at my eyes and got in my mouth and I began to cough and choke.

I got frantic, swatted at the flies, and spit them out. Bree grabbed me beneath the armpits, trying to help me up.

"Are you okay?" she said.

The dizziness eased. I nodded and began to struggle to my feet. But as I did, I saw that vortex of flies in a completely different way.

They weren't pouring out of the van. They

weren't pouring from the coffins. They were coming from beneath the vehicle.

"Wait," I said. I shook off Bree's help, sprawled on the ground to look underneath the van, and saw through the flies to the corpse I'd been smelling since the wind changed.

The deer, a doe, had died in the past day or two. A knife had split the guts wide open. The heat did the rest.

It was brilliant camouflage in its own macabre way: a vile-smelling deterrent to the nosy types who might second-guess their decision to investigate the mound of vegetation where something dead and putrid lay.

I jumped up and told Bree what I'd seen, then climbed into the van, only now seeing the full interior. Beyond the coffins were lighting equipment, tripods, and a blowup mattress. The walls to either side were fitted with brackets for hand and power tools.

My eyes went to the two portable drills, side by side in the brackets, both featuring large batteries and Phillips-head screw bits sticking out the noses. Bree and I grabbed them and got to work.

I started unscrewing the first box. With a screech and then a long whine, the screw was out. I paused and heard muffled screaming inside.

"She's alive!" I shouted and went at the screws with a fury I have rarely possessed. I paused as the next screw left the plywood lid and heard yelling from inside Bree's box. But nothing yet from the third.

We kept shouting to the girls inside the boxes that they were safe now, that Peters was dead, and we were coming to help them. As I removed the third screw on my box, Deputy Cafaro charged onto the scene and Bree yelled at her to call ambulances and medevac helicopters to land on the maintenance road.

A minute later, the last screw came up. I tried to lift the top, but it wouldn't budge. It had been glued shut. I found a crowbar that I used to pry it off.

"Helicopters on their way," Cafaro said, coming back.

I lifted and handed her the first lid, seeing poor Rachel Christopher inside the wooden box, naked, blindfolded, gagged, and bound at the ankles and wrists with silver duct tape.

Thrilled that Rachel was alive but wanting to spare her the embarrassment of being naked in front of a man she barely knew, I said, "Deputy Cafaro, there's a young lady in here who needs your help."

Then I turned and went with the drill to the silent third coffin and began to remove the screws. Bree used the crowbar to pry off the second coffin's lid.

"It's Tina," she told me, then reached into the box. "It's okay, honey. Let me help you."

Their blindfolds came off and then the gags. The Christopher twins were both shaking and sobbing as they sat up, their backs to me. Bree and Cafaro cut the duct tape from their wrists and ankles, freeing them.

The deputy ran back to her Suburban and returned with two space blankets to wrap around the girls just as I removed the last screw on the last coffin. In quick order, I had the lid pried off.

Dee Nathaniel was inside, bound, although not blindfolded or gagged. Her face and body had been beaten badly. Her eyes were swollen shut. There was a lot of caked blood from a gash on her head. And she wasn't moving.

I was starting to check her neck for a pulse when she shifted her chin, moaned, opened one of her eyes to a slit, then moved her split, swollen lips and whispered thickly, "I'm not dead yet, Dr. Cross."

"No, you are not!" I cried, pumping my fist and feeling like we'd triumphed over impossible odds. "You are alive, Dee Nathaniel! And you are going to the hospital and then home to your mom!"

CHAPTER
109

A MONTH LATER, I CLIMBED a steep, windy trail up Old Rag Mountain. It was the first of October, a Saturday, still hot but not intolerable, and there was a nice steady breeze blowing through the trees.

"How much farther?" asked John Sampson, who was leading.

"A quarter mile?" Bree said.

She was behind him. Bree looked over her shoulder at me and smiled.

My lovely wife had been doing a lot of smiling lately. She loved her new job. There was even talk of sending her to Paris on an assignment.

I smiled back, thinking about Ronald Peters and how we'd all overlooked him. Well, everyone but Randall Christopher, evidently.

We'd found phones and laptops that belonged to Christopher and Kay Willingham in the rafters of Peters's home in Takoma Park, Maryland. We also found a collection of videos and digital photographs on CDs that featured the girls he'd killed.

The Christopher girls had been traumatized by their abduction and captivity, but Peters had not sexually abused either of them. Dee Nathaniel, however, had twice been raped and filmed by Peters.

She had a broken jaw from his beating her after he realized that her phone had not been completely dead. She'd been able to turn it on when he left her alone briefly on the second floor of the old silica plant, where he'd kept them overnight. He'd broken two of Dee's ribs and her right wrist.

But when I'd gone to see her with Bree at home the other day, Dee said she was feeling much better. She was in therapy to deal with the experience and said that she was happy to report that Peters may have violated her body and messed with her mind, but he had not touched her soul.

"Not once," she said through the wires that held her jaw shut.

We all thought that was a beautiful place to start.

Peters had lured Dee out of her house after he'd seen her on the street earlier in the day and told her he might have found evidence on the

Maya Parker case that he wanted to show her. Dee said she felt comfortable doing it because she'd been around the man for years and he'd always been the same nice, homely guy.

The Christopher twins were lured into his van after the nighttime canvass with a promise of a quick ride home. Like Dee, they had known Peters for years. When the bodega owner got the girls inside the van, he'd sprayed them in the face with a chemical that knocked them cold.

Elaine Paulson was released the morning after we found her daughters. She and Gina Nathaniel were still thanking us for not giving up on their girls. And Analisa Hernandez had written me a touching note from Guatemala saying that through our work and in her heart, she was finally at peace with her daughter's death.

All of which made me feel pretty great as we climbed that trail in the Shenandoah. Still, I couldn't help feeling a little sadness for Kay and Randall Christopher. Not to mention all of the young women from Southeast.

Sampson got to the top of the trail first. The big man stepped out of the forest and onto the cliff; the national park was spread out below us on a bluebird day. Some of the swamp maples were already showing color.

"Beautiful," Sampson said. "Where are they going to do this?"

I pointed at the cliff edge. "Get on your belly."

The three of us got down and shimmied forward until we could see sixty feet to the bottom, where climbing instructor Tom Mury adjusted Willow's harness and then showed her how to rig the rope through her climbing jumar.

"Are you sure about this, Alex?" Sampson said. "I can't see Billie being happy about her little girl climbing a six-story cliff. Can't say I am either."

"The first time I watched Ali and Jannie do it, I almost threw up," I said. "But with the harnesses, you are safe. I mean, I got up this thing. Once."

"Don't count on seeing me doing it ever," Sampson said. "Someone built like a Clydesdale has no business climbing a cliff."

"I'm glad there was a trail up because I have no interest in it either, John," Bree said. "Oh, here she goes."

"On rope," Willow said, sounding uncertain.

"Say it like you mean it!" Mury said.

"On rope!" Willow shouted.

Her first three moves up the rock face, however, were tentative and stiff. Mury called up to her from below, "Relax, Willow, I've got you on the belay rope, so it's impossible to fall. Just relax and climb it as if you were the itsy-bitsy spider."

Willow laughed and from there Sampson's daughter moved more freely, gaining confidence with every hand- and foothold. We started cheering when she was ten feet below us. Her helmet and then her head and chest reached the lip of the cliff. John reached over and hauled her up by the harness and into his arms.

"I did it!" she said. "I did it, Dad!"

"You sure did," Sampson said, grinning and kissing her cheek. "You sure did."

Ali came next, followed by Jannie and then Mury, who basically sprint-climbed the cliff. We took pictures of everyone up there in a group with the lower flanks of the Blue Ridge Mountains behind us.

"It's so pretty," I heard Willow say to Sampson. "Mom would have loved it here."

Sampson squeezed her hand and looked off into the distance. "You're right. This was your mom's kind of place, the kind of place to feel heart coherence."

"What's that?" she asked.

John put his big hand on her chest and her small hand on his. "Breathe deep and slow and look out at the forest."

They did that for several minutes. "Feel that?" Sampson said finally.

Willow grinned. "I do."

"That's heart coherence. What we share."

After the kids had had a snack and a drink, they prepared to go back down.

Ali rappelled first, yelling, "Screamer!" He

descended the face in seven big leaps. Jannie did it in ten.

"Ready, Willow?" Sampson asked as Mury double-checked her rappelling rig.

Willow didn't say anything, but her lower lip trembled when Mury patted her on the shoulder and told her she was ready for liftoff.

"Scared?" Sampson said.

Willow shrugged and then looked at her father with teary eyes. "I just wish Mom could be here. To see me do this."

John got down on his knees next to her. He put one hand on his daughter's chest and the other on his own. "Willow, I promise you that your mom is here because she would not miss it. She's in your heart and in mine. She'll always be here, giving us strength and love and heart. You feel her?"

Willow smiled through her tears and nodded. She held tight to her rappelling rack and backed up to the cliff edge.

"Okay, Mom," she said. "Here we go!"

Willow grinned at us, kicked off the edge, and dropped away, screaming happily.

ABOUT THE AUTHOR

JAMES PATTERSON is the world's bestselling author and most trusted storyteller. He has created many enduring fictional characters and series, including Alex Cross, the Women's Murder Club, Michael Bennett, Maximum Ride, Middle School, and I Funny. Among his notable literary collaborations are *The President Is Missing,* with President Bill Clinton, and the Max Einstein series, produced in partnership with the Albert Einstein Estate. Patterson's writing career is characterized by a single mission: to prove that there is no such thing as a person who "doesn't like to read," only people who haven't found the right book. He's given over three million books to schoolkids and the military, donated more than seventy million dollars to support education, and endowed over five thousand college scholarships for teachers. For his prodigious imagination and championship of literacy in America, Patterson was awarded the 2019

National Humanities Medal. The National Book Foundation presented him with the Literarian Award for Outstanding Service to the American Literary Community, and he is also the recipient of an Edgar Award and nine Emmy Awards. He lives in Florida with his family.

For a complete list of books by

JAMES PATTERSON

VISIT
JamesPatterson.com

 Follow James Patterson on Facebook
@JamesPatterson

 Follow James Patterson on Twitter
@JP_Books

 Follow James Patterson on Instagram
@jamespattersonbooks

COMING SOON

The Last Days of John Lennon

The Russian

Walk in My Combat Boots

21st Birthday

The Red Book